W9-CBH-305

INITIATION NIGHT

Cassie watched with growing wonder and mounting terror as her best friend Robin was led to the center of the campfire circle. There Abigail, the most beautiful of the senior girls, solemnly hung a strangely shaped pendant on a silver chain around Robin's neck.

"Robin, don't . . ." Cassie whispered, hoping her voice would reach her.

But when Abigail slipped an arm around her and pulled her close, Robin didn't resist. They stood belly to belly in the scorching heat, Abigail pressing her hips against her. Then Robin closed her eyes and opened her mouth . . .

THE GLORY HAND

Paul & Sharon Boorstin

BERKLEY BOOKS, NEW YORK

THE GLORY HAND

A Berkley Book / published by arrangement with
the authors

PRINTING HISTORY
Berkley edition / April 1983

All rights reserved.
Copyright © 1983 by Boorstin Ink, Inc.
This book may not be reproduced in whole or in part,
by mimeograph or any other means, without permission.
For information address: Berkley Publishing Corporation,
200 Madison Avenue, New York, New York 10016.

ISBN: 0-425-06230-9

A BERKLEY BOOK ® TM 757,375
The name "BERKLEY" and the stylized "B" with design
are trademarks belonging to Berkley Publishing Corporation.
PRINTED IN THE UNITED STATES OF AMERICA

TO OUR PARENTS

PROLOGUE

They had spoken of love before, but now, in their struggle, words were forgotten. The man and the woman shed their tenderness, shed all emotion until only the hunger remained. Pleasure overwhelmed them like pain, their bodies gleaming with sweat from the fever, the heat fusing them into one—flesh into flesh, blood into blood, until they formed one creature, committing a mortal sin.

Forgive them.

Forgive.

On the stone mantel, like an altar in the room where they lay, the hand flared to life, five fingers tipped with needles of blue flame. A lump of flesh the color of tallow, imbued with a power beyond life, a portent of unholy revelations.

In their final, shuddering moment of release, the hand glowed with a power greater than either the man or the woman could have conceived, a spell overwhelming and eternal.

From the violence came the seed, a human life with a secret at its core, a mystery spawned at the moment sperm pierced egg, a riddle that would grow each day until it was inseparable from the child's being. Yet for all its terrible nearness, the future would be beyond the *child's comprehension, an enemy lurking within.*

So much that was unfathomable, unleashed in one final moment that looked strangely like murder. But in the aftermath, lying drugged side by side, the man and the woman knew nothing of what their hunger had spawned. They collapsed, victors and victims, lost in sleep, thinking the struggle had ended, when really it had yet to begin.

Forgive them.

Forgive.

THE GLORY HAND

Part One

THE BECKONING HAND

Chapter 1

~~~

"If your mother knew you were out here, she'd . . ." The wiry teenager ran his thumb across his throat, and scrambled a few more steps up the trail that cut a scar up the sheer face of the cliff.

"She won't find out," Cassie said, following him, but she chose her next handhold carefully. Moonlight bathed the surf 200 feet below in a glacial glow that flickered out when it hit the boulders, submerging the shore in a deeper night.

One slip and you'll fall, crushed on the rocks, like she warned.

"Careful," she shouted to him, "this is where it gets hairy."

"Give me a break," he laughed. But suddenly the root he was holding snapped. His feet were slipping, showering her with clots of dirt. He clutched at the cliff wall with his knees, groping for a rock to cling to as he slipped back towards the edge. *"Cassie!"*

She clutched his hand, but he still didn't have a foothold, and the weight of his body was pulling her down now too. "*Hang on.*" She could feel his fingers slipping from her grasp. "Over there!" She nodded to a faint niche in the granite, and he dug the toe of his boot into it, crawling back up onto a ledge.

She pulled herself up beside him. She wasn't even breathing hard, and her legs felt no strain. "You're lucky I'm in such good shape from dancing . . . *Mr. Macho.*"

"Shit . . ." His voice was lowered in embarrassment as he brushed himself off.

"You all right?"

With a toss of his head he swept his blond hair from his eyes and shoved his hands into the pockets of his parka, changing the subject: "How come your mom freaks out if you go near the water?"

"I don't know . . ." Her mother's fear of the sea— Cassie called it the Chill because of the way it seemed to creep over her until her hands went clammy and her teeth chattered and . . .

God, it pisses me off.

It was because of her mother's Chill that Cassie wasn't allowed to go out on Todd's catamaran . . . that she wasn't allowed to go down to the beach near their summer house, not even in broad daylight. Which was the reason why, even though she didn't lie to her mother, Cassie had lied to her tonight.

"I mean, what's she afraid of?" he pressed her.

To avoid answering, Cassie started up the trail ahead of him. She didn't know *why* the Chill had such a hold over her mother. All she knew was when it had started, and she wasn't about to tell Todd that. *When* had been that terrible night on the *Pandora* when she was four and her mother . . .

Get him off your back.

"Look, my mother's no crazier than your father . . . the way he freaks out when you put on your hang-gliding wings and jump off a cliff . . ."

"It's worth it."

"So was this." She looked back once more at the

waves, glinting like steel coils below. The last of the *scorpaena* had vanished. For two hours the phosphorescent plankton, galaxies of tiny diatoms, had impregnated the sea with a ghostly green glow. "It was unbelievable."

"Even my old man's never seen it," Todd said, "and he's lived on this island all his life."

Cassie glanced up to the top of the sheer rock face. Cliff's Edge, her family's rambling old summer house, loomed ahead, its three sharp gables like ship's sails stabbing into the night sky. She had never liked the way the three-story shingle and brick structure seemed to tilt crazily over her when she came upon it from the beach below. With the years, the wind and the sea had gnawed away at the cliff, bringing the weathered mansion perilously close to the brink. She hurried up the last few feet of the trail, feeling that one more moment beneath the brooding shadow of the house and it would topple to crush her.

A brass ship's lantern glimmered on the porch, but the leaded windows on each of the three floors were dark. If her mother was waiting up for her—and she always waited up for her—then why were all the lights out? Usually her mother left every light on when her father was away—Cassie had even teased her that without him, she was afraid of the dark. Then why tonight, Cassie wondered, when he was off for another round on the political glad-handing trail, did the house look as if it had been boarded up for the winter?

You're just uptight because you went out on Todd's boat instead of going over to Robin's like you told her, and you're afraid she'll find out.

Todd pulled her up onto the top of the cliff. The flinty escarpment softened into knee-high grass, and he loosened his grip on her hand as though afraid she might lead him somewhere even more precarious than the cliff trail. In the boat tonight he had been so confident, she thought, just as he was confident soaring in his hang-glider off the cliffs. But get him off of the water, or out of the sky, get Todd back on land, and he was shy about everything.

She was only shy with him. As they stepped onto the porch, that made them even.

Face it. You would have snuck out with Todd tonight even if the scorpaena *hadn't made its big once-in-a-lifetime appearance off the coast of Nantucket.*

Tonight was her last night on the island before spring vacation ended, before she had to return to Washington, and prep school, and the hassles that came from being a U.S. Senator's daughter. It was also her last chance to see Todd before summer. She intended to make the most of it.

But now that her time with him was ending, she froze. For once, *she* was the awkward one, not knowing what to say, what to do next. It struck her that what had been daring about tonight wasn't sneaking out to see the *scorpaena* or climbing the sheer cliff in the dark. It was facing this moment.

She hesitated before the oak door that had been hewn from the bulkhead of a clipper ship. It was unlocked—no burglar would bother to come out to this remote corner of Nantucket—but she didn't open it. Instead, she turned to face him.

It was one thing to be alone with Todd on his catamaran, or holding his hand as they climbed the trail in the dark. But standing so close to him, he seemed different, as though she hadn't spent every vacation with him on Nantucket since she could remember. Suddenly she didn't know Todd Stites at all. Though in August they had been the same height, barely seven months later she had to tilt her chin up to meet his gaze. The fine layer of brown hair on his upper lip—it hadn't been there in August, had it?

Zip-zip.

He was nervous, too, zipping and unzipping his red goose-down parka, his tongue flicking a toothpick from one side of his mouth to the other. The March night was balmy, even here on this promontory that was usually ripped by sea winds. So why had he worn the heavy jacket? *Zip-zip.* To defend himself from her?

She looked away from him, catching her fragmented image in the beveled glass of the foyer window. Her chestnut hair looked black in the shadows, her dark, almond-shaped eyes almost oriental, and the light from the ship's lantern on the porch accentuated her high cheekbones and long neck. People told her she was pretty, and she believed them, though she never believed them when they said she was as pretty as her mother.

Todd was staring at her in the window. "I'd better get back down to the boat," he said, biting down hard on the toothpick. "The tide'll take her right out."

"No, it won't." Cassie felt a twinge of panic: couldn't he see through her? Couldn't he see the confidence in her voice was just a sham? "Come here." Her breath caught in her throat, but not because of the steep climb up from the beach.

He took one step and stood facing her in the narrow pool of light at the front door. Sweat drenched her hands and she wiped them on her Levis. It frightened her: she put in two hours of ballet practice a day, watched what she ate, allowed herself exactly eight hours of sleep a night—all to keep control over her body. And now she was a basket case.

Zip-zip. Todd stepped closer.

He pulled the toothpick out of his mouth and slipped it into his pocket. *Zip.* The zipper stuck. Then, as if he had nowhere else to put his hands, he slipped them around her waist. He was so close she could smell him—salt spray and clean sweat.

She closed her eyes because that was the way they always did it in the books she had read, the way she had always imagined *she* would do it when the time finally came. At first it seemed strange that it should be happening with Todd Stites, but now that it was happening, it made perfect sense: better with the boy she had called her "summer brother" than with one of the preppies in her class at the Windward Country Day School in Washington.

Though their faces couldn't have been more than a few inches apart, it seemed as if they were approaching each other from a great distance, and Cassie felt as cautious, as tentative, as when she had been about to dip her hand in the water where the *scorpaena* glowed. No matter how carefully you held the luminous substance in your hand, it would slip through your fingers, a shimmer you could catch for only one moment in your life.

It took her a long time to reach Todd. Then suddenly her lips brushed against his. She wondered fleetingly if she had expected music (all right, maybe not violins), the kind of corny stuff that the movies and the books (even the good ones) had promised. But it wasn't like that, her first kiss.

Instead of music she heard a scream.

She opened her eyes. Todd's were still closed, his lips pressed against hers. He hadn't heard a thing.

Don't blow it.

The scream—what *sounded* like a scream—it must have been a gull wheeling in the sky (at *night*?) or the rusty squeal of the weather-cock on the roof (but there's no wind).

Why didn't Todd hear it?

If you stop now, he'll think you're chickening out.

She pulled away from him. "Can we go out on the boat tomorrow? I mean, I'm not leaving until evening."

He didn't let go of her waist. "What about your mom?"

"We can do it before she gets up. I finish practicing at eight."

"Eight. Down on the beach," he said, leaning closer her to kiss her again.

She pulled away from him and ran towards the door. The scream—it must have been an echo of her panic at being alone with him, she thought, for it faded as soon as she closed the door behind her.

The house was silent, but something was wrong. The house . . . like Todd, it seemed strangely unfamiliar in the dark. The darkened cut-crystal chandelier in the foyer seemed to hang down from the ceiling at an angle that defied the law of gravity, and the framed tintypes of her mother's ancestors, dressed in morning coats and taffeta dresses, tilted on the wall beside the staircase, as if the house were starting to list with age. As Cassie walked over the hooked rug, the floorboards groaned underfoot, like the deck of a ship on choppy seas.

Something glimmered in the dining room: two candles in silver sconces on the polished oak table. The tapers had burned down to stumps, and teardrops of wax spattered the wood, so that the high-vaulted room smelled like a church. The table was set for two, with gilt-edged Wedgwood china and Waterford crystal, and on the sideboard were silver platters holding an elaborate dinner that she had seen her mother preparing that day: boneless chicken breasts stuffed with tarragon from their herb garden, a salad of local vegetables, and a tart made with blackberry jam she and her mother had put up the summer before. *All of it*, she thought uneasily, *for you*.

She had promised that she would be home for dinner. How could she have forgotten? A dinner that had seemed so important to her mother, their last chance for some private time together, she had told Cassie, before they had to return to the hectic public life of a Senator's wife and a Senator's daughter.

And yet hadn't every dinner that her mother had prepared on the island in the past week been as elaborate? It had almost seemed to Cassie that her mother had been trying to keep her away from Todd and Robin by bribing her with food. Cassie had responded by eating only yogurt and drinking Tab, saying that professional dancers—she wanted more than anything to be one—

had to be thin. But her strict diet had really been to resist what felt like her mother's attempt to control her.

On her mother's plate was a single slice of chicken, untouched.

You told her you'd be home and when you didn't show, she couldn't eat.

Cassie picked up the meat with her fingers, but she felt no hunger. She felt guilt and only guilt, clinging to her, as clammy as her hair, wet with the salt smell of the sea.

A wine cork lay beside the plate, but there was no bottle on the table. The thought of her mother going upstairs to her bedroom when she hadn't come home, to drink alone, sickened Cassie. Had the *National Enquirer* been correct when it had printed its malicious "scoop" not long ago: *Ann Broyles* vs. *the Bottle?* Was that the real reason why her mother had been avoiding the public eye in the last few months? Why she had chosen to come out to Nantucket during spring vacation with Cassie, instead of following her husband on the political circuit that might edge him closer to a shot at the Presidency?

Cassie thought of adding the cork to the collection her mother kept lined up on the windowsill in the kitchen, mementos of the family dinners they had shared at Cliff's Edge over the years. But as she pushed through the swinging kitchen door, she threw the cork into the wastebasket instead, and slid the platter of chicken into the refrigerator.

Another scream.

This time it wasn't the cry of a gull or the screech of the weather vane rusting above the widow's walk. This time the cry Cassie heard wasn't an echo in her mind. It came from inside the house. Upstairs. And what had begun as a single shriek dissolved into a cacophony of voices.

She rushed over to a Currier and Ives print on the wall near the stove and pulled aside the frame. The tin mouth of the dumbwaiter shaft yawned open behind it, the dumbwaiter that hadn't been used since rats had gnawed through the pulley ropes years before. Cassie tore through a veil of cobwebs and leaned inside.

The noise that echoed off the tin walls—it sounded like voices on a record played at the wrong speed, racing with an urgency she couldn't understand. When rats scurried up the walls of the dumbwaiter shaft, their squeals might *sound* like voices, she thought.

But this wasn't rats. It was a woman's voice that echoed down the shaft. Her mother's voice.

Why did that startle her so? Her mother was the only person in the house, wasn't she? But she never raised her voice. Not at Cassie. Not at her husband—even when his Irish temper exploded. Ann Broyles kept her anger locked inside her, expressing it only in the brooding paintings at her easel on the second-floor landing. No, Cassie thought, her mother never shrieked like that.

And the words . . . Cassie could hear a few that bled through: ". . . *Bitch* . . . *you fucking bitch* . . ." It was her mother's voice, but her mother never talked like that.

Someone's up there . . .

Impulsively, Cassie grabbed a carving knife from the counter and pushed open the kitchen door into the hall. A garbled torrent of curses rang down the stairwell. She rushed up the stairs, the planking, warped from generations of footsteps, complaining underfoot. On the second-floor landing a grandfather clock chimed once, her startled face reflected in the swinging pendulum. She clutched the knife more tightly, raising it high, ready to . . . attack? She had no idea who . . . or *what* . . . was the enemy.

When she reached the third-floor landing the shrill, one-sided argument ended. The house was filled with a leaden silence, pierced only by the tick of the grandfather clock. She had expected to see a sliver of light beneath her mother's door, as thin as the knife blade in her hand. Instead, darkness.

Someone's in there with her. He heard you coming. He's waiting.

She hesitated to touch the old brass knob shaped like a lion's paw, as if it were charged with a powerful electric shock. Outside the leaded window at the end of the hall a foghorn moaned, and a light on a ship's mast bobbed across the horizon, like the North Star veering off-course.

She grabbed the knob and turned it. The corroded latch resisted stubbornly. She threw all her weight against the door. Grudgingly it creaked open.

Gauze curtains flailed in the breeze from the open window, catching the moonlight, and it looked for a moment as though the glowing *scorpaena* from the sea had filtered inside the bedroom. Reflections from the waves cast green flames across the oriental carpet, a warning to Cassie that something was terribly wrong. Her mother never pulled open the curtains that faced the sea, much less opened the window to admit the roar of the surf . . . and the Chill.

But tonight the window was open. Tonight, after so many years of being locked out of the room, the surf growled like an intruder.

"Mother?"

She was lying naked on the four-poster bed, a white sheet pulled tightly over her, her hair spread out on the pillow, deep as the night sea. Cassie scanned the room for a trace of movement in the shadows.

"I heard screaming."

Ann's face glistened with sweat, and she lay so still that Cassie feared she must be dead.

"Mom?"

In her haste to reach her, Cassie bumped into the dressing table, knocking a hairbrush to the floor. The way her mother's eyes snapped open at the sound told Cassie that she had only been pretending to sleep.

"What are you doing?" Ann sat up quickly, the glint of the knifeblade reflected in her eyes.

Cassie lowered the knife, but didn't let go of it. "I heard voices."

"Voices?" The parental tone made Cassie feel childish to be holding the knife, childish to have barged in at all. "You didn't hear anything."

Cassie didn't believe her—she *had* heard something—but she let her mother take the knife from her and lay it on the bedstand.

"Cassie . . ." The anger in Ann's voice vanished mysteriously and was replaced by an emotion that Cassie found harder to identify, a tenderness mingled with . . . "You'd better get to bed, honey." She beckoned for Cassie to hand her the quilted bathrobe at the foot of the bed, and slipped it on, stifling a shiver. It struck Cassie that she hadn't seen her mother naked since she was a child, not since before that night on the *Pandora*. Ann had gone to great lengths to hide the scars from the burns, as if she felt that the Chill—the other scar from that night—had caused her daughter enough pain.

Ann seemed surprised that the window was open and stood up to close it. Even at forty, even after what the tragedy on the *Pandora* had done to her, she still carried herself like a dancer, Cassie thought as she watched her glide towards the window in a single smooth movement. Before Ann pulled the curtains shut, Cassie glanced around the room. In the moonlight she could make out the emerald-green curve of a wine bottle on the bedstand.

So that was it, Cassie thought sadly: the screams . . . the curses . . . her mother had been shouting out in lonely, drunken rage at the darkness. If only she hadn't forgotten about dinner, Cassie thought . . . if only she hadn't snuck out with Todd, her mother wouldn't have taken the bottle up to her room, and all the strange and terrifying anger wouldn't have spewed out.

"It's late. Go to bed," Ann said.

Cassie hesitated. "I love you." It was what her mother had always said to *her* at bedtime. Why did

Cassie feel compelled to say it tonight?

Ann reached out and embraced her, held her so tightly that Cassie could feel her breath against her hair—no words, but a gentle rush of air that spoke to her. Her mother was clutching her, she thought, the way a frightened child clutches a doll. On her breath, Cassie expected to smell the sweet, familiar bouquet of wine. It would have explained everything.

But there was no hint of it. The wine bottle on the bedstand . . . Cassie took a good look at it: it was full.

Ann released her with a wisp of a smile. "Sleep tight."

Reluctantly, Cassie let go, and left the room. But as she started down the stairs, she felt a queasiness in the pit of her stomach, and looked back over her shoulder. Her mother had picked up the silver hairbrush that had been knocked off the dressing table, the Art Nouveau antique that had been her grandmother's. She brushed her hair in fitful strokes, her long black tresses crackling with electricity, sparks cutting blue question marks in the dark.

Chapter 2

⁓

Cassie could force what had happened last night out of her mind, but not out of her muscles. Her arms and legs ached as if she had fallen down that flight of stairs, instead of running down them, when she had left her mother's room. She pulled the purple leg-warmers up over her knees and started the record of *Swan Lake* again. Resting her foot on the *barre*, she leaned over her thigh and stretched until it hurt.

She stared at herself in the mirrors that lined the walls of the high-ceilinged room, but not with her usual eye to form. Her arms spread wide, her back arched, she gazed at her face, hoping that by studying it, she would somehow be able to decipher her feelings. It was too dark to see. She had pulled open the velvet drapes her mother insisted on keeping shut to block out the view of the sea, but outside a curtain of clouds stifled the first light of morning. All Cassie could make out was her slender, hesitant shadow in the mirror.

She bent her legs slowly in a series of pliés in each of the five positions, then did three pirouettes towards the center of the room, snapping her head around so that she didn't lose her image in the mirror, and ending with her arms curved overhead, her left foot on the parquet floor firmly in front of her right. She wasn't dizzy—she never got dizzy when she danced—but the troublesome thoughts lingered, like the salt smell which clung to her hair from last night.

With a nervous flick of her hand, she brushed back the chestnut wisps of hair that had loosened from the knot pinned on top of her head. Two separate anxieties were tugging at her—what to do about Todd, and what to do about her mother—and as if she were trying to perform two different ballet steps at the same time, it seemed impossible to resolve either of them.

Go up and check on her.

No, let her sleep. She needs sleep. You can be out on the boat with Todd and back before she wakes up.

Cassie raised her chin, then threw back her shoulders so that her tiny breasts pushed against the black nylon leotard, and imagined Todd was staring at her the way he had stared at her last night.

The door clicked open.

Todd . . . He must have been too impatient to wait for her on the beach. She arched her back, looking into the mirror to catch the expression on his face when he walked in.

"Cassie, we've got to go."

Her mother was standing in the doorway.

Go back to bed. Please go back to bed.

"What are you doing up?" Cassie asked.

"We're leaving."

In a long batik skirt over a leotard and tights, the outfit she always wore at Cliff's Edge, Ann Broyles looked like a ballet teacher. But something was different about her this morning: her raven hair, which was usually pulled into a tight bun, was wild and unkempt; her eyes were red (from sleeplessness or tears?), and her complexion . . . her complexion that had tanned so

readily in one week of sunshine, was as wan as the dawn
sky.

"Are you okay?" Cassie's cautious words were an
echo of last night. And like last night, her mother ignored them, pulling the velvet curtains back across the
window. She's shutting me in, Cassie thought. She's
always shutting me in.

"You'd better get dressed."

"What for?" Cassie walked to the Baldwin upright in
the corner, grabbed a towel from the piano bench and
wiped her forehead with it. "Our plane's not till tonight."

"We're due at Woods Hole in an hour."

"You've got to be kidding." Cassie threw the towel
on the floor and started the record again with an angry
scratch.

"Cassie, sometimes your father's needs come first."

"I thought he said we didn't have to go . . . He didn't
want us to go."

"It's important."

"Come on, you hate those dumb political things more
than *I* do. I thought the whole reason you came out here
was to get away from all that Senator's wife junk."

"Honey, we don't have much time."

Cassie turned her back on her to face the *barre*. She
balanced her leg up on it and stretched until pain shot
from her ankle into her hip. "You go ahead. I'll be okay
here . . ." (*With Todd.*) "I'll meet you and Dad at
Logan Airport tonight."

Ann didn't reply. Instead, with an urgency Cassie
couldn't understand, she grabbed her hand and led
her—*dragged* her—out of the dance studio and into the
hall.

Despite her sleeplessness, despite whatever had
afflicted her last night, her mother still had a dancer's
strength, Cassie thought, her grasp so tight that her ring
bit into Cassie's palm. The antique silver band was
shaped like a hand, with spindly fingers and pointed

nails that seemed to clutch her mother's ring finger. "You're hurting me," Cassie said.

"I'm sorry." But Ann didn't loosen her grip.

Cassie knew her mother would never deliberately hurt her. Whenever she held Cassie's hand so tightly that the ring stung Cassie's palm, it meant that she was afraid. "It's Dad, isn't it? You're worried something's going to happen to him."

"Not at all."

On the landing, an easel faced a corner window. Her mother had chosen to work here because it was the only window on the second floor of the summer house that faced away from the sea. After the fire on the *Pandora* years before had scarred her legs, she had stopped dancing and had begun painting the view from this window: scrub pines and cypresses, sand dunes tangled with heather and wild roses. Cassie resisted her mother's breakneck pace long enough to glance at the canvas on the easel, surprised to see that the half-finished work wasn't a landscape like the others that lined the hall, but a portrait: a young girl in a *tutu*, done in stormy blues that seemed to have been stolen from her mother's troubled eyes.

Cassie realized it was a portrait of herself as a child, melancholy and vulnerable. It galled her all the more— it was as if her mother were trying to keep her frozen forever at age four. "I know why you won't let me stay here by myself while you go to that thing today. You don't trust me!"

Ann stiffened. "Cassie, I know you went out on Todd's boat last night . . . and I know it wasn't the first time."

"Jesus!" Cassie exploded. "I'm thirteen years old. All the other kids my age go sailing . . . swimming. Why won't you let me?"

Ann searched Cassie's eyes. "It used to be that coming to Nantucket was a chance for us to be together. The dancing . . . the closeness . . . the dinners we used to have. You never minded spending time with me here then.''

"Things are different now.''

"You used to like staying in the house, dancing while I played the piano, or looking at those art books downstairs . . .''

That was before your Chill ruined everything, Cassie wanted to say. *That was before your obsessive, consuming fear of the sea kept me here*. And yet, Cassie didn't open her mouth. For her mother was limping. Whenever the scars on her legs gave her trouble, Cassie backed off. "I was with you, don't forget." She chose her words carefully: "The horrible stuff that happened on that ship . . . it didn't hurt me like it hurt you.''

"You were young . . . children can be very resilient. I'm grateful you haven't suffered the way I have.'' Her weary tone reminded Cassie they'd been over the same ground countless times before. "I wish you understood it's only because I care about your safety that I've made these rules.''

"It is not!'' Cassie shot back. "It's because you're afraid. And not just of the sea . . . That's not the reason you don't like me spending time, with Todd. You're afraid of what I'll do with him!'' She ran across the hall into her bedroom.

The pink-wallpapered room was crammed with childhood mementos. An oak cradle held frayed stuffed animals; tiny costumed mice filled a miniature Victorian house, and Princess Alexandra dolls wearing taffeta dresses trimmed with rabbit fur were lined up on the window seat where Cassie had left them the summer before. Signs of her more grown-up passions seemed to conflict with them—the chrome-framed posters of Nureyev and Baryshnikov, the black stereo speakers stark against the floral wallpaper; paperback novels by Vonnegut and Salinger scattered across the four-poster bed, their colors clashing with the patchwork quilt.

Ann followed her inside with a sigh, as if yielding to

her daughter's anger. "I'm sorry. Look, I don't mean to ruin things for you and Todd. It's just . . . I don't know, it just seems like such a long time since we were together as a family. All the talk about Clay's Presidential chances . . ." She lowered her voice, as if mentioning a terminal illness. "He can't get out to the island so easily anymore. I thought, since he was going to be on the Cape today—so close—that maybe it would be nice if we went to Woods Hole, to be with him." She reached out to hug her, but Cassie squirmed away.

Clay Broyles' face smiled down from the collage of Senatorial campaign buttons and bumper stickers that she'd tacked above her bed. "Sitting on some stage in front of hundreds of people . . . That's not being with him! We might as well watch him on TV!" Cassie stripped off her leotard and stood naked, defiant, in front of her, as if to say that at least her mother couldn't control her body, that she was growing into a woman, and if that meant growing away from her, there wasn't a damn thing her mother could do about it.

Ann averted her eyes as if to avoid facing the reality, and reached into the closet. "It's a good thing I remembered to pack this." She pulled a pink dress from a hanger, the Florence Eiseman she had bought for Cassie's thirteenth birthday in the children's department at Saks, though Cassie could have fit into a Junior size. Pearl buttons in the shape of hearts adorned the bodice, and hand-appliquéd roses trimmed the prim white collar.

"*Cute*." Cassie made a face.

Ann lay the dress carefully on the bed. "Be ready in fifteen minutes . . . please."

Ann walked slowly out of the room and Cassie felt the urge, as she always did after such clashes, to apologize. "Mom . . ." As usual, it was too late. Ann was halfway down the stairs. It didn't make sense. Hadn't her mother always encouraged her to express her feelings? So why, when Cassie vented her anger, did it only make both of them feel worse? They never used to hurt each other like this.

She could hear her stop on the landing and call to someone coming up the stairs from below: *"Cassie's got to leave in five minutes."*

"No problem, Mrs. Broyles."

A girl with frizzy blonde hair walked into Cassie's bedroom. "Jesus . . . Todd said he could hear you two bitching at each other all the way down on the beach. What's going on?" She pulled a pack of Virginia Slims from under her "Save the Whales" T-shirt and lit up.

Cassie clutched her throat in mock agony. "Robin, *must* you?"

The blonde snapped her bathing suit around a protruding crescent of buttock and exhaled luxuriously: "It's not dope. Don't sweat it."

"Is that what they teach you at boarding school? You'll stunt your growth . . . stunt *my* growth . . . turn me into a dwarf or something."

"Pardonnez-moi. I'd hate to screw up your gorgeous dancer's bod." She was about to tap the ash onto the carpet when Cassie motioned her towards the bathroom. Reluctantly, Robin went in and tossed the cigarette into the toilet without flushing it. On her way back to the bedroom, she stopped in front of the mirror, tried to suck in her softly rounded stomach, gave up and flopped down onto the bed. *"Shit!"* She pulled a copy of *Watership Down* out from under her. "How can you read stuff for school on *vacation*?"

"It's a good book."

Robin rolled her eyes and blew an imaginary smoke ring. "The dancing . . . the homework . . . How do I tell my best friend she's turned into a *masochist* this past year. You'll be burnt out before you get to high school! I mean, don't you ever relax?"

Cassie smiled. "Maybe I don't know how."

Robin took an Almond Joy out of her backpack and offered Cassie a bite, but Cassie shook her head:

"You're too much. Here I am fighting battles with my self-control day and night, and all you do is stuff your face. And the worst part is, you don't even feel guilty . . ." She eyed her friend's body enviously. Since last summer, Robin had lost her baby-fat, and had developed full breasts and shapely hips. Watching her polish off the candy bar, all Cassie could come up with was: "You're going to get zits."

Robin brushed a crumb of chocolate from her baby-smooth cheek. "At least I've got tits!" They both laughed. "Cass, you worry too much."

"That's what I just said to my mom."

Cassie padded barefoot into the bathroom and switched on the shower. Stretching a plastic shower-cap over her hair, she stepped under the spray and turned it as hot as she could stand.

Robin leaned in the doorway and raised her voice to be heard over the rush of water. "She hassling you about Todd?"

"You name it." Cassie squirted Vitabath on a sponge and lathered her body. "I thought you were supposed to get more freedom when you got older . . . you know, that they trusted you more. I think my mom trusted me more when I was four." She rinsed off quickly and stepped out of the shower. Robin handed her a yellow towel and she rubbed herself down. "God, it's like she's pulling in the reins or something."

"Where's she making you go today?"

"You won't believe it . . . I mean, I have one day left before I have to go back to Washington, right? And she's making me blow it on one of those dumb political things." She chose a pair of pink lace bikini panties from the dresser drawer and stepped into them, then pulled on a bra, though it was clearly more a sign of hope than a necessity. "I wish I knew what her problem was."

Robin joined Cassie at the mirror and licked her finger, then tried to smooth down her eyebrows that had been plucked to a ragged line. "Maybe it's menopause or something. My mom's been acting weird lately, too. Only with her, it's like she can't *wait* to get rid of me.''

"Don't I wish.''

"*Cassie*?'' Ann didn't have to shout: voices carried in the old house like cold drafts from the cellar.

Cassie picked up the Florence Eiseman from the bed and held it up in front of her in the mirror. Then she threw it down and plunged into the closet, pulling out a red sundress of sheer Indian cotton, with a scoop neck and spaghetti straps that tied at the shoulder.

"I thought your mom made you return that,'' Robin said. "I thought she said it was . . .''

"*Obscene*.'' Cassie laughed and pulled the dress on over her head. The filmy cloth stretched taut across her hips and breasts, accentuating them.

"Now into your Sunday School dress before your mother has a cow.''

"*Cassie?*'' from downstairs.

"Take off your shoes,'' Cassie said.

"What?''

Cassie pulled off Robin's high-heeled white sandals and slipped them on. She unclasped the barrette that held a bun neatly on her head and shook out her long chestnut hair, letting it cascade around her shoulders. With a flick of a finger, she adjusted a wave seductively over one eye.

"Your mother's going to *shit*,'' Robin said.

Chapter 3

~

Cassie strained against the seatbelt for a last glimpse of the island out of the porthole: Nantucket lay on the ocean a thousand feet below, soft and warm in the sunlight, like a puppy asleep on a porch. Woods Hole would be cold and dank, she brooded, gray with the thick fog that hugged the south coast of Cape Cod until the beginning of summer. The riveted steel walls of the helicopter confined her like a prison, and she wished she could turn on a blast of air, the way she could on a jet. But Navy helicopters had no such luxuries, she knew from the tedious journeys she'd taken on them with her father. They weren't designed for comfort—just to get you there.

If she and her mother really *had* to go, they should have taken the ferry across Nantucket Sound—it would have been a lot easier on her stomach. But of course her mother never would have agreed to that. Cassie glanced over at her: judging from her tense squint, her drawn lips, even a thousand feet high was too close to the sea for comfort.

Ann's left hand rested on Cassie's, as cold as the silver ring on her finger. It seemed she was staring out a private window only she could see through, as if today the Chill arose from a place closer than the sea, from inside her. It didn't make sense—she hadn't noticed the dress Cassie had worn, or Robin's high-heeled sandals . . . not even the lipstick and rouge. Nothing seemed to get a rise out of her, and that troubled Cassie. It was as though the familiar part of her mother, the part that she thought she understood, had gone numb.

Ann seemed just as oblivious to her own appearance. Her makeup, usually meticulous, understated, when she was to appear in public beside her husband, had been carelessly applied: the mascara was smeared below her eyes, the rouge on her cheeks streaked. And though she wore a beige-linen Givenchy suit from the "right" boutique in Georgetown (with opaque stockings to hide the scars on her legs) she had forgotten to wear the simple gold necklace and diamond-stud earrings, the orchid-patterned Gucci silk scarf, accessories that the media man on the Senator's staff had recommended "to project the right image." It seemed the only thing she *hadn't* forgotten was the antique silver ring in the shape of a hand, the ring Cassie hated.

Maybe she's freaking out. Maybe she's played the role of Senator's wife once too often, and it's finally gotten to her.

Cassie knew her mother had only endured the Washington luncheon circuit, the vapid Senators' wives, out of love for Clay. She had often wondered if Ann Cunningham had known what she was getting into when she'd gone to Cliff's Edge after graduating from college and had fallen in love with a Nantucket "lifer," a man she had once thought of as the kid who repainted her father's boat every summer. The Cunninghams had disowned her—until Clay had started to "make it." The rest was crazy, Cassie thought: the more Clay Broyles' political career had taken him away from the island, the more her mother had wanted to spend time there.

Which made her decision to leave Cliff's Edge today all the more puzzling.

Ann was squeezing her left hand into a fist, clenching it so tightly that the ring's pointed silver fingers must be hurting her, Cassie thought. Yet the way Ann continued to stare straight ahead, her eyes dulled, it was as if the discomfort were insignificant compared to some deep, unspoken pain.

"Mother?"

Ann turned to Cassie, her eyes slowly focusing, as if the dark meanderings of her thoughts had led her back to a single concern. "Your hair . . . We've got to do something about your hair, Cassie." She fumbled under the seat, but before Cassie could protest, Ann's voice faded: "I must have left my purse back at the house . . ." She retreated again into herself, the matter apparently forgotten. Cassie stared into her eyes for an explanation—they were the gunmetal gray of the ocean sky that looked as though it could shift violently to a storm at any moment.

The helicopter shuddered in a downdraft, and Cassie's stomach turned over. Her mother's depression —if that was what it was—Cassie couldn't help but hold herself responsible and wonder whether what had happened last night had pushed her over the edge. If she hadn't snuck out with Todd . . . if she had come home for dinner with her mother . . . would that have made the difference?

The helicopter plummeted into a maze of armor plate and barbed wire. The Woods Hole Naval Shipyard seemed to Cassie like a confusion of sharp steel edges at war with each other, like her feelings. Even from a hundred feet in the air, one rumpled figure stood out among the immaculate white uniforms, and the sight came as an enormous relief.

God, I don't get enough of him.

She had inherited Clay Broyles' stubbornness—"pig-headedness" his opponents in the Senate had called it—but thank God, he had always joked, she hadn't inherited his looks: the pugnacious, out-thrust jaw that dared an adversary to land the first punch, the saddle-nose that had been broken three times when he had boxed in the Navy. He was heavy and thick-boned where her mother's features were fragile, aristocratic, and he still looked like a fighter, Cassie thought, though judging from the paunch he'd acquired over the years in Washington, a fighter who'd broken training. With her mother suddenly a stranger to her, Cassie longed for the directness of his flag-blue eyes.

Buffeted by a stiff breeze, the helicopter settled to earth with what seemed to Cassie an agonizing slowness. Below, her father shifted from one foot to the other on the cement, and turned up the collar of his tweed jacket against the gale from the chopper blades, his red hair flecked with gray blowing wildly. The rough edges that made him look and act like a Washington outsider had worked to his advantage, Cassie knew. An upstart lawyer in Nantucket, then District Attorney in Boston, he had defeated the slick four-term Senate incumbent in a groundswell of anti-Washington sentiment. Now, even after almost two terms, he still didn't *look* like the Washington politician. Cassie smiled: his pants were too baggy, his shoes scuffed. He tugged at his unfashionably wide necktie to straighten it, but only succeeded in pulling it more askew. Before the rotor blades stopped spinning, he was running over to the helicopter, surprisingly light on his feet for a man who was a good twenty-five pounds over what he called "fighting weight."

God, I don't get enough of him.

The hatch of the helicopter swung open, and to Cassie's surprise, her mother rushed down the aisle ahead of her into his arms. Ann had always been reluctant to show affection in public, yet despite the TV cameras focusing on them, she held him tightly, her eyes closed as if to shut out everything but the feeling of his body against hers. His bear-hug seemed to revive her smile, bring the color back to her cheeks. It must have been Clay—or the lack of him—Cassie thought, that had troubled her mother so.

When he held Ann at arm's length his smile faded. "Are you all right?"

"I'm fine."

"But . . . I wasn't expecting you."

"Surprise," she said with a brittle laugh.

It did nothing to erase the puzzled look on his face. Despite the camera lenses targeted on them, he spoke with his usual bluntness: "Ann, what the hell's going on?"

When her reply was an unconvincing smile, he turned to Cassie and swept her up in his arms: "Cassandra!" He stood back to get a good look at her, raising an eyebrow at the skimpy dress, the makeup. She felt ashamed of her appearance, ashamed to have embarrassed him in public. But he didn't mention it. "What in God's name ever got you off of the island? Did Todd run off with Robin, or what?"

Cassie glanced towards her mother.

He took Ann's hand as if he understood her neediness, if not the reason for the sudden visit. "Come on," he whispered as he led Cassie and her mother past the honor guard standing at attention on the asphalt apron. "Let's get this damn thing over with."

It was only when they had left the helicopter pad that Cassie realized the gray structures towering over them weren't buildings, but warships, as gigantic and as cold as icebergs. The searing yellow flames of acetylene torches were welding steel into cruisers and destroyers in dry docks ten stories high. Ahead of them, poised on a launching ramp and draped with red, white and blue bunting, was a submarine as sleek as a shark. An audience of Navy men faced it in reverent silence, like a congregation before an altar in church.

To reach the reviewing stand, they had to walk along the breakwater, so close to the water's edge that Cassie could taste the salt spray. Her mother must have been desperate to be with Clay, she thought, to risk the Chill that surely lay in wait for her here. She glanced over at her: Ann had slipped on her best wife-of-the-Senator smile for the cameras.

An Admiral with bushy white eyebrows and a stoop shook Clay's hand, and when introduced to Cassie and Ann, gave the expected *what a lovely family* response before seating them on folding chairs beside the Joint Chiefs of Staff. Gripping the podium like a pulpit, the Admiral lauded the "Space Age" submarine behind them, thanking Cassie's father, Massachusetts' "favorite son," who had pushed through its funding (over $600 million), and patting himself on the back for seeing the project through. Cassie scanned the audience that sat stiffly before them. They were the same faces she had seen at other such tedious rituals; "filler," she called the bureaucrats and military men who got paid as much for suffering through these meaningless speeches as for *doing* anything.

She read the name on the prow of the submarine: U.S.S. WILL ROGERS. Hadn't Will Rogers said, "*I never met a man I didn't like*"? It was her father's favorite quote. To name a ship designed to *kill* people after the man who had said that was *sick*.

The Admiral droned on, and Cassie tuned out. Her mother could make her sit here, but she couldn't make her listen. Her eyes were drawn to the ocean, and she strained to see Nantucket across the sound, but the sea and the sky had clamped together, an identical battleship gray, welded into a seam at the horizon.

I could have been out with Todd on his boat right now, and . . .

The odor of "Old Spice" brought Cassie back to the reviewing stand. Wayne Runtledge, her father's new "assistant," smiled ingratiatingly and sat down beside her. She avoided his gaze. Runtledge had first been introduced to her at a speech her father had given at the Rotarians' convention two weeks before in Boston (she had only agreed to go along because it was a chance to

visit Robin at boarding school nearby). Though Robin
had thought Runtledge was sexy, Cassie hated him immediately, because she was sure he wasn't really one of
her father's assistants at all. The truth was painfully obvious: the other members of the Senatorial staff were
smooth Ivy Leaguers who wore muted pinstripes and
carried hand-sewn leather attaché cases, but Runtledge
had a crewcut so short his scalp showed through, a
Marine tattoo on his wrist . . . and a telltale bulge under
the left armpit of his rumpled sharkskin suit. Cassie
wondered if her father's closed-door Senate hearings
into organized crime had put him in some kind of
danger, or if it was just his sudden prominence as a
Presidential hopeful that explained why he had been
assigned a bodyguard. In either case, she resented the
way Runtledge intruded on what few private moments
with her father she had left. For revenge, she had
branded him "Runt." The label stuck—even her father
had started calling him that behind his back.

Runt squirmed in his chair and she folded her arms
tightly over her chest to keep him from getting a look
down her dress.

Polite applause told her that the Admiral had ended
his speech, and when her father stood up and walked to
the podium, Cassie joined in the standing ovation.

But Ann wasn't clapping.

As soon as Clay left their side, Cassie saw dread creep
into her mother's eyes. Her lips were drawn tight, her
body stiff and tense . . . Cassie wondered whether her
mother was listening to the same shrill voices in her
mind that had clashed last night.

She was grateful when her father cut his remarks
short, and began following the Admiral up the wooden
steps of the scaffolding to a wind-whipped platform
that extended out over the waves, facing the prow of
the submarine. The Navy band struck up "Anchors
Aweigh," and Cassie winced. Band music was just
noise, she and her mother had decided at another,
equally tedious patriotic event (was it at Newport News?

Annapolis?)—the only real music was what you could dance to. She turned to her mother to exchange the undercover grimace they'd perfected to elude the eyes of the cameras.

But her mother wasn't listening to the music. She was halfway across the reviewing stand, heading towards the scaffolding.

"Mother . . ." Cassie stood up, but didn't follow. Ann had to be with him, she realized, even if it meant climbing a precarious staircase, teetering dangerously close to the water.

Ann was forcing herself up the stairs of the scaffolding, both hands on the bannister, one painful step at a time—as if the limp, that vestige of the tragedy aboard the *Pandora*, had suddenly gotten much worse. She was trying to focus her eyes straight ahead, perhaps to avoid looking down through the wide spaces between the steps, but as if against her will, her eyes were drawn to the water. The sight seemed to afflict her; she stopped and rubbed her leg as if it smarted with pain.

Cassie ran towards her.

The steps were slippery with ocean spray, and the flimsy scaffolding swayed in the wind. Cassie wished she hadn't worn Robin's high-heeled sandals that wobbled beneath her, or the skimpy dress that was whipping above her knees. A hundred feet below, water frothed, the poisonous amber of gasoline, and the hiss of blowtorches, the whine of blades sawing through armor plate in the dry docks threatened to throw her off balance. Yet she reached out to her mother, grabbed her hand.

The wind flailed Cassie's hair against her cheeks, shook the planking beneath her feet, but escorting Ann onto the high platform, she felt a surge of exhilaration —her mother had needed her and she had helped, and the relief on her father's face told how much he appreciated what she had done.

Close up, the submarine seemed even more enormous, more awesome, than it had from the reviewing stand. A bottle of Moët & Chandon dangled by a satin ribbon from its prow, puny beside the wall of steel. The Admiral shook hands with Cassie's father for the benefit of the cameras below, then picked up the bottle. A drumroll and a fanfare of trumpets echoed off the hull of the submarine as the Admiral turned and held out the champagne.

"Mrs. Broyles, we are delighted that you could be with us to do the honors."

Ann said nothing. She stood, wooden, at Clay's side, as if after all it had taken to reach him, she had no intention of moving.

The Admiral leaned closer to give her the bottle, but her hands were limp, her eyes looking right through him. She was staring out at the sea, seemingly hypnotized by the shattered rainbows floating on the oil-slick waves.

Take the bottle.

Cassie tried to focus her mind, to concentrate hard enough to make her mother read her thoughts: *Take it.*

Her father cleared his throat, and Cassie's skin beaded with sweat under the gaze of the TV cameras, the eyes of the crowd.

Everybody's watching.

She was sure she could hear cruel whispers from the audience: gossip of a drinking problem . . . rumors of a candidate's wife cracking from the strain . . .

Take it. They're watching.

"Mrs. Broyles?" The Admiral licked his lips and glanced nervously at the Senator.

Impulsively, Cassie snatched the champagne out of the Admiral's hand, the bottle so cold and wet it almost slipped from her grasp. Ann didn't seem to notice, but Cassie sensed a flicker of gratitude on her father's face. He smiled down at the audience, as if this had been the plan all along.

What have I done?

The bottle wavered in Cassie's hands. She stepped towards the submarine, too nervous to summon up the smile she knew was expected of her.

What do I do now?

The wind whipped her sundress above her knees, and she felt the urge to drop the champagne and run down the steps. She glanced behind her: her mother's lips had set into a drunken smile that was even more disturbing than the dull stare. And her father—he was nodding to Cassie, urging her forward.

She stepped to the edge of the platform. A dozen feet away, across a watery chasm, the hull of the submarine glinted dully in the sun. The crowd hushed, and as she weighed the bottle in her hand she found herself raising her chin, straightening her back, her feet moving instinctively to the third ballet position. For one fragmented moment she was performing a role in a ballet before an audience, and this time, as the band struck up "Anchors Aweigh," it was the New York Philharmonic, playing Tchaikovsky. Her mother would have been proud of her poise, she thought—if only she had been watching.

Cassie pulled back the bottle, took aim at the seam of rivets that stitched a scar up the prow. Then she rose up on her toes and hurled the bottle in what she hoped would be a bold, yet graceful movement.

The bottle seemed to hover in the air, and she held her breath, fearing she hadn't thrown it with enough force. Then it shattered against the hull in an explosion of foam.

With a whine, pneumatic sledges thrust the submarine backwards, down the launching ramp. The platform shuddered underfoot and Cassie struggled to keep her balance as the hull slammed into the water. In her exhilaration, the spray that drenched her tasted like champagne.

The band must have started playing, for she could see the drummer's arms flailing, the trumpeter's cheeks bulging as he pressed his instrument to his lips. But all she could hear was the din of the submarine's twin turbines rumbling to life. Red, white and blue balloons exploded in the sky, along with a blizzard of confetti.

Beaming, she turned to the crowd, expecting applause for her performance.

But no one—no *one*—was clapping. They were gaping at the other end of the platform.

She whirled around: the pride was gone from her father's face, replaced by . . . She didn't recognize the emotion because she had never seen it there before.

Oh, God.

Anointing her mother's forehead, like a Hindu holy mark, was a single red droplet.

"No!"

Ann's knees were buckling, but with a twitch of recognition, she reached out. Cassie lunged for her, clutched her hand and held on, even when the sharp, pointed fingers of her mother's ring cut into her palm, even when she felt her hand sticky with blood from where the ring had pierced her skin.

The wake of the submarine churning across the harbor slammed against the scaffolding, and Cassie slipped. The sea wind was pulling her mother away from her, wrenching her out of her grasp. The jewel on her forehead, which at first had been so precise, was trickling over the bridge of her nose, down her cheek, a red tear. With a vicious gust, the wind threw Ann against the railing of the scaffolding and it broke with a sickening snap.

"Mother!"

Slowly (*Don't let go!*), slowly (*Wait!*), her mother's grasp loosened in Cassie's, until the pain from the ring ceased. Ann's eyes turned the green of the sea.

Don't leave me!

At first Ann's body soared out over the water, drifting in an upcurrent of wind, like a gull.

Then she fell straight down.

Cassie lunged into thin air. First her left foot, then her right, stepped free of the platform, stepped into the void to follow her.

Something hit her in the chest hard, wrenching the breath out of her. When she opened her eyes, burly arms clutched her. Runt had grabbed her, dragged her back onto the scaffolding. But instead of gratitude, she felt rage, fury at him for not letting her reach out to her mother, to save her.

Or join her.

"Let me go!"

She fought to tear free of Runt's grasp, her eyes frantically searching the water for some trace of her mother. The froth shimmered with the flare of the blowtorches in the dry docks, waves that swirled and writhed and ate each other, a cauldron of luminous green.

"Let me go!"

Runt pinned Cassie's arm and carried her across the platform, rushing her down the stairs, holding her as brutally as if *she* were the murderer, and suddenly the fear gripped her: *They've killed Dad, too* . . .

"Daddy!" She strained to pick him out in the blur of uniforms on the reviewing stand below.

"Cassie!"

The unruly mop of red hair, the rumpled tweed coat —he was flailing out with his fists, trying to fight his way over to her. But it was no use: he was swept away by military police and hustled into a helicopter.

"Daddy!" the hatch slammed shut, and the rotor blades roared to life, strangling her cries as the helicopter lifted into the sky.

Cassie kicked her legs, beat her fists against Runt's chest as he dragged her off of the reviewing stand and carried her across the concrete breakwater. The audience was fleeing, too, their folding chairs scattered across the ground like broken toys. They didn't care what had happened to her mother; they were running in sheer terror, and she hated them for that.

Another helicopter touched down and Runt threw Cassie inside, then jumped in beside her. The pilot pulled up on the stick, nosing the helicopter into a steep turn that sent her falling back into her seat.

Over the din of the rotor blades, the radio crackled from the cockpit: *"They've recovered the body* . . .

*wound inflicted by . . . it's hard to tell . . . maybe a
small caliber . . ."*

The pilot interrupted: "Whatever it was that got her,
I'll lay odds it had the Senator's name on it . . ."

Cassie pressed her hands to her ears: as long as she
blocked it out, she could convince herself that it wasn't
true, that nothing had happened. She tried desperately
to recall her mother's face, to breathe it back to life in
her mind: *the gray, almond-shaped eyes, the graceful
neck, the high cheekbones of a dancer*. She buried her
face in her hands and tasted blood from the cut the
silver ring had made in her palm.

The blood . . . The single droplet on her mother's
forehead dissolved the tranquil vision of the face in
Cassie's mind. Her thoughts churned like the water
beyond the window as the helicopter gained altitude, her
emotions tearing at each other, clashing like gulf-stream
currents: disbelief . . . fear . . . rage.

Guilt.

Tears were streaming down her cheeks, trickling into
her mouth, as hot and salty as blood. Runt gripped her
shoulders. "You're going to be okay," he mumbled in a
gravelly monotone. "You're safe now."

"Safe?" She shaped the word with her lips, but no
sound came out. Runt's square, pock-marked face
showed no trace of sympathy, and his indifference
sparked fury. She struck out at him with clenched fists,
and he sat there without trying to stop her, as if it were
part of his job, as if it were easier to take her punishment than to comfort her.

She pounded Runt's massive chest until her arms
ached and her hands were sore, and even the sight of the
bloodstains on his shirt from the gash on her palm
didn't stop her. As she lashed out at him, she realized
she was shouting for her mother, that she had been
shouting her name for a long time, crying out in a little
girl's wail. She collapsed into sobs and pressed her face
against the glass of the helicopter window. It was as cold
as a knife blade.

With enormous effort she opened her eyes: out the window the ocean spanned the horizon. She closed her eyes, but the sea followed her, a night sea under a starless sky, storm clouds and wind raising tidal waves. When she cried out for her mother now, it no longer sounded like her own voice. It sounded as if it came from somewhere outside of her, somewhere far away, a voice echoing down the dumbwaiter shaft at Cliff's Edge. Like her mother's voice last night, cursing the darkness.

Her mother had been right, Cassie thought as she brushed the last of the confetti from her hair. Her mother had been right to fear the sea. It was there that the danger lay. She stared out of the window, gazing down at the black and fathomless deep, fascinated and repelled by its lethal magnetism.

And for the first time she, too, felt the Chill.

Chapter 4

EXCERPT FROM THE CONGRESSIONAL REC-
ORD: Proceedings of the Joint Select Committee on
Assassination. May 12, 2:38 p.m.

*Representative Stennis O'Conner of Alabama,
Chairman, and Senator Clayburn Broyles, senior
committee member, receiving testimony from Sey-
mour Hutton, Ph.D., Chief of Ballistics, Federal
Bureau of Investigation.*

*REP. O'CONNER: . . . and you have examined the
body of the victim, Dr. Hutton?*
DR. HUTTON: Yes, sir, I have.
*REP. O'CONNER: When and where did the exam-
ination take place?*
*DR. HUTTON: In the morgue at the Woods Hole
Naval Hospital, approximately three hours after
the time of death.*

SEN. BROYLES: Please explain your findings to the committee.

DR. HUTTON: Well, as the report you have before you indicates—

SEN. BROYLES: The report doesn't indicate a damn thing.

REP. O'CONNER: Senator Broyles!

DR. HUTTON: As the report concludes on page eighty-six, our findings were—inconclusive.

SEN. BROYLES: Were the findings inconclusive, or was the staff who assembled them incompetent? The Bureau has spent over a month and God knows how much of the taxpayers' money!

REP. O'CONNER: Senator, please. We know you have no intention of personally accusing—

DR. HUTTON: No, it's all right. It's understandable—the results must look questionable. But to be totally frank, I've never seen a case quite like this one.

REP. O'CONNER: You'll have to be more specific, Dr. Hutton.

SEN. BROYLES: Try confusing us with a few details, why don't you?

REP. O'CONNER: Senator—

DR. HUTTON: As the report explains, we used the most sophisticated techniques in our ballistics analysis. But there are rules of physics, gentlemen, and, well—

SEN. BROYLES: Well?

DR. HUTTON: There are laws of nature, if you will, laws which can never be broken: a piece of inert matter, a lump of lead impacting on a living thing, should behave a certain way. But our findings—well, they don't seem to follow those laws.

REP. O'CONNER: Which means—?

SEN. BROYLES: Which means that Hutton and his staff can't hack it.

REP. O'CONNER: Senator Broyles, if these out-bursts don't cease, I'm afraid I will have to request that you excuse yourself from this committee.

SEN. BROYLES: But we're talking about my wife!

DR. HUTTON: Senator Broyles, please under-stand that I share your frustration. I've been on the Bureau for thirty-two years and I have never seen a case where the cause of death was quite this—problematic.

SEN. BROYLES: Problematic? Jesus Christ!

REP. O'CONNER: With all due respect to the ef-forts of your staff, Dr. Hutton, the Senator has a point: this is not the organized presentation that we were promised when the Director appeared before our committee on April 27th. We were assured there would be a complete analysis of the evidence, with relevant details clearly spelled out: caliber of bullet, direction of trajectory—type of weapon. Facts that can be put to use in an investigation.

DR. HUTTON: I understand. But the details are the whole point. It doesn't appear—I say appear—from the evidence that there was a bullet.

REP. O'CONNER: But she—the victim—was shot through the head. That was in your preliminary report.

DR. HUTTON: At first glance, yes. There appears to be an entry wound, like that made with a .32-caliber slug. But there was no exit wound. No sign of a bullet within the body. And—from the cause of death determined by the coroner in the autopsy, it was—well—it wasn't really as if the victim had been hit by a bullet at all.

REP. O'CONNER: I'm afraid you lost me, Dr. Hutton.

DR. HUTTON: You see, a bullet didn't seem to be the cause of death. It was cardiac arrest. Her heart just stopped. It was as though—as though she had been struck by lightning.

(EDITOR'S NOTE: At this point in the proceedings, Senator Broyles, evidently distraught, requested to be excused. Shortly thereafter, Representative O'Conner declared a recess until Dr. Hutton and his staff could arrive at a more satisfactory report.)

Chapter 5

~————

The Burning Man. Even before she knew the ship was on fire, Cassie saw him, a dark and fiery angel. And the faster he ran along the deck of the Pandora, the faster his cloak of flames engulfed him.

The decks were slick with oil, like the blood of some enormous butchered creature, and smoke gushed out of the portholes. Cassie was only four years old, and she couldn't see the flames at first, just women and children screaming as they clawed their way to the lifeboats. The ship was screaming, too, electrical wires sizzling, planking warping in the heat. When her mother turned to grab life jackets, Cassie was swept along by the stampeding crowd.

The Burning Man . . . everyone else was fighting to get into a lifeboat. Why was he fighting to reach her? She cried out in panic, and for a moment the Burning Man and her mother were both grabbing for her, his face so close that his breath scorched her skin. Then her mother clutched her hand, the sharp pointed fingers of

*her silver ring cutting into her palm. She dragged Cassie
towards the railing.*

*In the water below, the light from the flames engulf-
ing the* Pandora *gleamed in confused pools of magenta,
scarlet and indigo. One by one the passengers leapt into
the night ocean, escaping the stench of sulfur, the acrid
smoke, helpless as a swarm of drowning insects. Only
their heads showed above the water black with oil,
heads that looked as if they had been severed from their
bodies, screaming.*

*Cassie and her mother teetered at the railing over-
looking the water, and the Burning Man seized on that
moment of hesitation to make one final lunge.*

*Her mother shielded Cassie's body with her own, let
the flames from the Burning Man lick at her, crawl up
her legs, as Cassie watched in horror. Before the fire
could reach Cassie too, Ann snatched her in her arms
and jumped.*

The shock of cold.

One look back to see the Pandora *turning over, like
an old horse dying, the boards splintering as it groaned
over on its side. Her mother was swimming, dragging
her frantically away from the boat so they wouldn't be
sucked into the vortex of the whirlpool as the ship began
to sink.*

*The Burning Man—he stood alone on the tilted deck,
the flames engulfing him. Why didn't he jump into the
water like the others?*

Then he was swallowed up in smoke.

*A gasp, and the sea swallowed Cassie, too. She floun-
dered in the icy swells, water streaming into her mouth,
her nostrils, and down her throat, infecting her with the
blackness that she was certain must be death. The Chill
was pulling her down, dissolving her in its acid, filtering
into her veins, a transfusion with the blood of a corpse.*

*Even with her eyes closed she could feel them sinking,
away from the smoke and oil and screams, down to
death-still depths. It seemed hopeless: her mother strug-*

*gled to claw her way back, fighting painfully upward,
but the fiery shimmer of the surface was impossibly far
away.*

*They had to make it. They had to. For even in the
depths she feared that she could not escape the Burning
Man, that even down there in the darkness, he would be
lying in wait.*

Cassie turned her face up to the gentle sunshine to
escape the memory. The wind tangled her hair, whipped
the long batik shirt she wore over her leotard against her
legs, and she gripped the railing of the aft deck more
tightly. It was always the same—first the memory that
had haunted her since her mother's death, then the Chill
shooting through her veins like a stream of needles,
followed by a lingering nausea that left the bitterness of
poison in her mouth, the sea-taste of bile. She had tried
to bury the memory, but like a drowned corpse, it
always floated to the surface. And only when the
memory had spent itself, wound down like a dying
clock, only when she felt her eyes rolling up into her
head, on the verge of losing consciousness, did she feel
the Chill ease its grip on her throat.

It was not an uncommon phenomenon, the psychiatrists in Washington had explained to her and her
father: the death of a parent triggering a repressed
childhood memory, linking it with a recent trauma. But
they hadn't been able to explain why it was the same
memory that had once paralyzed her mother, why the
Chill that had afflicted Ann Broyles now afflicted
Cassie. Since Cassie had watched the waves swallow up
her mother at Woods Hole, her mother's sea phobia had
seemed both reasonable and wise. And now that the
tumor had lodged in her mind, she was sure nothing
could remove it, certainly not the fruitless hours with
psychiatrists she had suffered through.

The phobia had worsened, until Cassie dreaded sleep,
fearing that if she closed her eyes she might drown under dark fathoms, trapped too far beneath the surface

to claw her way up for breath. In their apartment in
Georgetown, she had left the light on in her room at
night, and had started rocking in bed, cradling herself
with the rhythm her mother had once used in her
lullabies, the tempo of a heartbeat. But still the memory
had seized her. And though in reality she and her
mother had finally been rescued from the icy waters by
the Coast Guard, in Cassie's mind it no longer turned
out that way. The memory had warped insidiously, so
that the way she remembered it now, at age four she had
drowned.

We should never have taken the ferry.

In summers past, they had taken the New England
Airlines turboprop to Nantucket. Her mother had insisted on it. But Cassie had assured her father that she
could handle taking the *Nantucket Queen* for this first
trip back to Cliff's Edge since her mother's death. From
a distance, landlocked in Washington, it had seemed
safe, but the moment the boat had churned away from
the pier at Hyannis Port, into the moss-green waves,
nausea had welled up, the taste of brine.

We never should have taken the ferry today.

The *Nantucket Queen*, molded of powder-blue fiberglass, had hard plastic seats like those on a bus. It could
hardly have been more different from the *Pandora*, a
floating antique of varnished mahogany and polished
brass that had taken vacationers to and from the island
for generations. That night nine years before, she and
her mother had been guests on the final, gala voyage of
the old steam ferry, before it was to have been turned
into a dock-side restaurant and amusement arcade.
Cassie's mind circled fitfully over the memory, a confusion of first-hand sensations dimly remembered, and
newspaper clippings she had assembled much later.
(According to the *Nantucket Standard*, the disaster of
the night of July 13, 1972, had been sparked by the fire-
works launched from the *Pandora*'s aft deck. The
rescue of Cassie and her mother—the only survivors—
had been termed "*miraculous*.") Her mind wheeled,

like the gulls over the ferry's wake, and she wondered if they were at the very point—about five miles out from the mainland—where the *Pandora* had gone down in fifty fathoms.

Like the cycle of a cruel mechanical toy, the Chill ground to a halt with a click and a stutter that caused a twinge of pain in the palm of Cassie's hand. She ran her thumb across the skin, searching for the scar. The wound from her mother's sharp ring that night on the *Pandora* had dwindled to a white line across her palm. The wound from where the ring had pierced her skin three months ago, on the scaffolding at Woods Hole, was still raw and red, slow to heal.

She ran a finger over the two scars. They intersected, like two snakes entwined on her palm. What would a palm-reader say, looking at her hand? she wondered. That her lifeline was longer than her mother's? Or that it, too, foretold death by drowning?

The two scars in her palm—there was one important difference between them. On the *Pandora*, the ring had cut her because her mother had refused to release her, because she had not allowed anything—not the flames, or the Burning Man, or the sea—to snatch Cassie out of her arms. But at Woods Hole, when Cassie could have saved her mother, the pain from the ring had made Cassie let go . . .

She ran her palm along the ferry's smooth fiberglass railing and the recent wound stung from the salt. She looked out into the waves, hunched against the wind like an old woman. "I should have held on . . ." She spoke softly, her lips barely moving. "I never should have let go of her."

"Don't." Her father put his arm around her. "You didn't let her fall. You couldn't have stopped her from falling. She was already dead." He sighed, and the guilt in his own voice surpassed Cassie's: "That bullet . . . *whatever* it was that got her. It was meant for me . . . She was only standing there because of me . . ."

"She *wanted* to be there," Cassie cut him off. "I

don't know what was going on with her, but it was like she *had* to be with you. Sometimes I think Mom knew . . . I think she knew something was going to happen to you."

"So it happened to her instead!"

"She loved you."

"A lot of good it did her."

It had become a ritual with them, Cassie knew, the father forgiving the daughter, the daughter forgiving the father, and none of it did a damn bit of good. But that didn't stop the ritual, or the need for it. "Don't come down so hard on yourself," she said.

He raked his fingers through the reddish stubble of his beard, a beard he had grown, she thought, to hide behind. The disguise hadn't worked. The hair had grown in raggedly, and it only made him look unkempt. "Why the hell shouldn't I be hard on myself? I only got to the Hill in the first place because of her . . . Her confidence in me . . . Christ, when I was D.A. I put away some of the biggest racketeers in the country, but I can't do a goddamn thing to find the son-of-a-bitch that killed her . . ."

"You've done all that anyone could do." But Cassie knew it was too easy to say that. So she blurted it out: "What difference does it make if they find out who did it or not? Nothing can bring her back . . ." As soon as the words escaped her lips, she was sorry. For she knew that it was the pressure of the investigation, however futile, that had kept her father going, the slender hope of revenge that kept him sharp and energetic, instead of letting him sink into self-pity or depression, as she had. He said nothing, clenching and unclenching his fists, the knuckles black and blue from pummeling the punching bag in the Senate gym. "I mean, look at you. You've worked your way down to fighting weight."

He smiled bitterly at the term, which he had taught her. "Fighting weight?" He stared at his hands. "To fight what? I'm just shadowboxing, that's all. All my life I've tried to win by a knockout—when I boxed in the Navy, when I was D.A. That was the way I won my elections—landslide. I hate split decisions . . . photo finishes. But this damn FBI thing . . . it's so gray . . . inconclusive. Dragging on and on without a definite suspect. For me, that's the worst . . ."

The island of Nantucket lay ahead on the water, a warship cruising towards them in the midday glare, and he slipped an arm around her. "It'll be okay, once we get there," he said, and Cassie thought it was to reassure himself as much as her. He had wanted to board up the summer house for good, she knew, and she suddenly wondered if it had been wrong of her to beg him to take her there, wrong to wrench him away from the investigation. He had only agreed because she'd been so insistent. But maybe, she thought, as the boat neared the shore, her need to return to the place where her mother had been the happiest could only end in failure—as futile as her father's search for the murderer.

Runt dragged their luggage over to the gangplank. Like her father and herself, Cassie thought, the bodyguard seemed burdened by his guilt. He kept even closer to them than before, a brooding presence in his wrinkled sharkskin suit. It struck her that each of them who had been with her mother at Woods Hole that morning felt that the guilt was his alone. Her steps were hesitant as she filed down the gangplank after her father, over the brackish water at the dock. She remembered reading about a place somewhere, called Devil's Island, where guilty people were condemned for life.

If Cassie had thought that the weathered lobster boats bobbing at anchor in Nantucket Harbor, the nets drying in the sun, would somehow soothe her with their picture-postcard charm, she had been mistaken. Her gaze crept insidiously over the side of the pier, to the gutted fish that slapped against the pilings, eyes bulging and jaws agape, as though poisoned by the sea.

Her father insisted on taking the wheel of the rented Buick that was waiting for them, leaving the bodyguard to sit in the back seat with Cassie. It was his fighter's instinct, she thought, that made him drive so recklessly over the narrow road snaking away from the harbor up the coast, as if he were lunging to take the first punch at an opponent. A sharp curve, and Cassie slid across the vinyl seat, against Runt. She had refused to speak to him since her mother's murder, and he had responded with an equally brutal silence.

Clay didn't slow down as the car shuddered over a cobblestone street, where saltbox houses hugged the rim of an inlet. Cassie pressed her cheek to the window as the clapboard home where Clay had grown up rushed by. Her grandfather had been a staunch Yankee freethinker, a bearded fisherman who liked to tell her that any man who had seen the monsters of the deep and weathered the gales of the North Atlantic could never believe in God. Cassie barely remembered her grandmother Broyles, a gentle woman who had expressed herself with a needle the way a writer might with a pen, sewing comforters to sell to summer tourists. Hannah Broyles had seen no reason to leave the island. On Nantucket, she'd said, there was always enough cloth, always enough thread. When she died, her husband's cynicism had turned to despair. He had joined her within the year, as if he lacked the will to endure life without her. Cassie tried not to think how much Clay might be like his own father.

Clay gunned the car out of town and Cassie looked back to see the lighthouse dip beneath a sand dune where the wind rippled the marsh grass. The road climbed over chalk-white cliffs, then leveled off as they reached the northern tip of the island. On the rocky promontory, the waters of the Atlantic met those of Nantucket Sound to spawn fierce riptides, their fury echoed by the wind that threatened to blow the car off the road, flinging a barrage of sand against the windshield. Though oak trees had been planted here a hundred years before as a windbreak, they were still as stunted as saplings.

It had always puzzled Cassie that her great-great-grandfather on her mother's side had chosen to build a home on this precipice, away from the grand whaling-captains' mansions near the harbor. Perhaps the very violence of the place was what had attracted him. "Black Jack" Meacham had by all accounts been a violent man, a whaler who would pursue his prey far out into the Atlantic if his first harpoon missed its mark, and take out his rage on his family and crew if a whale eluded him. When his ship, *The Harpy*, had broken up in a gale off of Point Fear, there had been few mourners.

With its three steep gables, and its Widow's Walk for sighting ships on the horizon, the hundred-year-old house stood out boldly against the sky, like a beached schooner. Though he had built Cliff's Edge in the Victorian era, Captain Meacham had refused to allow it to be festooned with gingerbread latticework like the other sea captains' houses on the island. He had kept its lines sharp, angular, like a harpoon thrust into the sand, and that was fitting, she thought, considering it had been paid for with murder. She wondered how many whales the captain had killed to buy it.

They climbed out of the car and walked hastily across a lawn choked with weeds. The wind fought their every step, assaulting the brick walls and the Welsh slate roof like a cat raking its claws across a dollhouse. The waves bombarding the beach beneath the cliffs seemed to roar more fiercely than Cassie had heard them before, and she glanced towards her father: his gait, the way he clenched and unclenched his fists, said he was reluctant—perhaps even afraid—of what he would find inside the house. She hesitated, too. It struck her that maybe she hadn't come to Cliff's Edge for comfort, but to punish herself for her guilt.

The lock of the heavy oak door was rusty, and Clay had to twist the key violently before the door finally yawned open. Sand had seeped under the door, and when they walked inside, it grated underfoot on the warped floorboards. The air in the foyer bore the damp weight of winter, defying the June warmth, as if, Cassie thought, after the chill of her mother's death, it hadn't been able to thaw. She felt as though she were walking into a house that had just been burglarized, looted of something terribly valuable that could not be replaced. She walked cautiously to the foot of the stairs as if fearing that the burglar might still be inside.

No sooner did Clay walk in than he snatched the telephone off of its walnut table, as if reaching for a lifeline. "I'll just check in."

"Sure."

Checking in . . . She knew it meant calling the FBI to ask if they had any news on the investigation. He checked in as often as he might have phoned for an update on election night.

Cassie went into the parlor and began tugging off the white coverlets from the furniture, not wanting to face the green velvet sofa where her mother had liked to sit at cocktail time, with a glass of white wine. The captain's chest before the Queen Anne chair was scuffed from where, in more leisurely times, Clay had put his feet up when he had joined her, sipping his Scotch straight up.

The parlor was a room of compromises, Cassie thought. Her father had insisted on keeping "Black Jack" Meacham's scrimshaw, the crossed harpoons and grappling hooks mounted along the walls, and though her mother had called them "bloody trophies," she had left them on display. But he had compromised, too. He had let Ann take down the seascapes he loved, to put up her own brooding paintings, and he had let her replace the Captain's sea charts in the lacquered Japanese cabinet with art books: Degas, and more Degas, for his dancers.

Cassie glanced uneasily at the one heirloom that neither of her parents had wanted, but which hung over the mantel with a malevolent life of its own—the figurehead from Captain Meacham's ship, *The Harpy*. The rotting wooden carcass, its steel breasts pointed like the tips of two harpoons, had been washed ashore at Point Fear after the ship had sunk, and been returned to the Captain's widow, Cassie's great-great-grandmother, Zena Meacham. The face had been modeled after Zena, Cassie had been told. If so, it was a cruel likeness, its nose a hooked beak, its eyes luminescent blue stones that gave the weathered visage a vengeful intensity. Her mother had called the figurehead "Neptune's Whore," ridiculing it, Cassie thought, the way she made fun of things that scared her. Cassie had never understood why her parents had left it there. She snuck a backward glance at the Harpy as she left the room: it almost seemed that the stone eyes of the figurehead were gloating in triumph, as if it took a perverse pride that the sea had claimed her mother the way it had claimed the Captain. That the Chill had won.

Clay was still on the phone when she returned to the foyer. He cupped his hand over the receiver. "Want to go into town? Get some lunch?"

"But the lobsters . . . I thought we were going to broil them."

"Okay," he said after a moment's hesitation that told just how eager he was to escape from the house.

"It'll be fine," she said, and she felt as if she were reassuring him not just about the meal, but about their having come here at all.

The draft from the foyer didn't follow her into the kitchen. Unlike the parlor, it was warmed by a southern exposure, sunlight filtering through panels of yellow stained glass that edged the bay windows, gleaming in the copper pots that hung from a rack over the butcherblock counter. Cassie strained to smell some trace of the fresh bread that her mother used to bake here, but all she could smell was garlic: the knot of bulbs hanging over the door—"to keep away vampires," her mother had joked—had shriveled into husks.

Lining the windowsill overlooking the beach was the collection of wine corks her mother had saved, as though to hoard the memories of dinners at Cliff's Edge. Dried wishbones filled a Mason jar beside them, "for emergencies," Ann had said.

The door to the dumbwaiter shaft was open, and Cassie slammed it shut, as if to shield her ears from her mother's screams that might still be echoing inside. The Wedgwood plates and Tiffany silver from that last, uneaten dinner were stacked by the sink. Cassie couldn't bear using them for lunch and replaced them in the locked cupboard, removing two simple ironstone plates and stainless flatware instead.

"I don't give a good goddamn who the Director's in a meeting with . . ." Clay was shouting into the phone. *"What the hell have your people been doing . . . Playing with themselves?"* She turned on the faucet so that she wouldn't have to listen. Over the running water she could hear the receiver slam down on the hook. "I'm going out for awhile," he called to her from the hallway, his voice lowered, she knew, to hide his rage.

By the time Cassie had unwrapped the three five-pound lobsters the market had split for broiling, Clay had changed into his white shorts and Golden Gloves T-shirt (he was an honorary member) and was clattering down the stairs. The door banged shut behind him, and she watched him through the window as he descended the steep, rocky trail that slashed down the cliff face to the beach. From the look on Runt's face, the bodyguard was none too pleased. Usually he tagged along when the Senator jogged through Rock Creek Park in Washington. But after that phone call, Cassie decided, her father had felt the need to escape the house, and his shadow. Runt perched sullenly on the edge of the cliff, following Clay's run down the beach with his binoculars. At least for once, she thought, her father would get a moment's peace, the freedom to sweat out his anger.

Cassie picked up the lobsters, scrubbing the shells quickly and scooping the gritty eggs from the tails. As she dumped the roe down the drain she remembered how her mother had tried to avoid this part because she hated the smell of the sea on her hands.

When she had dotted the lobsters with butter and slid them under the broiler, her eyes were drawn back out the window. She tried to catch sight of the red sail of Todd's catamaran on the water, hoping that he somehow knew she was here and would come to see her. But looking at the sea . . . For a moment, in the sun's glare off the surf, it looked as if the tide were rushing in, slithering all the way up the cliff to inundate the house.

Clay was coming back up the beach, the sand scattering behind his feet in little bursts, running at a cruel speed as he punished the last breath out of himself. His silhouette stood out so boldly against the shimmering sand . . . On the wide beach that ran between the cliff and the crashing surf, he was visible for miles, an easy target. The sun burned in her eyes, like the blowtorches from Woods Hole, where she had learned that the water's edge could be a killing ground, as lethal as the open sea. He was taking a terrible chance, she thought. Thank God he was almost through. The tension eased from her muscles, and she waved to him through the window. But he wasn't looking up towards the house. Instead of heading up the trail, he pulled off his sweat-soaked T-shirt, kicked off his Adidas, and . . .

Cassie's throat tightened: he was running towards the surf. With an exuberant leap, Clay dashed into the breakers and dove into a tower of foam. *He's gone.* Cassie's fingers went numb, and the knife she was rinsing clattered into the sink. She wanted to cry out, but the words wouldn't come.

He's going to drown himself . . . he's going out there to join her, the way his father joined his mother . . .

Where was Runt? Why didn't Runt stop him? Cassie spotted the burly figure on the edge of the cliff, his elbows raised awkwardly, watching the sea through his binoculars without so much as a nervous twitch.

Cassie's mind spun. The sea had taken her mother . . . now it was taking her father, and . . .

The sea . . . the whitecaps gleaming like the eyes of the Harpy figurehead, shining with vengeance and joy.

Icy tendrils began creeping up her back. She was starting to shake, as if she were plunging into the water after him, the cold numbing her to the marrow.

Then the razor edge of the Chill. *She was staring out of a porthole into an inferno . . . People were floating, their heads bobbing on the night waves, as if they had been severed from their bodies, and this time her father's head was among them.*

The waves blurred, the blinding glare of the surf suddenly a cascade of flame. Cassie tried to move, but it was all she could do to support her weight on the rim of the kitchen sink with her hands. Her elbows locked against her stomach to keep her knees from buckling, and she could smell smoke, feel heat singeing the hair on her arms. It was more than a memory. The smoke billowed, and she started coughing uncontrollably.

A hand gripped her shoulder, a man's arms held her tightly and she opened her eyes. The smoke was coming from the oven beside her. In one quick movement, her father pulled out the pan and dumped the charred lobsters into the sink.

"I ruined them!" Cassie's chest was heaving, sobs buffeting her in waves. "I ruined everything!" Tears suffocated her, blocked off the words before she could say them: *She's dead and I wanted to take care of you the way she did, but I can't . . . I can't!*

He pressed her to him, his beard wet and shaggy against her face, but she squirmed out of his arms and ran into the hall.

"Cassie!"

She clattered up the stairs, her hand, wet with tears,

slipping on the bannister. For a moment it felt like the railing on the *Pandora* the night of the . . .

Or was it the scaffolding at Woods Hole the morning her mother . . . ?

She stumbled, then scrambled back to her feet, running upstairs on blind instinct.

Cassie had no idea where she was until she slammed the door behind her and wiped the tears from her eyes. The windows smothered with velvet drapes, the mirrored walls . . . She switched on an old whale-oil lamp that had been converted to electricity, but it did little to relieve the gloom. Her reflection echoed between the two mirrored walls into infinity, as if she were chasing herself in a hopeless pursuit.

The studio . . . Cassie hadn't danced since the morning her mother had dragged her out of here to Woods Hole. She doubted she would ever dance again. Her body felt leaden, too heavy to spin across the floor, burdened with a weight that kept her from transforming her feelings into movement. She stared into the mirror and felt as if she were teetering over a deep reflecting pool where she might drown.

She forced herself to study the figure in the mirror. The skirt strained at her hips; whatever curves she had begun to acquire had disappeared with the ten pounds she had gained since her mother's death. The hem of her batik skirt—Ann's skirt—brushed the floor. Face it, she brooded, coming here with your father, trying to cook for him, trying to take care of him—you were just a little girl playing dress-up.

She slumped to the floor. Why had she run away from her father when she wanted so desperately to please him? Because she knew she couldn't give him what he needed?

Her eyes escaped her gaze in the mirror, drawn to the piano in the corner, remembering the afternoons her mother had played the Baldwin upright while she danced. But the scuff marks on the dusty floor were all that was left of the dancing, and the piano that had once been brought to life by her mother's touch was shrouded in shadows, like a black jack-in-the-box that concealed a frightening surprise. She walked over and ran a finger along the keys. The notes had gone flat.

On top of the piano . . . What was it? A leotard? An old pair of leg-warmers?

A purse. The purse her mother had forgotten to take with her on the helicopter. Cassie picked it up cautiously, uneasy with a reminder of the day she wanted to forget. But the suppleness of the black calfskin under her fingers was strangely inviting. She opened the gold clasp. Greedy for something she couldn't put into words, she slipped a hand inside.

The hairbrush, the art nouveau antique backed in silver that her mother had been looking for that day on the helicopter . . . Strands of her mother's hair were still trapped in the bristles, and as Cassie carefully pulled them out, she remembered how her mother had brushed her hair that last night, crackling blue sparks in the darkness. She set the hairbrush down on the dusty piano top.

Deeper inside the purse, a lipstick, the neutral shade her mother had used to soften her lips, rather than to color them; a champagne cork, for good luck . . .

And a letter.

It was addressed in her mother's flowing handwriting with the broad strokes of her gold-tipped Mont Blanc pen. The name, "Miss Grace," was one Cassie had never heard her mother mention, nor did she recognize the rural address in Maine. A stamp had been attached, but the envelope was unsealed, as if her mother had meant to read it one more time before she mailed it. And then she'd forgotten her purse . . .

Cassie slipped the letter from the envelope, and unfolded the cream-colored stationery monogrammed *ACB*.

"Dear Miss Grace,

"I hesitate to write you at this late date, and I hope

you will forgive me for my tardiness. But then, I'm sure you will remember that I was always the artistic one, that planning ahead was never my strong point. I'm writing because I realize that you were right, of course— just like you were right when I would come to you with problems at Casmaran. My daughter is precious to me, but I've been selfish. She's on the verge of becoming a woman, and she doesn't need me in the way she used to—the way I admit I wish she still did. It feels as if she's been slipping away from me this past year, and yet, as you warned once, trying to hold on to her hasn't been healthy for either of us. As you said years ago, there comes a time when mothers and daughters—all women—must share a bond based on mutual love, rather than dependence. That's something I learned at Casmaran, of course, but I guess I'd forgotten."

Cassie glanced up at herself in the mirror, then looked quickly away. Her mother had understood all along what she had been feeling. Why hadn't they been able to talk about it?

"I know it may be impossible, so close to opening day, to find Cassie a bunk." Bunk? Cassie looked again at the address on the envelope: Maine. Casmaran had to be a summer camp. But why hadn't her mother mentioned going there? *"She's really quite special, and I'm sure she would be an asset to any cabin. I know how much it would mean to her if she could experience what I treasured at Casmaran: the endless fields of flowers, dancing near the lake, meeting lifelong friends. And getting to know you, Miss Grace. Casmaran changed me more than I can say—I know I haven't been a very loyal daughter of Casmaran all these years, but if you could find a spot for Cassie I would be forever in your debt. And I know that Cassie would be, too. Because whatever happens, this is her summer, Miss Grace. It has to be.*

　Love,
　Ann."

Cassie's eyes strayed from the letter to her face in the

mirror. Her expression startled her. The despair had left her eyes, replaced by a serenity, a calm she would have thought impossible when she had run up the stairs a moment before. Her mother had understood. She had understood that another summer together at Cliff's Edge would only have made Cassie resent her more. And, Cassie realized, it had been just as wrong to come here without her. She would only be trying to take her mother's place, and that would be a burden she could never bear, a burden neither her mother nor her father expected of her.

"Whatever happens," Ann had written. Cassie wondered if her mother had suspected (could she have *known*?) that she was going to die that day. This letter . . . was it her mother's last wish for her? She slipped the letter back into the envelope, feeling (*but how could it be*?) that her mother *hadn't* forgotten the purse that morning, that she had deliberately left it here, where she knew Cassie would discover it, a clue to how to survive the ache of her death.

As Cassie raised the envelope to her lips, licked the seal, then smoothed it firmly shut, the door to the studio creaked open behind her. The shadowy silhouette of a woman hovered at the threshold, and Cassie was seized by a giddy panic that her mother had been summoned here by her reading the letter. She shoved it quickly into the purse, as if she had been caught stealing.

"Cassie?"

It was Robin.

For a moment, neither of them moved. They were painted on the mirror, caught in an uneasy balance. Then Robin rushed over to her.

"Cassie, I'm sorry."

"Sorry for what?" Cassie hugged her.

"I wanted to write you . . . about your mother. It must have been so terrible for you. But I couldn't make it sound right. You're so good about putting your feelings into words, but I . . ."

"It's okay."

"I thought you'd never forgive me . . . for not coming to the funeral. I've been such a lousy friend."

"You're a good friend," Cassie said.

"I'm really glad you came back." Cassie didn't reply. "Aren't you?"

"I don't know. Maybe I thought that being here would make everything the way it used to be." Cassie shook her head. "Or maybe I thought I could take her place."

"What matters is, you're here."

Cassie ran her foot along a scuff mark on the floor. "I shouldn't have come."

"Why not? We can be together all summer. You, me . . . Todd."

"No, it won't work for me here anymore. Even if my mother were alive, it wouldn't have worked."

"I don't get it."

Cassie thought of showing Robin the letter, but realized it would be like giving away a secret her mother had meant only for her. "My father," she said. "I can't give him what he needs. He should be in Washington. The investigation is what he lives for, what keeps him going."

Robin pulled away from her. "But you can't leave now. I don't want you to . . ."

"There's always Todd." It was a bad attempt at a joke, Cassie knew, and neither of them laughed.

"Anyway, what would you do in D.C. all summer? It's the pits."

Without answering, Cassie took the letter from the purse and tucked it into the pocket of her skirt. "Look, we'll see each other . . . maybe this fall. I'm sure Dad will be going up to Boston."

"Sure."

They hugged again. When Cassie pressed her cheek against Robin's, she could feel that her friend's was wet. Cassie took her arm and they walked down the stairs.

Clay was sitting in the Queen Anne chair in the parlor in his wet jogging shorts, his feet propped up on the captain's trunk, next to a glass half-filled with Glenfiddich. The fire in the hearth gleamed in the opalescent eyes of the figurehead over the mantel, and it was as though the Harpy's presence prevented the crackling flames from taking the chill out of the room.

"I guess I'd better go." Robin brushed her hand across her eyes, then turned abruptly, her rubber zorries slapping against the wood as she ran down the steps. Cassie let out a sigh when the screen door banged shut. Better to part quickly, than face the thought that she might never see Robin again.

When Cassie walked into the parlor and sat down on the arm of her father's chair, she saw that he was twirling a wishbone from the jar in the kitchen. "Ann liked to save up her wishes," he said. "She should never have done that."

"It's not going to work here, is it?"

He looked up, surprised, yet seemingly relieved that she had said it first. "What do you mean?"

"You should be in Washington. Your work is there. And the investigation . . ."

"But you wanted to come here so much . . ."

She didn't answer. Instead, she took the wishbone from him, and held it by one prong. "Wish?"

He took hold of the other end and they both closed their eyes and pulled.

With a snap, the bone shattered into a dozen pieces.

"It looks like neither of us won," he said.

"Maybe . . ." She could feel the letter in her pocket. "Maybe we both did."

Chapter 6

~

Todd hovered eight hundred feet up, with nothing between him and the jagged cliffs but air. And that was the joy of it. Lying prone, he moved forward in the harness and pressed on the control bar with both hands, swooping down, the red wings of his hang-glider riding an air current off the sea, his speed building until he hovered in a stiff up-draft. Like a sea bird, he thought. Or an angel.

The cliffs on the remote, desolate north end of Nantucket, near Point Fear, were perfect for soaring. Once he strapped himself into the hang-glider, all it took was a running leap off the granite escarpment and he was airborne. It called for the same talents as sailing, really —the wings of the hang-glider were even sewn from the same Howe and Bainbridge dacron as the sails of his catamaran. And like sailing, you had to know how to read the wind, its whispers and its howls—even its lies—the way a seemingly innocent freshet could betray with its telltale scent of brine that it was really the advance guard of a gale. Sailing on Nantucket Sound had taught Todd how to harness the wind, but this giddy ride was so much freer, so much more exhilarating, than being tied to the water. Up here, you could dive and soar, and the birds accepted you as one of their own.

He glanced at the air-speed gauge attached to one of the aluminum spars: thirty miles per hour. Too risky. He leaned back on the control bar, raised the angle of attack of the wings against the wind, and gaining altitude, slowed to 25.

He gazed down at the white strip of beach, the sand dunes, the scrub pines that formed a ragged windbreak along the shore. Was that his father digging in the rocky soil on the edge of the dunes, trying to uproot the weeds that overran the lawn around the clapboard church? It was a futile task, Todd knew, but he was grateful that at least it would divert his father's eyes from the sky. If Parson Jedediah Stites saw him hang-gliding it would mean the inevitable sermon on his return: *"Remember Lucifer—even angels can fall."*

Fallen angels were his father's specialty, Todd brooded. Jedediah saw evil everywhere: on the radio, on television, in the movies and newspapers and magazines. Which was why he never left the isolation of Nantucket, and why he expected Todd to be a Nantucket "lifer" too. His father had spent so many years seeking out evil, it was no surprise that he always found it. Before his father was through, even things that weren't evil, he *made* evil, Todd thought, with his hatred. Parson Stites had championed a God so vengeful and unforgiving that he had driven away his congregation, but the preacher hadn't seemed to mind—it had only proved to him that his worst vision of mankind was true.

Todd looked down at the church: his father had deliberately let it decay, as if to prove the power of the evil forces against him. The roof was pocked with broken shingles, the paint was peeling, and the once-gilded cross on the steeple had tarnished black.

The echo of a gunshot. Todd glimpsed the faint puff

of smoke. Maybe it was because he had no more parishioners at which to level his wrath, that his father had taken up his shotgun, polishing and caring for it as lovingly as he used to pore over the doom prophecies of Jeremiah, or the mystical prayers of the Book of Revelation. The evil he had once hunted with his Bible he now stalked with his 12-gauge Browning.

A second echo. His father must have spotted a bird of prey. Each day he would search the skies for the ospreys with their six-foot wingspans and their hooked beaks, that hovered on the thermals, swooping down to seize fish in their talons. Both judge and executioner, his father had branded them evil, like so much else. As Todd wheeled in the air, a giant bird with red wings, he wondered if that was why he had chosen to soar like this—because he wanted to join the enemy, to become one of the wild, free ospreys that circled just out of firing range, taunting his father.

But today Todd hadn't come up here to escape. He had taken to the air to think, to decide whether or not what his father had told him last night was just another of his paranoid visions.

But what if it was true?

Parson Stites knew about evil, there was no denying that. And if there was even the slightest chance that he'd told Todd the truth . . .

How can you possibly believe him? Usually you laugh at his prophecies of doom. What made you listen so carefully last night?

Maybe, he thought, because last night his father hadn't launched into one of his usual tirades, but had spoken with calm certainty. Maybe because this time his father's eyes hadn't been wild with rage, but cool with reason, the way they were when they sighted down the barrel of his gun.

No, that wasn't why his father's words had troubled him so. It was because what his father had said had to do with Cassie Broyles.

In the sky, you didn't have to ponder even the toughest questions for long. The answers just came, as sure and swift as the wind. Already, Todd had decided what he had to do.

There was still enough time to hitch a ride up to Boston, where Cassie was meeting the bus for camp. At first, when she had written that she hoped he would see her off, he had sworn he wouldn't go—not after she had chosen to go to Casmaran instead of spending the summer on Nantucket with him. But after he had mentioned Casmaran to his father, and after his father's warning, he knew he had to go to Boston. To stop her.

A push forward on the control bar was all it took to descend towards the sand dunes behind the church where he had landed dozens of times before. But in his eagerness to get to Cassie, he was letting the dunes rush up towards him more rapidly than usual. (*Take it easy.*) He leaned back on the control bar to ease his descent.

And then . . . it didn't make sense. Another wind was blowing at him, a tail wind, sweeping him towards the cliffs. The sudden fierce turbulence—it must be a shear line, he thought, the clash of two weather fronts that could spawn a wind as fierce as a riptide. *Ride it out— You've got no choice.* He turned into the wind to reduce his speed, and looked for a safe landing place.

The winds on Nantucket—Todd thought he knew them all. But this one wasn't a sheer line, he realized now. This wasn't a wind he had sparred with before. This alien wind smelled different from the morning freshets that blew off the Sound, different from the chilly gusts that telegraphed a gale in the North Atlantic. The wind that howled in his ears blew hot, like the siroccos he had read about that came off the Sahara. He stared up at the sky: if the wind that was toying with him now was so strong, why weren't the clouds moving?

He leaned forward in the harness, pressed down on the control bar with all his weight, to force the glider into a steep dive towards the sand dunes. The air-speed gauge on the aluminum spar pushed 45 miles per hour, his maximum possible speed, but it wasn't enough to free him from the wind's grasp. The gale was sweeping him away, hurling him upwards into the air in a shift of altitude so painfully sudden that his nose started to bleed.

Then, with a sickening snap, the wings of the hang-glider crumpled, like a crushed umbrella. (*Impossible*, he told himself. *The aluminum spars were stress-tested to 6 g's.*)

Todd wasn't soaring anymore. He was falling.

As he streaked to earth, the red wings streaming behind him like the tail of a meteor, he thought he could hear his father's voice resounding from the pulpit, echoing off the cobwebbed pews, speaking of his son as though he were already dead: *"The angels that fall are forever lost."*

In the dizzying acceleration downward, Todd could feel the droplets of blood oozing out of the tear ducts of his eyes, and yet he didn't black out. He could see he was hurtling towards the power station on Point Fear, racing towards a pylon, its girders upthrust like the stark fingers of a hand against the sky. Before he hit the black power cables that snaked to the tips of the steel fingers, a thought raced through him with its own electricity: had his father's vengeful wrath been wise and sane after all? Had he been right, all these years, that dark forces were gathering to dominate the earth?

And he feared for Cassie Broyles.

Then, all of a sudden, the warning that had been so terribly urgent for him to tell her seemed of no importance at all. The hang-glider rammed the high-tension lines, its aluminum spars glowing from the heat, igniting the fabric of the wings. Ten thousand volts of electricity jolted through Todd's body, jerking him like a marionette on a string, endowing his body with movements so lifelike that even the ospreys that wheeled nearby did not swoop in to tear at him with their hooked beaks. The hungry birds of prey would wait until the wind swept the smoldering corpse into the sea, before they devoured it.

Chapter 7

~~~~~~~

"Judging from the clientele," Clay said as he scanned the group that had gathered at Gate 12 of the Boston Municipal Bus Terminal, "Casmaran will probably have Gloria Vanderbilt sheets."

Runt unloaded Cassie's new aluminum footlocker from the trunk of the limousine on the curb and heaved it beside a dozen others that were scuffed and dented, plastered with blue Casmaran decals, as if they had made the same trip for countless summers. Girls in blue shorts and white Casmaran T-shirts were helping each other throw their luggage into the hold of the bus, while others leaned out of the windows, shouting out to late arrivals. *They all know each other,* Cassie thought. *Old friends don't need to make new ones.* She zipped up her hooded sweatshirt to hide the fact that she was wearing a Joffrey Ballet T-shirt instead of the one they wore. She had been admitted to Casmaran too late to order a camp T-shirt of her own.

Clay read the anxiety on her face and put his arm

around her. "You'll meet some kids you like. I'm not worried about that. But the parents . . ." He frowned. "That's another story." He nodded towards the adults who stood in an uneasy line-up against a tile wall sprayed with graffiti. "The president of Mobil . . ." He nodded towards a tall redhead with an expensive Nikon draped over her shoulder. "And that used car salesman she's talking to is the Secretary of Defense . . ."

"*Dad* . . ."

"The blonde with the horn-rims . . . She's some kind of honcho in that think tank at MIT . . ."

"I get the general idea." Cassie hadn't recognized all the faces of the campers' parents, but their uniform was familiar enough: the mothers in silk blouses and Cartier tank watches, the fathers in bright Lacoste shirts, Brooks Brothers slacks, and hand-sewn loafers. At least her father, in his faded Levi's and sweatshirt, hadn't knuckled under to their "*casual chic*," she thought, even after ten years of wielding as much power as they had. "Guess you'd better go over and shake a few hands," she said.

He considered it for a moment, then turned his back on them. "To hell with it."

They walked across the main concourse where clusters of children in camp T-shirts ("*Oiwassa*," "*Tegawitha*," "*Teela-Wooket*") were piling onto buses in a noisy exodus, as if it were a crime to be under sixteen and caught in Boston for the summer.

The humidity was stifling. Clay mopped his brow and led Cassie over to a bench where a sailor was asleep, a copy of *Hustler* over his face to shut out the glare of the fluorescent lights. "Reminds me of the days when I used to take the ferry over from the island, then catch the bus up from the Cape. The 'Combat Zone' . . . that's what they used to call it in Boston . . . where the action was." He glanced back at the Casmaran parents, who were chatting among themselves as if they were at a cocktail party, oblivious to their children. "When do you think was the last time any of *them* set foot in a bus station?''

''When was the last time *I* did?''

''Where have I failed?''

''Face it. You raised me like a rich kid.''

''Correction. Your mother was the one with the money. When *I* went to camp they picked us up in an old army truck. Marine Basic would have been cushier. Talk about tacky. We had to sleep in tents that leaked when it rained, and the cook never bothered to fish the maggots out of the stew.''

''*Please!*''

''At twenty-five bucks a summer, the price was right.''

''Twenty-five dollars?'' Cassie had seen the check he had mailed to Casmaran the week before, for fifteen hundred.

''My folks couldn't even afford that. Camp Cottonwood—we used to call it *Rotten*wood—let me in for free.''

''You almost sound like you wished I was going there.''

''No. That's not it, Cassie.'' His direct blue eyes concealed nothing. ''I don't want you to go. Period.''

''*Dad* . . .''

''I mean, it would be fine with me if you just decided to chuck it and come back to Washington. When I'm not busy we could take off, and . . .''

''You know you're always busy with the investigation.'' Her answer was the same as it had been whenever he had broached the subject. ''I'm going. Mom would have wanted me to.''

He shook his head. ''One thing I *do* know—once a Cunningham woman's got her mind made up, it's better to just . . .''

''Stay down for the count.'' She smiled a little sadly. It was what he had always said when he had yielded to her mother.

''Still,'' he nodded in Runt's direction, ''I'd feel a

hell of a lot better if you'd let me send him along."

"No way! What do you think's going to happen to me? Everyone up there is the kid of someone even richer and more *famous* than you are!"

He laughed. "Thanks!"

"I'll blend in with the crowd. Really."

"I suppose that could be a good thing."

He walked over and slotted a quarter into a Coke machine. It took the coin, but denied him the bottle, and as if to express his anger at more than that petty theft, he banged the machine with his fist until finally the Coke clunked out.

He popped it open, and when Cassie refused his offer of a sip, he nursed it philosophically, staring at the campers and their parents. "Christ, I can't believe I'm doing this. I mean, I would have put up with staying out on the island if that's what you had wanted. Now you get it into your head that you've got to be independent, and what does it mean? I won't see you all summer." He downed the last of the Coke and made a face, as if it were cheap whiskey.

"Casmaran didn't do mother any harm."

"No. She turned out pretty damn well." He looked at the empty bottle before he threw it away, like the last of his objections. "I won't argue with that. But Ann went there twenty-five years ago. If you get up there and find it's a slum . . ."

"You worry too much." She was going to say, *You worry too much, like mother used to*, but stopped herself. The sadness she thought she had under control was starting to well up in her throat, and she didn't want to cry, not when she wanted him to think she had made the right decision.

The yellow school bus with a "Casmaran" sign in the window began to rev up, and it hit Cassie with the engine's roar—she was leaving her father for a place where she wouldn't know a soul.

"Cassie!"

A familiar figure barged through the crowd.

"Robin!" Cassie ran over and hugged her.

"Come on. I saved you a seat."

"But what . . . ?"

"You didn't expect me to stick around Nantucket after I heard where you were going . . ."

"But how . . . ?"

"Are you kidding? My mom's been bugging me to go to Casmaran since *last* summer. She's been driving me out of my gourd, telling me what a great time *she* had."

"Your mother went there, too?"

"Dahling, the girls from *all* the 'right' families wouldn't be caught dead anywhere else." Robin put the back of her hand against her forehead in mock agony: "What I go through for you."

"I'm counting on you to keep Cassie out of trouble, Robin," Clay said. "You're supposed to be the responsible one." At the mention of the word "responsible," the two girls looked at each other and broke up.

Three deafening blasts from the bus horn, and the campers squirmed away from their parents' hasty kisses. Cassie searched for a face in the crowd.

Robin laughed: "You waiting for Todd to come kiss you goodbye?"

"I wrote him . . . I hoped he'd see me off . . ." Cassie said.

"He must be royally pissed. Anyway, how does it go? 'Absence makes the heart grow . . .' " Clay wrapped his arms around Cassie, and Robin stopped herself. "You two are unreal." She climbed into the bus. "If you're thinking about changing your mind, Cass, forget it. I'm not going without you."

Cassie hugged her father tightly. She didn't like the feeling, the two of them balancing in each other's arms, as if one of them were about to fall from a high place. With her eyes closed, the diesel fumes and the din of the jostling mob wrenched her back to another time, another frantic moment. She couldn't block out that other goodbye high on the shuddering scaffolding, so cruel, so unexpected. To escape the memory, she pulled away from him and climbed into the bus.

You chose to do this, she tried to comfort herself as she fought her way down the crowded aisle. *It's what she wanted for you.*

Part Two

THE WARNING HAND

Chapter 8

Cassie tried to figure out how long it had been: the campers had worked their way through "Ninety-nine Bottles of Beer On the Wall" so many times she had lost count, the song a monotonous counterpoint to the knocking engine and the rattle of empty Tab cans rolling back and forth in the aisle. Enough peanut butter cups and Hostess Twinkies had been consumed, their wrappers hurled out of the windows, that they could have used the litter to retrace their route all the way back to Bangor, Maine.

But by now, the girls' voices had grown hoarse, and they stared dumbly ahead, their faces sickly in the pine shadows. The New England brick houses, darkened with coal soot, the lath and plaster English Tudor tracts in the suburbs, had long since given way to a never-ending wall of trees. They had seen their last house, their last person, at the "john" stop an hour ago, and the forest, miles and miles of it, made Cassie begin to wonder whether she had done the right thing to talk her father into letting her go.

Her back ached. The seats of the rickety yellow school bus were little more than benches; their springs —had rusted years ago. In a tight Casmaran T-shirt that showed off her bust and fashionably oversized sunglasses, the counselor who drove hardly turned the wheel at all. The bus sped along, as if it knew the way by heart.

Robin was slumped against Cassie's shoulder, asleep, a smile on her lips. Cassie envied her friend for being able to shut her brain off at moments like this. Hers was always switched on, darting, weaving, twisting around corners like the bus, racing down dark roads before she quite had time to know where she was going, or even where she had been.

The bus jolted through a pothole and Robin woke up. She looked out the window at the same wall of trees that had been there when she had dozed off. "If Casmaran turns out to be the pits," she said, "it's your ass." To distract herself from the thought, Cassie opened the copy of *Cat's Cradle* she had brought along, but the brooding, endless corridor of trees meant that even at noon it was hard to read.

Robin picked up the brochure Cassie had been using to mark her place, the brochure that had come in the mail along with Cassie's acceptance letter, and read it aloud in a melodramatic baritone: " *'The oldest girl's camp in America . . . In operation under the same management since 1889.'* Great. I bet they've also got the same plumbing. *'What began as a retreat devoted to training daughters of prominent New England families in deportment, the household arts, and lawn sports . . .'* Are they kidding? *'. . . now offers a progressive program in a setting of ten-thousand unspoiled acres . . .'* " Robin stuck a finger down her throat as though she were trying to puke.

"Give me a break."

"You won't believe this: *'Casmaran's three C's— Citizenship, Camaraderie and Courage—have remained our hallmark since its founding.'* " Robin turned the brochure over. "No photographs. Are they trying to hide something? Or are they just cheap?"

"They don't need pictures," Cassie said. "Anyone who'd need a brochure to learn about Casmaran wouldn't stand a prayer of getting in anyway."

Robin handed Cassie back the brochure and closed her eyes again. Cassie tried to focus on the forest, but the sunlight strobed through the pine boughs, blurring the trees together into one continuous flight of crows. The forest was so dark that even in daytime, Cassie thought, night bristled here like a thorn thicket, taking root in the rocky soil. When the road narrowed from two asphalt lanes to a single, gravel one, it seemed as though the walls of evergreens would slam shut in a dead end.

The girls behind her broke into song: "*We're here because we're here, because we're here, because we're here . . . !*"

Robin opened her eyes and stretched. "It's about time."

Suddenly the unrelenting wall of evergreens gave way to poplars and birches, and the pine scent dissolved into the aroma of rain-fresh grass. Maples arched their boughs over the road to form an arbor of sun-dappled green. And through the trees, an image shimmered like a mirage, ethereal as a memory. Washed-out in the sun like a faded sepia photograph, were old buildings, but upside down, as if they had been projected out of Cassie's mind's eye. She realized she was seeing a reflection in a lake, the picture so sharp because the water was perfectly still, a mirror-image of the camp. She wondered whether her mother had felt this same exhilaration when she had seen Casmaran for the first time.

The bus doubled back behind a grove of pines and they lost sight of everything. Then the gears whined and clanked as the bus lurched down a final steep grade, the tires churning off the gravel onto dirt. *Casmaran— Founded 1889* a sign scorched on a knotty-pine board announced, and the bus barreled through open split-rail gates. She glanced over her shoulder: the picturesque wooden fense was edged with barbed wire.

The bus rumbled out of the shade into blinding sunshine, and with surprising suddenness, Cassie found herself in the midst of the picture she had glimpsed from a distance. She realized she must have expected a hodgepodge of jerry-built tent-cabins and outdoor privies, like the camp her father had attended. She couldn't have been more wrong. Lining both sides of an impeccably trimmed lawn were freshly painted white clapboard cabins with gingerbread latticework around the eaves, and forest-green windowboxes overflowing with geraniums. Even the smallest of the cottages was solidly built, as if from a time when everything was constructed with a loving attention to detail. At the head of the lawn, austere and dignified between the two rows of cheerful cabins, an enormous windowless structure of ivy-covered granite seemed all the more imposing because it was built up on fieldstones six feet above the ground. Behind it, near the woods, were two smaller, but equally severe granite-faced facades that reminded Cassie of the shelters built to withstand blizzards, where mountain climbers found refuge on Alpine slopes. It seemed as though the buildings—all of them—had been here so long that they had taken root, as natural, as permanent, as the forest. The deep green of the lawn ended in the turquoise blue of the lake. Limpid and serene, the water was a far cry from the brooding, hungry sea, she thought, water that was too clear to hide the ocean's secrets.

The bus lurched to a stop in the dust before the brass-bound doors of the massive stone building which, Cassie guessed, must be the main lodge. The campers shoved their way down the aisle, exploding onto the lawn.

"Please claim your baggage, girls. Every camper is responsible for her own baggage . . ." A counselor in a Lacoste tennis dress and spotlessly white tennis shoes,

with gold ear studs to match the gold chains around her neck, spoke with a politeness that didn't jibe with the bullhorn in her hand.

"If I'd wanted to suck up to debutantes," Robin said, "I would have gone to Newport for the summer."

"Come on, she was probably a camper here herself once," Cassie said.

"That's what I'm afraid of."

Half a dozen other counselors in equally stylish sports clothes waited on the porch of the main lodge as the campers spewed out of the bus, their manicured fingers toying nervously with the whistles on lanyards around their necks.

"*Campers are requested to locate their counselors immediately for bunk-up . . .*"

Clipboards on their hips, the counselors descended the steps of the lodge to the lawn with what Cassie thought was considerable reluctance. The counselors directed, rather than helped, the campers heft their footlockers out of the baggage compartment of the bus, and Cassie edged away from them, starting cautiously across the lawn, as if to get her land legs.

Daisies and snapdragons overran the grass in bright constellations, up to the forest's edge a hundred yards away. Cassie remembered that her mother had mentioned the flowers in her letter, and knelt down and touched the pastel petals. They dissolved between her fingers like sherbet.

Then she stood up and turned slowly, taking it all in: the main lodge, like a fortress, the two smaller, equally severe stone structures behind it, the cheerful white clapboard cabins flanking the lawn. The cabin closest to the lodge was for the seven- and eight-year-olds, she guessed, from the swings and slide beside it. A weathered shed extended out over the lake—probably the boathouse—and half-hidden by a stand of pines was a rambling red barn. Somehow they all seemed in harmony, tied together by the ivy and the wildflowers, the lush grass, and the glittering sweep of the lake. Her mother had been right to think she would love it, she thought.

"This place looks prehistoric," Robin groaned.

"Campers report to their cabins at once, please. Bunk assignments are made on a first-come, first-serve basis . . ."

Cassie ignored the bullhorn, and grabbing Robin's hand, led her away from the cabins.

"You act like you've been here before," Robin said.

"I almost feel like I have."

Behind the lodge, at one end of a baseball diamond, was a square enclosed by a white picket fence, the grass inside mown as smooth as felt.

"Croquet!" Robin shook her head. "Looks like it's going to be one hell of an exciting summer."

Cassie laughed and headed towards the two small stone buildings behind the lodge. One smelled of turpentine and leather, and a frost of sawdust coated the leaded windows. Above the door hung a sign: *"Idle hands are the Devil's workshop."* "Arts and Crafts?" Cassie peered inside through the open door. A rack along one wall gleamed with the blades of a surprising number of chisels and knives.

"Very convenient . . ." Robin pointed to the adjoining granite building, identical, except for the red crosses painted on its shutters. "If you lop off your pinkie with one of those knives in Arts and Crafts, you only have to carry it a few feet to have it sewn back on."

Cassie read a cardboard sign someone had tacked to the infirmary door: *"Germ City."* A lizard scurried up the tiled wall of the waiting room where an aqua vinyl sofa was stacked with dog-eared copies of *Today's Health*. Beyond it was a row of spartan army cots. A tray on a chipped enamel table held a syringe.

"Reminds me of this movie I saw on the late show," Robin said. *"The Torture Chamber of Doctor Sadism."*

"I bet it keeps the kids from getting sick."

"Get this . . ." Robin was studying a chart posted on the door: "*To Tell Whether a Snake is Poisonous.*" Diagrams compared the scale formations, head shapes, and fangs of different species. "God, this is confusing," Robin said. "By the time you figured out if the snake that bit you was poisonous, you'd be dead!"

The trail behind the infirmary weaved through a grove of pines. "What the hell's that?" Robin stopped and gripped Cassie's arm, pointing out a silhouette dimly visible through the trees, a creature about four feet tall, crouched on its haunches. They approached cautiously, pushing aside the pine boughs.

"*Weird.*"

The wooden sculpture had been carved from a single log with crude strokes, like primitive idols Cassie had seen in *National Geographic*.

"A wolf?" Robin ran her fingers over the raised hackles on its back. Cassie stepped closer. Its teeth were bared, and its eyes . . . they were ice-blue luminescent stones, like those on the *Harpy* figurehead that hung over the mantel at Cliff's Edge.

"*Cute,*" Robin said.

Cassie read the plaque at the base of the statue: "*To Soledad, Casmaran's beloved mascot, in fond remembrance (1945–58). Gift of the Seniors, 1958.*"

"Hell of a lot of work for one dead dog. I mean, why didn't they just have him stuffed?"

"You're gross!" Cassie laughed, but she avoided glancing at the statue again.

The trail led them back to the lawn, where a forty-eight-star American flag snapped in the breeze on a flagpole in front of the lodge. Cassie stared down at the sundial at the base of the flagpole. Its copper face had oxidized green with age, and the Roman numerals and signs of the zodiac etched around its edge were barely legible. She read the inscription: "*And at my back I always hear, time's winged chariot drawing near . . .*"

"It's busted," Robin said.

"Come on."

"Seriously." Robin checked her digital watch. "It's 4:58. But this thing thinks it's still noon."

Robin was right. The blade of the sundial shot a shadow over the twelve. It seemed to Cassie as if at Casmaran, time had ground to a halt, as if everything were frozen the way it had been when her mother was there.

"Well, it's been a gas." Robin yawned. "Let's find our cabin and break open the Famous Amos I stashed in my bedroll."

"You go ahead," Cassie said. "There's someone I've got to see."

Miss Grace . . . Cassie wondered why the Director hadn't been there to greet the bus, why she hadn't seen the Director's office among the camp buildings. When she asked a group of campers playing catch on the baseball diamond where to find her, the girls rolled their eyes and laughed. Finally one of them pointed to a trail leading into the woods.

Cassie followed it around the corner of the lodge where an herb garden behind a chicken-wire fence rustled in the wind. She recognized most of the plants: basil and tarragon and flowering sage—herbs her mother had grown on Nantucket—but there were others with red-tipped leaves and barbed branches, their smell so foul she couldn't imagine they could be used in cooking.

The sun hung low over the lake, and in the gathering shadows, she stumbled among a ragged row of granite slabs that thrust out of the ground. It took her a moment to realize that they were headstones, that she was walking through what had once been a cemetery. But why was there a burial ground at a girls' camp? She picked her way through the petrified thicket, squinting to make out the inscriptions. The names of the dead had been worn away by time, no doubt dissolved by a hundred harsh winters along with the bones buried beneath them. On only one stone could she decipher the words:

"Choose Death." Choose death over what? Cassie wondered.

When she emerged from the graveyard at the edge of the woods, and turned back for one final look, something struck her as odd. There were no crosses on the headstones. It looked as though someone had broken them off.

The trail led into a corner of the forest where she hadn't been with Robin. A yellow light in the distance tipped the pine needles with gold, and she headed towards it.

The cottage where the light burned seemed too small to be an adult's house. Sturdy yet whimsical, it looked more like a playhouse built for a child by a wealthy, doting father, the chocolate-brown shutters stenciled with cupids, the door carved with the signs of the zodiac. Dovecotes cut in the shape of rabbits and squirrels adorned the steep, peaked roof, but she could see no pigeons roosting there. Nestled among the trees, the cottage looked like an illustration from a book of Grimm's fairy tales, as cozy as a childhood memory.

She stepped onto the porch, where a single wicker rocking chair creaked in the breeze through the sighing pines. A broad-brimmed straw bonnet hung from a peg on the wall beside an umbrella with an ebony handle. The birdhouse swinging from the eaves was an exact copy of the cottage, right down to the tiny rocking chair on its porch. She gripped the brass knocker on the cottage door and let it fall with a sharp clap. With a flurry of wings, a crow that had been plundering the birdhouse darted away.

She waited. Listened. No answer. She knocked again.

No sign of life. Only the flicker of the gas flame in the coach lamp at the threshold. She tested the door with her toe, and it creaked open.

Inside the cottage, under the low-beamed ceiling, night had already fallen. Heavy lace curtains veiled the windows, smothered the air in their shroud. It felt as if it had been night here for years. "Miss Grace?" she

called, but not too loudly, suddenly unsure whether it
had been right to barge in like this. A grandfather clock
ticked in the stillness, its pendulum missing every third
beat, like a failing heart. She called again, and was
relieved when there was no answer.

Her eyes adjusted to the dim light and she could make
out the flocked wallpaper, a love seat covered in blue
velvet, with wooden legs carved into lions' paws, and
two matching wing chairs, their lace antimacassars
yellow with age.

And everywhere—on bookshelves and table tops and
inside display cases—were fragile porcelain figurines:
Royal Doulton clowns and children with soulful eyes,
Toby mugs winking and leering, and a white unicorn
like the one she had seen in a Cybis ad in the *New
Yorker*. A handful of clay animal figurines, evidently
made in Arts and Crafts, nestled among them, horribly
crude by comparison.

"*I could eat you up!*"

The shrill voice startled Cassie, and she spun around.

"Cassandra Broyles!" A figure hunched motionless
in the shadows before the cold hearth, like one more
porcelain figurine too fragile to touch. With an electric
hum, the wheels of her chair began to turn and it rolled
slowly towards Cassie. "You look just like your
mother!"

Cassie was astounded. How could the old lady know
her name? She had said it with a sigh of satisfaction, as
if relieved to see a long-lost friend after a painful sepa-
ration. "Miss Grace?"

A brittle laugh from the wheelchair. "You expected
Casmaran's Directress to be young, fast on her feet, did
you?"

"No, I . . ."

"Not to worry. I have everything well under control.
Delegation of authority, that's the key. My counselors
are first-rate. But then, why shouldn't they be? They
were Casmaran campers, every last one of them!"

Cassie felt ashamed of herself for having been frightened. Miss Grace was ancient, and a cripple. It had been cruel of the campers to make fun of her. "I wanted to thank you," she said. "For letting me in so late, I mean. I know you turn down a lot of girls, and . . ."

"It was my pleasure, child." She chuckled. "I knew that we would get you at Casmaran sooner or later."

The wheelchair rolled over a floor switch and a fringed Tiffany lamp on a side-table blinked on. Cassie could see Miss Grace more clearly, her skin almost transparent, a thin membrane revealing veins and arteries beneath it, like frayed wiring, her dark red lipstick outlining lips that had all but vanished with age. A hairnet as fine as a spiderweb held her silken-white chignon in place, and the robe wrapping her frail body was as silvery as her hair, the heavy satin, Cassie thought, that you were either baptized or buried in. Cassie's own maternal grandmother had never looked that old, not even at the age of ninety, when Cassie had visited her in her sickroom on Beacon Hill. The senile old woman had so hated facing her deteriorating body that she'd ordered all mirrors removed from the house.

"I do wish I could welcome you with a big hug. But *quel dommage*," Miss Grace sighed, "I'm as good as dead from the neck down." Her hands lay still in her lap, their faded lace gloves revealing patches of flesh as yellow as the fabric covering them. Miss Grace smiled gratefully as Cassie took her hand. It felt terribly light, as if the old lady's bones were hollow, like a bird's, and Cassie set it down carefully, afraid the least pressure would break it.

"To see you at long last . . ." Miss Grace's voice trailed off. Her eyes were clouded with cataracts, as glazed as the eyes of the Toby mugs lining the mantel, and Cassie felt as if the old woman's distant stare was really seeking out the spark of her mother within her, poring over memories: "What a gift to be able to lay eyes on you before . . . Well, none of us is going to be here forever, are we, Cassandra?"

Cassie sensed the old lady was fishing for a compliment. "You look very well to me."

"Your mother wasn't much of a fibber, either," she chuckled, "but thank you, dear. Thank you, anyway." Her laugh ended in a dry cough. "You know, child, your mother was one of the sweetest young ladies ever to bunk up with us at Casmaran. The horrid event that took her—*quelle tragédie*—it was like losing a daughter. But then, she must have told you how fond we were of each other."

"Oh, yes." Cassie thought of the letter. Her mother *had* been writing her like a daughter. But why hadn't she ever mentioned Miss Grace—or Casmaran—to her?

"I feel I'm in the strangest sort of limbo," Miss Grace murmured. "Betwixt and between. Right now I'm with you. Tomorrow I may be traveling over to join your mother, on the Other Side."

"Don't talk like that," Cassie said, feeling it was expected of her.

"Well, when I do make the journey, I'll tell her just how splendidly you turned out." Cassie squirmed, and as if sensing her discomfort, Miss Grace sealed her thin lips. She twitched her head, and Cassie realized she was gesturing to the table beside her. Careful to avoid knocking over a sculpture of etched glass—Jonah inside the whale—Cassie picked up a china cup of what smelled like green tea and raised it to the old lady's lips. "I must make a pretty picture . . . a fine sight!" Miss Grace said, the liquid dribbling down her chin. "Growing old is never beautiful, Cassandra. The tragedy is not that one feels old—but that one feels young!" Cassie wiped the corners of Miss Grace's mouth with the hankie on her lap. The lipstick left a dark stain on the lace. She wanted to ask about her mother, wanted to hear what she had been like when she was her age, but Miss Grace rambled on: "I'd like to be right out there with my girls, of course: soccer and swimming and riding . . . I was quite an equestrian in my day. Now . . ." She shot a glance towards a brass telescope on a tripod by the window. "I still keep an eye

on things. But every year the woods grow thicker . . ."
She laughed. "Pretty soon all I'll be able to see are the
crows in the trees!" Cassie offered her another sip from
the cup, and tea dripped from the old lady's mouth onto
Cassie's hand. Cassie wiped it away quickly, as if old
age might be catching.

"I used to have Soledad to keep me company, bless
his soul . . ."

"Your dog?" Cassie remembered the wolflike statue
in the woods, with its shimmering eyes.

"The girls wanted to buy me another pet after he
passed on, but I don't have to tell you, Cassandra, how
once you lose a loved one, it's impossible to try to
replace it."

Cassie squirmed at the awkward comparison to her
mother, but excused it—the old woman must be senile.

"Don't misunderstand me, Cassandra. My life isn't
as lonely as it sounds. I have many wonderful com-
panions." With an electric hum, Miss Grace's chair
whirled around and Cassie followed her out of the
parlor into an alcove bare of furniture. Its walls were a
mosaic of photographs of campers from floor to ceiling,
a shrine in faded sepia, black-and-white, and color,
each picture framed in wood or mother-of-pearl or
sterling silver. *"This,"* Miss Grace's eyes widened,
"This is my immortality."

Cassie stepped closer. In a sepia photo girls were wading in the lake, wearing bloomers that extended to the
ankles, but with looks of daring on their faces, as if they
were being photographed stark naked. In another, a girl
in a striped cape, the word "Liberty" lettered on a tinsel
crown, held a wooden sword to the throat of a kneeling
girl dressed as the Kaiser.

"We've given the Republic doctors, lawyers, judges
. . . Leaders in business. Three first ladies," Miss Grace
said. "Behind many an important man, there's been a
Casmaran girl." She made a little smacking sound with
her lips, and Cassie guessed she was relishing a sermon
she repeated to everyone who had ever visited her here.

"We were preaching equality long before all this Women's Lib nonsense. Our girls have always been doers—not just a bunch of empty-headed debutantes. They marched in the vanguard of women's suffrage and the Temperance crusade, though I must confess I always found the Temperance thing a bit silly . . ." She continued without taking a breath: "Of course, Casmaran can't take *all* the credit. Our campers have always been of good family . . . the *finest* families. They come to us girls, and they leave young ladies."

Cassie was scanning the pictures on the wall. "Is my mother here?"

With a sudden hum of the motor, Miss Grace edged her wheelchair forward until her forehead almost touched a photograph in a baroque gilt frame. "Don't you recognize her?" Cassie studied the three girls in leotards sashed with chiffon scarves who were standing beneath a pagoda roof, their arms encircling each other's waists. The girl in the middle—Cassie felt as if she were looking at a photograph of herself. "Quite a remarkable resemblance, isn't it?" Miss Grace chuckled. Cassie nodded: the high cheekbones, the almond-shaped eyes, the long neck—a dancer's neck— were so like her own. "Your mother danced the solo on Visiting Day that year . . ."

"A solo?"

"I don't think I can recall a more enchanting performance before or since," Miss Grace said. "I was the dance instructor then, of course."

"You were?" It seemed impossible that this old lady could ever have danced. To be trapped in a wheelchair . . . For a dancer, Cassie thought, it must have been like a death sentence.

"I hear you're quite a ballerina too, Cassie."

"I used to be. Since she died, I . . ."

"Think how proud your mother would be if you danced the solo this year, just like she did back then. Right in her 'ballet slippers,' so to speak."

"No, I . . ."

"It won't be easy, of course. Several of the other girls are quite talented, I'm told. They ought to give you a good run for your money, competing for the part. But you, my dear Cassandra . . . it's in your *blood*!"

Cassie studied her mother's picture again. Something troubled her about it. Her mother had always said that the expression on a dancer's face was as important as the movement of her body. Yet something about her expression in the picture—it seemed so out of harmony with her graceful pose . . . Was it a look of longing?

Or fear?

Before Cassie could be sure, the Tiffany lamp switched off as Miss Grace's wheelchair glided out of the alcove, denying Cassie a final look at her mother's face.

The grandfather clock chimed five times. "*Tempus fugit*," Miss Grace sighed, her chair whirring over until it nudged the back of Cassie's legs. "Your counselor will be cross with me if she finds out I kept you here during bunk-up."

Cassie followed her to the door: "I'd like to come back sometime. I'd like to talk to you about . . ."

"Your mother?" Cassie nodded. "I knew her well, child. In some ways, I suppose you might say I knew her better than anybody. Come any time. Any time at all." When they reached the door the old woman cleared her throat. "Haven't we forgotten something?" she murmured in a coy singsong.

The way she tilted her head and closed her eyes told Cassie that the old lady was expecting a kiss. She leaned towards her, close enough to smell Miss Grace's hair. It had a strangely seductive scent, the odor of musk. How bizarre, she thought—how *wrong*—for so old a woman. Cassie forced her lips towards Miss Grace's cheek.

But the old woman's head twisted. Her mouth joined Cassie's and . . . was it only Cassie's imagination?

No, she could feel it. Taste it.

Miss Grace's tongue flicked into her mouth.

Cassie straightened up and Miss Grace smacked her

lips as if she had just had dessert. "A pleasure to meet you at long last, Cassandra. And when you come next time, I'll tell you all about your mother." Cassie was backing toward the door. "Rest assured. You'll have a wonderful time at Casmaran. You'll love it every bit as much as she did. One summer with us and you'll be a changed girl!"

Chapter 9

Sunset stained the western sky scarlet, like a telltale smudge of Miss Grace's lipstick. In her breakneck dash through the woods from the cottage, Cassie glimpsed a swarm of bats spinning up from the eaves of the lodge, spiraling into the dark, a corkscrew of doubt twisting into her mind. The taste of Miss Grace's kiss soured in her mouth. How could her mother have loved the old woman with her scent of musk, and her horrible scarlet lipstick, and . . . How old had Miss Grace said she was? At her age it would be surprising if she *weren't* a bit unhinged, Cassie comforted herself, relieved to see the lipstick-red smudge in the sky fade to gray. But the gathering dusk brought an indistinct recollection. The dark scent as she ran from the cottage through the pines . . . The dark scent . . . It was the smell of her mother's coffin.

Her father had only let her look inside it after she had begged him—her mother wouldn't look the same as she had in life, he'd warned—but Cassie had insisted on one last glimpse, to seal the memory. When they opened the half-lid lined with quilted white satin, she had turned away quickly. Not because the embalmers hadn't done a good job hiding the damage. They had done their job too well. Lying on the satin pillow, with her hands folded over her chest, Cassie's mother had been reduced to a marble statue, hard and cold.

Her pace slowed. The pine scent permeated her clothes, her hair, and the smell was an unsettling reminder: nothing could free her mother from the pine box.

As she neared the lake, Cassie suspected that she had not left the Chill behind in Nantucket. It had caught up with her, ambushed her here. At least you knew the dangers when you plunged into the sea, she thought; the sharp horns of the whitecaps, the roar of the breakers gave warning. But the lake was deceptively innocent, concealing its own sea-chill.

And yet, what was she afraid of, really? A crippled old lady? She knew what her father would have said about Miss Grace: "*When you're poor, they call you crazy, but when you're rich, they just call you eccentric.*" Eccentric . . . that was the word for Miss Grace, eccentric, and undoubtedly senile. But why should the kiss of a crippled old lady instill her with the Chill?

Cassie looked up to see that she had wandered away from the cabins and was standing at the lake's edge before an open-air pavilion painted Chinese red, with the upturned roof of a pagoda. One end jutted over the water, while the other thrust into the forest, where the pine trees provided a green backdrop. A woman in a black leotard, her legs bare, spun across the stage in circles, as if dancing to the rhythm of the waves that lapped at the pilings below. Cassie stopped to watch her, realizing that this was where the photograph of her mother had been taken. The openness, the lofty trees, the breathtaking vista of the lake . . . Cassie could understand why her mother had danced here.

When the woman saw her, she tossed her long white-blonde hair behind her shoulders and walked to the edge of the stage. Back-lit by the sunset, her lithe legs and slender arms seemed silvered with a faint layer of down. Her delicate features, her pearl-gray eyes that reflected the water, made her seem vulnerable, despite her confident smile. "Cassie Broyles?" she called to her.

"How did you know my name?"

"It's my job. I'm Sarah, your counselor." She pulled on a baggy sweatshirt. "Everyone else is already bunked up . . . I thought you'd taken one look at Casmaran and turned around and hitched a ride home . . ."

"No, I . . ." Cassie decided not to tell her about visiting Miss Grace. "That was nice . . . the dancing," she said.

"You think so? I dance at Bennington nine months a year. Up here I just fool around. But I figure I might as well take advantage of my last free summer. After I graduate, I'll have to head for New York and see if I can make it."

"The ABT . . .?"

"Or the New York City . . . or the Joffrey . . . whoever will have me." She held out a hand and boosted Cassie onto the stage. "Anyway, this is still my favorite place to dance." She did a quick series of jetés across the polished wood floor. "Maybe the reason I like it here so much is that I don't have to compete with anybody. I don't even have to have an audience if I don't want. There's only one problem," she laughed. "If you mess up on a sequence . . ." She stopped herself short on the brink of the lake. ". . . you end up doing *water* ballet." Cassie managed a laugh, but kept her distance from the edge.

Though her feet were planted on the floor, Sarah's body was swaying, as if she were fighting the urge to dance. Her mother used to do that, Cassie remembered, her body responding to the rhythm of the music even when her legs could no longer perform with agility.

Cassie ran a cautious foot across the floor and Sarah noticed: "It's amazingly smooth, isn't it? At least the ice was good for something."

"Ice?"

"This is where they stored it. The ice wore the floor down over the years."

"I don't understand."

"Before the Sisterhood started a camp here, Lake Casmaran was an ice settlement in the winter. That's why some of the buildings, you know, like the lodge and the other stone structures—this one, too—were built so high off the ground."

"Why?"

"To be above the snow line. Some winters the drifts get five . . . six feet deep."

"But the ice . . . what did they want it for?"

"In the late 1800s, before refrigeration, there used to be a lot of money in it. Men would actually come all the way up here to live in the dead of winter. Can you imagine? When it was twenty, thirty below, they'd be out there on the ice, driving horses dragging these huge plowlike contraptions . . . The runners had jagged blades, like saws, to cut into the ice. They had to criss-cross the lines, slice deeper and deeper until the huge chunks finally broke apart. Then some poor guy had to go out there with a big hook, pry the blocks out, drag them across the ice and dump them into an insulated storage shack . . ." She pointed across the lake. "You can still find a couple of the old shacks over there. When spring came, they'd stack the blocks of ice here, for shipping out."

"To where?"

Sarah was squinting out at the water, as if trying to look back in time. "There's no telling how many poor souls lost arms or legs when the saws slipped, or how many drowned out there—or froze to death. Just so people in Boston and New York could have ice cream in the summer."

"Ice cream?"

"Until somebody, I forget who, invented the refrigerator."

"I think it was Edison," Cassie said politely.

"It turned this place into a ghost town. The Sisterhood must have picked it up for nothing. To save money, they even used some of the original buildings . . ."

"Like the lodge?"

Sarah nodded. "All they had to do was put up a few cabins, with the appropriate Victorian gingerbread trim, and they had a camp for *proper* young ladies." The way she emphasized the word made Cassie laugh. "The old biddies who started this place were convinced that city life was corrupting the flower of America's womanhood. They wanted a camp to foster the right values . . . especially virginity."

"I don't suppose they ever thought of making it coed."

"Are you kidding? I don't think a man's set foot here since the last ice cutter left. No boys' camp across the lake, like every other girls' camp in Maine. Not even a gardener. Miss Grace would never stand for it. Someone told me once that she's been here since day one. Anyway, she's ancient . . ."

Cassie laughed: "Prehistoric!" Somehow, seeing how offhandedly Sarah dismissed the old woman reassured her.

Sarah put a hand on Cassie's shoulder as they climbed down the steps of the pavilion. "It's not as bad as it sounds, though. The boy thing, I mean. When I was a camper here, it was a relief to get away from that kind of pressure for a few weeks."

"I know what you mean."

"Do you dance?"

"I used to. Before . . ."

"I know about your mother. I'm sorry." Sarah quickened her pace, as if she understood the subject was a painful one, to be passed over briskly. "I teach some modern dance, some ballet. Mostly it's just . . . I guess you'd call it *'free expression.'* That may sound hokey, but it isn't, really. This place seems to inspire it." She glanced back at her. "Maybe you'll join us . . . try out for the Visiting Day Show." She laughed. "It isn't exactly the Joffrey. But it's a pretty big deal in this part of Maine."

"Maybe . . ." Cassie looked over her shoulder. The dance pavilion had already vanished among the trees, like another of her mother's memories. "Maybe I will."

Only one more cabin, its roof of blue slate, its tidy windowbox overflowing with geraniums, was left before the lake. "Is this ours?" Cassie asked.

Sarah kept on walking. "You're in luck. You're in Lakeside."

The building that Cassie had guessed was a boathouse jutted over the water. Its planking had weathered gray and it had none of the gingerbread trim, none of the bright red flowers, that gave the other cabins their charm. As she walked up the ramp over the shore bristling with cattails, she could smell the rotting pilings in the lake-bed. Her stomach rocked with a sudden queasiness, an early warning of the Chill.

Sarah misread her discomfort. "I know, Lakeside's not as cutesy from the outside as the other cabins. We don't have the fresh paint. But we've got *atmosphere*." The floorboards creaked underfoot as they stepped onto the porch, and Cassie grabbed the railing to keep her balance. "In case you didn't guess, this used to be a boathouse." Sarah held the screen door open for her. "Another one of Miss Grace's bright ideas to save a few bucks, no doubt."

The pandemonium inside the barnlike room cut her off. Half a dozen girls were cheering on a camper with a single blonde braid who was swinging from a rusty chain that hung from the rafters. As the chain reached the peak of its arc, she took a flying leap onto one of the top bunks.

"Jo!" Sarah called, and the cheering died. "Those

were for hanging boats, not campers." She gazed up at the roof, where more rusty chains were knotted to the rafters. "How did you get it *down*?"

"Easy," Jo said. "All I did was . . ."

"I don't want to know." Sarah leveled a commanding gaze at the girls. "Casmaran has never had a camper seriously injured, and I don't intend to let the first be one of mine. I guess the best way to discourage you is to remind you that the nearest hospital—the nearest *anything*—is 150 miles away."

"There's always 'Germ City,' " a voice from the rear of the cabin called, and the girls laughed.

"*Ladies*, I'd like you to meet the latest addition to our motley crew . . ." Cassie tensed, expecting the inevitable. "*the Senator's daughter whose mother was tragically . . .*" Instead, Sarah introduced her simply as "Cassie Broyles." No one seemed the least bit impressed. They were daughters of famous parents, too, she reminded herself, and she tried to figure out whose child each of them was. She stopped herself: that was exactly what they'd come here to escape.

The girls returned to their unpacking with a vengeance, piling the shelves between their bunks with bikini underpants and copies of *Seventeen*, taping up posters—Pelé, Rick Springfield, a soulful basset hound. No snapshots of boyfriends, Cassie noticed, and wondered if that was because no one wanted to expose herself to the teasing that would bring.

The two bare bulbs that burned overhead revealed the walls were hung with varnished oars and red, orange and green signal flags, but it was hard to tell whether the nautical gear had been put there for decoration, or merely for storage. In either case, it did little to cheer up the cavernous room. Neither did the two old lifesavers under the windows, stenciled "U.S.S. LAKESIDE."

Cassie spotted Robin sprawled on a lower bunk in the corner, furtively nibbling a chocolate chip cookie from the bag concealed under her pillow. She started towards her, but Sarah took her arm.

"I'd like you to meet Chelsea Winfield, Cassie. We don't get many girls from Los Angeles."

"*Beverly Hills*," the girl in blue plastic rollers and a flowered kimono corrected her.

"Chelsea tops Casmaran's best-dressed list. She always comes to camp with enough clothes to last *two* summers, and enough *Chanel Number 5* to fill Lake Casmaran." Sarah patted a well-worn teddy bear on Chelsea's pillow. "And she only sleeps with what's-his-name . . ."

"Pooh," Chelsea said. "As in Pooh-ber-ty."

When Cassie held out her hand, Chelsea fluttered her fingers without taking it. "The nails." They glistened with wet polish, a frosted purple.

"*Summer Fling*," Sarah read from the bottle of nail polish, and the others in the cabin hooted appreciatively. She nudged Cassie to the next bunk: "This is . . ." A wave of static drowned her out. A girl with frizzy russet hair, in a Wings T-shirt, was fiddling with the dial of a transistor radio.

"Melanie, would you *mind*?" The girl switched off the radio and pulled a mini-TV from her footlocker. Though she clicked from channel to channel, the screen was filled with snow. "Melanie goes into withdrawal every summer when she comes up here," Sarah said. "No radio. No TV. She keeps hoping that civilization will creep a little bit closer, but it never does. Besides, Lake Casmaran is sitting in what was once a volcanic crater. The hills around us were the rim. They block out everything. Even if there *were* someone out there beaming Rod Stewart at us, or 'Dallas,' God forbid, we wouldn't be able to receive it. Sorry, Melanie, but it's strictly live entertainment from now on."

"Next year I'm bringing Pac-Man." Melanie stashed the TV back in her footlocker, then slumped down beside the girl with the blonde braid who was playing blackjack against herself. "Deal me in."

"Jo McGuire," Sarah said to Cassie. "Resident card shark." Jo dealt the cards, and even before Melanie

could rearrange hers, fanned out her own winning hand.
"Just because your father wheels and deals on Wall
Street, Jo, doesn't mean you can pull that stuff here."
She eyed the six Hershey bars they were using as the pot.
"And no selling candy, either, okay?"

A reluctant echo: "Okay."

"What do you expect?" someone called. "McGuire's
practically part Jew."

"If she was," another voice added, "she'd never be
at Casmaran."

Jo didn't so much as look up as she dealt another
hand, shielding her cards, but Sarah scooped them up:
"I'll just put these somewhere nice and safe, in case you
get desperate later." She took the cards to the cot by the
door and opened a worn wicker trunk, dropping them
inside.

"This is *my* space." Sarah took some dried herbs
from a tin canister in her trunk and pressed them into a
tea strainer. "I don't want anyone messing with it." She
dropped the tea strainer into an earthenware cup and
poured in steaming water from an electric teapot on the
floor. "And another thing. I don't care if you find a
corpse hanging from one of those things . . ." She
pointed up at the sharp hooks of the boat chains dangling from the ceiling. "I do yoga at dawn, and I don't
want anyone bugging me till I'm through. Not that any
of you characters will be up that early." As an after-
thought, she added, "Did you meet everyone, Cassie?"

Chelsea blew on her nails. "I don't think Cassie met
our *scholarship girl*."

"That's right." Sarah's tone grew gentler, as if she
were talking about someone who bruised easily. "Iris
Paletti is new this summer, too," she said, gesturing
towards a bunk in a shadowy corner.

"Charity case," Chelsea mumbled under her breath,
and Sarah shot her a look.

"Maybe it would be nice if you went over and talked
to her," Sarah said to Cassie.

Lakeside's "charity case" looked different from the

Waspy girls in the cabin, Cassie thought. Iris' eyebrows were thick, and almost met above her nose, and her skin was so sickly pale that it made her deep-set brown eyes seem almost black. She wore a faded Red Socks T-shirt and Madras bermudas, obvious hand-me-downs a size too large for her, which made her look even thinner than she was. Iris had the body of a ten-year-old, Cassie thought.

But her face—there was something about Iris' face that made her seem very old, her eyes an old lady's eyes, sad from memories. Sitting on her bunk in the corner, staring out at Cassie with those big, dark eyes, she reminded her of a trapped, frightened animal. Remembering that her father had been a "charity case," too, Cassie extended her hand. "Hi."

"Hi." Iris' clasp was weak, and her faint smile revealed crooked teeth. Probably the only girl in camp who hadn't gone to an orthodontist, Cassie thought. When Iris spoke, her voice was faint, but the words tumbled out, as if she were afraid that saying them too slowly would leave them open to criticism. "I was very sorry to hear about what happened to your mother. I . . ."

"Thanks." Cassie wanted to cut it short.

Iris didn't take the hint. "I read about it in the paper. I mean, even before I knew that you were going to be at Casmaran, I prayed for you. The Lord took your mother away from you so suddenly, it must . . ."

"It wasn't the Lord! It was some bastard with a gun."

"I'm . . . I'm sorry." Iris' voice shrank to a whisper. "I said the wrong thing."

"She's real good at *that*," Robin said from her bunk across from Iris'.

"You can sleep with me if you want," Iris said to Cassie. "My bottom bunk's free. I mean, I don't wet my bed or anything." When nobody laughed, she bit her lip.

"Thanks, but I'm bunking with my friend." Cassie

hefted her sleeping bag onto the mattress above Robin.

"If Iris starts in with the 'Hail Mary's' after lights-out," Chelsea said, "she's going in the lake."

Iris turned away from them to face the crucifix she had tacked over her bed: Christ contorted in agony, the gilt edges of the cross gleaming. As far as Cassie was concerned, religion was a crock. Sure, her family had made a production of Christmas gifts. But Clay's father had been a staunch freethinker who had refused to set foot in a church. The only time Clay went to services was right before an election—it was the one really hypocritical thing she had ever seen him do. Cassie had never thought much about God. Not until her mother's death. Since then, she had decided that if God could have permitted someone like her mother to be murdered, He was a shit.

As she watched the frail girl cross herself and mumble a prayer, Cassie allowed herself the luxury of anger. At least it kept her from feeling like an outsider. Compared to Iris, she belonged.

When she climbed onto Robin's upper bunk, her friend grabbed her foot playfully. "No rocking."

"Come on." Cassie lowered her voice, looking around to make sure no one had heard. "I don't rock anymore."

She was lying. After her mother's death she had returned to the childhood habit of rocking herself to sleep, moving back and forth on the mattress to the rhythm of one of her mother's lullabies. Not that it had done much good. She hoped she wouldn't feel the need to do it here.

Cassie climbed onto the bunk, unrolled her sleeping bag and smoothed out the down quilting, then sprawled on top of it, bone-weary. Her gaze was drawn to the rafters. From among the sharp boat hooks that dangled on rusty chains, two yellow eyes stared down at her. She sat up with a start.

"Hey, take it easy," Jo laughed from a neighboring bunk. "That's just Midnight, the camp cat. She must be looking for a place to have her kittens. She has a litter every summer, like clockwork.''

When the cat with thick blue-black fur and a stub of a tail crept into the shadows, Cassie sank back onto the pillow, but more cautiously. Casmaran hadn't been the way her mother's letter had promised . . . not quite. She could still taste Miss Grace's kiss in her mouth, and wondered whether she had been too impulsive, deciding to come here. *But your mother loved Miss Grace,* Cassie thought. *She loved it here.* Wasn't that enough to forgive what had happened in the cottage? Besides, there was Sarah, she told herself. Her counselor—her friend, she hoped—would more than make up for the eccentric old lady.

Still, she wasn't ready to close her eyes, not yet. The cabin had a strange smell: the musty odor of rotting wood and stagnant water. The sharp boat hooks clanked together gently in the rafters as waves slapped against the pilings, and for a moment it felt as if the whole cabin were a boat, far out at sea.

Chapter 10

"Bug juice?"

Jo slid a pitcher down the redwood table and Cassie peered inside. Warily, she poured herself a cup of the inky fruit punch.

"Mystery Meat?" Melanie passed a platter of gray roast beef, and Cassie helped herself, realizing that she hadn't eaten anything since the donut she had split with her father that morning. As she speared a piece with her fork, she felt as though someone were watching her hungrily from behind. It was the stuffed animal heads that lined the masonry wall, a dozen of them—elk and deer, and a mangy fox—their gláss eyes aglow with light from the wagon wheel chandeliers that hung from the high wood rafters.

The shouts and laughter of eighty campers, the clatter of melmac plates, echoed in the barnlike lodge, and Chelsea leaned towards Cassie and Robin to be heard: "You new guys better chow down. After the first day, this slop gets worse."

The others at the table started wolfing down their food, but Iris stopped them with a birdlike flutter of her hand. "We haven't said 'grace.'" She folded her hands on the edge of the table and closed her eyes.

"What does she think this is?" Jo mumbled, her mouth full. "The Last Supper?"

The campers laughed and continued eating, but Iris furrowed her brow and closed her eyes, her lips moving in a silent prayer.

Jo put her hand to her mouth and made a farting sound. Iris bit her lip and squeezed her eyes more tightly shut, continuing her prayer. But when Melanie and Chelsea began a raucous chorus of *"Onward Christian Soldiers,"* she looked like she was about to cry.

"Leave her alone!" Cassie said, surprised that she had been the one to come to Iris' defense, uncomfortable to receive her grateful stare.

"Well, what do you know?" Chelsea licked gravy from her fingers. *"Two* Jesus freaks."

Don't blow it, Cassie warned herself. *Here you've begun to feel as if you might actually fit in at Casmaran, that your cabinmates might accept you—even like you. Why risk it all by siding with a loser—a girl you can't stand yourself?*

Iris' lips formed *"Amen,"* and slowly, deliberately, she made the sign of the cross over her chest.

"Hallelujah!" Jo flailed her hands over her head, minstrel style. *"Praise de Lawd!"*

"Will you just *can* it?" Cassie cut Jo off, and the others stared at her. She knew now why she felt so protective of Iris. Iris looked as painfully sensitive, as vulnerable, as Cassie felt, a reflection of the small, scared part of herself. The more the others picked on Iris, the more it threatened her—she could so easily be their next target.

"Can we help it, Cassie," Chelsea said, "if God is dead at Casmaran?"

"He's not dead," Melanie interrupted her. "He just couldn't get in!"

"It *is* kind of weird," Cassie said. "I mean, a camp as tight-ass as this . . . you'd think they'd have some kind of chapel or something."

"We're sitting in it," Iris said.

"What?"

"This building. It used to be a church."

"Sure it was."

"Right, Iris."

"Really." The sudden certainty in Iris' voice forced the others to pay attention. She pointed to the raised platform at the end of the room where extra dining tables and benches were stacked. "There's where the preacher stood. And the pews were here . . ." Little holes, like animal tracks, extended across the wood-planked floor, as if nails had been ripped out. "It wasn't a *Catholic* church, of course," Iris continued. "It would have had much more elaborate detail: vaulted ceilings, stained-glass windows . . . that kind of thing. This church had no windows at all. It must have been built by one of those rigid, old-time Protestant sects. Maybe even Puritan."

"If this was a church," Chelsea said, "where's the 'Big C'?"

Iris pointed to the wall above them. An elk's head, its antlers laced with cobwebs, peered down at them with glazed eyes.

"Good one, Iris."

"She's right," Cassie said. "Look." Partly concealed by the animal's head was the silhouette of a cross, a shadowy afterimage, like the mark left when after years of hanging in the same place, a picture frame is removed from a wall.

"Now I know how Iris won the scholarship," Robin said. "She's smarter than all you dipshits put together."

Iris started to smile, but Chelsea cut it short: "She may have a 175 IQ, but she's only got a twenty-eight bust."

"Just cool it!" Cassie said. This time the others didn't laugh.

"Why would anyone build a church in the middle of nowhere?" Robin asked.

"The ice men," Cassie said.

"The what?"

"Sarah told me about them . . . these guys who used to work up here in the winter, a hundred years ago, before Casmaran was started. They would cut the ice up with these huge blades, and sell it in the cities during the summer. A lot of them must have drowned in the lake—or frozen to death. That explains the old graveyard out back; they probably needed a church for all the funerals."

"The church must have been abandoned when they left," Iris said, gazing up at the spot where the cross had hung.

Cassie looked at the leathery meat on her plate. "Casmaran seems to have a thing about leftovers, even leftover buildings." The girls at the table laughed, and she was glad for the chance to distance herself from the religious talk. She had avoided churches since the memorial service for her mother in the Capitol chapel, where the minister's words had echoed hollowly off the statues of the saints lining the vaulted nave. His assurances of Eternal Salvation had sounded as empty to her as campaign promises.

Melanie passed a plate of Oreos around the table, and the girls stuffed handfuls in their pockets for later. But Iris toyed with the cooked carrots on her plate.

"What's the matter?" Chelsea looked Iris' frail body up and down. "On a diet?"

"She pigs out on Communion Wafers . . ."

Iris hunched on the bench as if bracing for another barrage.

"Watch this!" To stop the taunts, Cassie grabbed a straw, bit off the end of the wrapper, then dipped it in the mashed potatoes. She tilted her head back and blew—the wrapper sailed up towards the stuffed elk's head and stuck on its nose. The girls stamped their feet and shouted encouragement, but before she could do it again, a hand snatched the straw from her mouth. "You're a regular riot."

It was Sarah.

The others plunged their straws back into their fruit punch, awaiting Cassie's punishment. But instead, Sarah offered her a hand up from the bench. "You've got a call."

"How does *she* rate?" Chelsea exploded. "I thought we weren't allowed to use the phone up here!"

"It's an emergency," Sarah said.

"So? My boyfriend's an emergency."

Robin eyed Cassie suspiciously: "If it's Todd I'll kill you."

But Cassie didn't hear her. She was already halfway to the phone, her mind racing. *Something's happened to daddy. I should have stayed with him . . . now they've got him, too.*

The phone hung on the wall of the Library Corner, where three unraveling wicker chairs faced an L-shaped bookcase lined with dusty Nancy Drew books, and a complete set of *The Book of Knowledge*, 1948 edition. Cassie grabbed the dangling receiver and stood on tiptoe to reach the mouthpiece of the old-fashioned wall phone.

"Hello?"

"Cassie!" It was Clay's voice.

She realized that she had been holding her breath, and let it out in a long sigh. "Are you okay?"

"What about you?"

"You scared me. They said it was an emergency."

"It is. I miss you!"

Cassie laughed with relief. "I miss you, too." The words had spilled out automatically, but she realized as soon as she'd said them that they weren't true.

"I've been thinking, honey . . . I know you thought camp was a good idea at the time . . ."

"*You* did, too!" She knew what was coming.

"But maybe this summer . . . I mean, wouldn't it be better if . . . ?"

"I'm fine here. Really."

A pause on the other end. She knew he was rethinking his strategy, formulating a new argument. "Honey, it would be okay with me if you invited Robin to come down to Washington. We've got plenty of room, and . . ."

"I want to stay, Dad. The kids are great, and the counselors are neat, too." The silence on the other end of the line told her he wasn't convinced. "Can you do me a favor?" she added. "I forgot my ballet shoes. They're in my closet. Do you think you could mail them up here?"

"You're dancing! That's great!" The elation in his voice said that he'd let her stay. "You'll get them day after tomorrow. Special delivery."

"You'll come up and see me, won't you? On Visiting Day?"

"Visiting Day?"

"They put on this program . . . Mom danced in it, and I . . ." She stopped herself, fearing that she might not get the part.

"I wouldn't miss it, honey."

"I'll see you then." A sudden silence in the lodge startled her and she turned around. The girls had stopped eating. They were staring at her, all eighty of them, gazing at her as if she had committed some terrible crime. Her voice rang hollowly in the stillness: "Dad, I've got to go."

"I'll call again tomorrow."

"No, don't. Please." She glanced nervously at the sea of faces. Everyone in the room was staring at her: the campers, the counselors, even, it seemed, the stuffed animal heads on the wall. "They don't like us using the phone."

"So . . . I'll tell them it's . . ."

"No emergencies! No one *else* has their parents calling."

A pause. "I understand."

"But I'll see you on Visiting Day. Okay?"

"Of course . . . I love you, Cass."

"I love you, too," she said quickly, then hung up the phone.

The click of the receiver on its cradle echoed off the walls. So did her footsteps as, eyes lowered to avoid the stony gaze of the others, she started back to her table.

"*Cassie is a Daddy's Girl . . .*" The chant began softly at first, "*Cassie is a Daddy's Girl . . . Cassie is a Daddy's Girl . . .*" The girls began pounding their mugs on the table in rhythm: "*Cassie is a Daddy's Girl . . . Cassie is a Daddy's Girl . . .*" They stomped their feet, shouting the words: "*Cassie is a Daddy's Girl!*"

Cassie's face flushed hot and she forgot where her table was. The floor shook under her from their stamping feet. "*Cassie is a Daddy's Girl . . .*" She sidestepped between two tables and someone stuck out a foot, sending her sprawling on the hard wooden floor.

"*Cassie is a Daddy's Girl . . . Daddy's Girl . . . Daddy's Girl . . . !*"

"Lay off her!"

The voice rang out from the far end of the room and the others hushed. Cassie scrambled to her feet, but she couldn't see who had spoken—a camper? a counselor? Someone who had stopped the jeers cold. By the time Cassie found her table and sat down, the campers were eating dinner as if nothing had happened.

"Abigail saved your ass," Jo said.

"Abigail?"

"She's a senior," Melanie said.

"She thinks she's hot shit," Chelsea added.

"Face it," Jo said. "Abigail *is* hot shit."

"Seniors get the best table, the best cabin. They even get their own shower." Chelsea pointed a finger at the table in the corner near the fireplace, as if she were aiming a pistol.

Even though Cassie knew Casmaran allowed no campers over fifteen, from the well-developed bodies of the girls sitting there she would have guessed that they were seventeen or older. One tall blonde wore a halter

top that barely covered her cleavage; a redhead in short
shorts had long, slender legs; and all of them had on
lipstick and eye makeup. But it was more than that.
There was something else about them, something Cassie
couldn't quite put her finger on, that made the seniors
look different: the self-confidence on their faces, a self-
confidence bordering on arrogance.

"Which one is Abigail?" she asked, but before anyone could answer, Cassie knew. It had to be the girl sitting at the head of the table. Her nose was perfectly
straight (Cassie considered her own turned-up nose
much too girlish for a dancer) and her skin was tanned
nut-brown (Cassie knew she wouldn't be able to match
that tan in an entire summer). Abigail had the slender
but finely-muscled body of a dancer, yet Cassie thought
she looked more exotic than a ballet dancer. She reminded Cassie of the dancers from India she had seen
perform at the Kennedy Center, who had been supple
and feline—controlled, yet somehow spontaneous.

Their eyes met, and Cassie shot Abigail a look of
thanks. The senior returned it with a wide and generous
smile before turning to the other girls at her table, who
all seemed to be courting her.

"Everybody loves Abigail," Melanie said. "Even if
you hate her, you love her."

Chapter 11

Abigail's face was painted white, her eyes outlined in black, so that in the glow of the candle she held, she looked both ghostly and chaste, like a pale statue of a forgotten saint. In her black turtleneck, her long raven hair flowing over her shoulders, she stood perfectly still before a wooden podium at the end of the main lodge. Cassie guessed it must have once been the church pulpit, and the cold wooden bench beneath her made her feel as if she were sitting in a pew. She straightened up, like her cabinmates who were seated beside her—six of them in the shadowy, cavernous room, facing Abigail and a dozen flickering candles of black wax.

It was hard to hear. Abigail spoke softly, and her voice echoed off the rafters. At first Cassie could only pick up snatches of her speech: "A privilege . . . Tonight . . . Consecration . . ." Cassie glanced up at the stuffed animal heads on the walls. The candlelight sparkled in their eyes, endowing them with a glimmer of life, as if they were listening, too.

"This is your year to face the test of Consecration,"

Abigail said, "just as the girls of Lakeside have always done . . ." The reverence with which she spoke, the combination of awe and respect, compelled Cassie to listen. "Tonight will be an initiation, yes. And for those who can make it to the end, a legacy. We seniors will entrust it to you, just as the seniors entrusted it to *us* when we bunked up in Lakeside. Next year, when you're seniors, you'll carry on the tradition with the younger girls, to continue the chain, unbroken."

Hokey, Cassie thought. It all sounds incredibly hokey. So why were the girls from Lakeside sitting here so politely, so wide-eyed? Why wasn't Chelsea groaning, or Melanie rolling her eyes or Robin sticking her finger down her throat as though she were going to puke?

Abigail raised her left hand: "Take the Vow. Swear your loyalty to Casmaran, that you will uphold the legacy. Swear that once you enter the forest tonight, you won't leave until you have been consecrated in the name of the Sisterhood. And that you will tell no one—*no one*—what you have seen and heard."

They raised their left hands, murmuring their assent, and for a moment, Cassie wondered why she had joined in so instinctively, without so much as a twinge of doubt. Then she understood. She didn't know about the others, but for herself, at least, swearing loyalty to Casmaran meant making the same pledge her mother must have made.

"You have taken the vow," Abigail said. "Now take the journey!" The girls squirmed on the bench. "I know what you're thinking." Abigail smiled. "You're thinking you'd have to be out of your mind to go into the forest at night. But even that fear is part of the tradition, part of what the girls from Lakeside have always had to go through, since there's been a Casmaran."

"Everybody loves Abigail," Cassie remembered someone saying at dinner, and she could see why. The way Abigail smiled, it seemed she was reaching out to make

her a special friend, and yet, from the rapt expressions on the faces of the girls beside her, she knew that each thought Abigail was speaking only to her.

Abigail nodded to Cassie, as if she would understand what was expected of her, and awkwardly, Cassie rose to her feet. She took the six candles Abigail held out to her and passed them out to her cabinmates. One by one, Abigail lit them with her own. "Let your candles burn with your loyalty to Casmaran. As long as they burn bright, you'll be safe. But if they go out . . ." She paused. "The woods are dark."

Abigail lit Cassie's taper last, staring at her long and hard, as if there were some special bond between them that Cassie did not yet understand. Cassie followed the others to the door, the glow of her candle dancing in the glass eyes of the stuffed animal heads, like the spark of a sudden awareness.

On the porch of the lodge, the night breeze threatened to extinguish the fragile flames, and Cassie cupped a hand to shield her candle. It glowed through her fingers like a trapped firefly. The lights in the cabins lining the lawn were out, and clouds obscured the stars. In the all-consuming shadows, the candles shed the only light.

Robin caught up with Cassie. "If you ask me, this initiation stuff is a crock."

Jo cracked her gum. "That bit about loyalty to the Sisterhood . . . Do you think the seniors are a bunch of dykes or something?"

" 'Consecration' . . . 'vows,' " Melanie said. "She talks like we're in a fucking convent."

"Yeah," Chelsea added. "Iris must really get off on it."

Iris' wrinkled brow said she was so nervous she hadn't even heard the dig. "It's irresponsible of them to expect us to enter the forest after dark. We won't be able to see the poison ivy . . . or the poison oak . . ."

"I think that's the whole idea," Robin said.

"And *snakes* . . ."

"Would it kill them to let us take flashlights?" Melanie whined.

"It's all bull," Jo said. "Let's head back to Lakeside for some five-card stud."

Cassie surprised herself by speaking out: "If it's all such bull, Jo, then what are you afraid of?"

Jo flinched as though hot wax from her candle had dripped on her hand.

Melanie picked up on it. "Since when are Lakeside girls chickenshit?"

"We gave our word," Cassie said. To come to Casmaran and not experience what her mother had experienced, especially something this important . . . No, she would have to go. And she had no intention of going alone.

"Sorry, but I just washed my hair." Chelsea started down the steps, towards Lakeside.

"Better hurry." Abigail appeared behind them on the porch of the lodge, pointing to a flickering trail of candles that led into the forest. "Once they burn out, you'll never find your way back." Cassie clattered down the steps onto the vast, dark lawn, and her bunkmates followed.

With nightfall, the balmy temperature had plummeted, and dew drenched Cassie's legs as she waded through the weeds beside the graveyard. She could hear something pursuing her through the darkness—was it the hum of Miss Grace's wheelchair? No, it was just a mosquito. Why hadn't she noticed any of them during the day? She slapped one on her neck, and felt the sticky moistness of her own blood. She glanced uncertainly back towards the porch.

Abigail was gone.

Details of the camp that Cassie might have ignored in daylight possessed an exaggerated significance at night. The archery targets on the lawn stared at her like hungry eyes, and the tumbled-over gravestones behind

the lodge looked like the bones of some extinct creature
too complex and puzzling to ever piece together into a
logical form. She glanced down towards the lake, to the
rocky promontory where she was sure the statue of Miss
Grace's dog had crouched, but she could no longer
detect it among the trees, as if nightfall had breathed it
to life, freed it to set out on the hunt. Her body tried to
overrule the thoughts, to sweat them out of her as she
broke into a run towards the flickering trail of candles.
But the green lump in her stomach wouldn't go away.

She stepped into the forest. Instead of the soft cush-
ion of pine needles and dead leaves Cassie remembered
from that afternoon, tonight the path was unyielding
underfoot, as if at sunset a carapace of sharp rocks had
thrust up through the earth's crust. A few candles had
been nailed to boughs to make a sketchy trail, and as the
girls passed the sputtering tapers one by one, their faces
glowed eerily before sinking back into shadow.

"It's dark as hell," Melanie said.

"No kidding."

Iris peered into the sky. "It's a special night."

"What's that supposed to mean?" Robin said it as
though she didn't want to know.

"The summer solstice . . . the shortest night of the
year." Iris paused. "The shortest, but the darkest." She
crossed herself.

Cassie caught her arm. "Don't be such an old lady."
Iris *did* look like an old lady, her brow wrinkled into
little furrows, her lips pinched. Iris crossed herself
again.

The wildflowers were brittle in the candlelight, yellowed like the waxen ornaments on the funeral urns
Cassie remembered from the cemetery where her mother
was buried. The flowers in the forest seemed to have lost
their scent at night, the perfume of forsythia and gold-
enrods transformed into a miasma of stagnant water
and dead leaves.

"Shit," Chelsea groaned as they trudged through the
muck of a dry creek bed. "I'm *destroying* my espa-

drilles.'' Candles shimmered on the boughs of a towering pine up ahead, and she stopped. "What's that?"

"It looks like icicles," Cassie said.

"Ice?"

They stopped dead: glittering slivers dangled from the branches, hundreds of them, as sharp as splinters of glass.

"Impossible," Iris said. "For water to freeze it has to be below 32 degrees Fahrenheit, and . . ."

"Are you brain-damaged or what?" Chelsea cut her off. "We know it can't be *real* ice."

Abigail's voice rang out from among the trees.

> *"The ice men came when winter raged*
> *And left with the first spring rain.*
> *They stole the ice to turn to gold*
> *But they paid a price in pain . . ."*

A dozen feet ahead, a waterfall shimmered in the candlelight. Cassie found the sight reassuring until she was close enough to see . . .

"It's red," she said. "The water's *red*."

"It must be dye." Iris knelt beside the stream, as though to test it with her hand, but seemed to think better of it. "It's much too bright to be real . . . *It can't be real* . . ."

No one said the word "blood" aloud.

Again Abigail's voice from the dark, ringing so clear and strong, the rush of the red-stained water couldn't drown it out.

> *"In the final blizzard many ice men died*
> *And when spring came, only two remained.*
> *Their fingers were lost in the killing frost*
> *Their eyes were wild and their legs were lame."*

The girls rounded a bend in the trail and faced a sight that froze them in disgust: ice picks impaled squirming rats and lizards against a tree trunk, the blood of the animals mingling as it trickled down the bark.

> *"Through bitter months the ice men ached,*
> *Suffering hunger's sting.*
> *Until the June when camp began*
> *With many a sweet young thing.*
> *Then the hunger of the ice men took its bloody toll:*
> *Hunger of the body*
> *Hunger of the soul!"*

A light flicked on, and Iris screamed.

The severed head of a long-haired girl lay in the middle of the trail, her face ghostly white like Abigail's; her tongue lolling from the side of her mouth.

The light flashed off.

"What the hell was that?" Robin whispered.

Cassie felt Iris grab her sleeve, and it was as if the timidity of the others emboldened her. "Come on!" Cassie said. "Don't let them get to you. Can't you see that's what they want? It was just one of the seniors, sitting in a hole."

They pushed deeper into the dense thicket, but Abigail's voice followed them:

> *"The ice men violated hallowed ground*
> *Ravaging innocent daughters.*
> *They brought down a curse upon the land:*
> *Spring against winter. Woman against man.*
> *Let no man harm a child of Casmaran!"*

A sudden gust of wind blew out all their candles.

"We're screwed," Robin whispered, her voice magnified by the total darkness.

"No shit!"

"We can't be more than half a mile from camp," Iris murmured hesitantly. "If we can spot the North Star, then we can calculate our bearings, and . . ."

"Oh, shut up!"

"Keep together," Cassie said.

They moved towards each other in the darkness, their feet crunching across dead leaves until their hands touched, all of them as slippery with sweat as Cassie's own. They formed a chain, with Cassie taking the lead, feeling her way, as if wading through a deep, murky pool. She picked her way over tree stumps, her legs scratched by prickly bushes that she hoped weren't poison oak. Then the path flattened out, and she led them gingerly along a smooth trail.

Suddenly Iris whimpered, as if she had been struck. *"Look!"*

Cassie strained to make out the silhouettes before them: two hulking human forms, hanging by ropes from an enormous tree, creaking as they swung in the wind. Bodies, heavy with a weight that only came when you were . . . She felt something wet on her face and looked up—something was dripping from the bodies.

"Blood!" Iris screamed.

This time when Abigail's voice rang out of the forest, it was strident, vengeful:

> *"The vow was kept*
> *The death sentence sealed*
> *The threat to Casmaran forever repealed.*
> *Begin the Women's hour. Begin!*
> *All hail to Casmaran's power!"*

Flashlights flicked on, aimed by seniors crouching on the enormous branches of the oak. The beams transfixed the bodies dangling from the hangman's ropes— the "corpses" were only crude effigies of straw.

> *"Begin the Women's hour. Begin!*
> *All hail to Casmaran's power!"*

Abigail straddled the bough above the effigies,

drenching them with liquid from a rusty can. The odor smarted in Cassie's nostrils.

"Gasoline!"

Abigail pressed her other hand between her thighs. "This is the fertile crescent where all life begins . . ." She rocked back and forth on the branch, moving her hand up to caress her breasts, and the seniors echoed her words.

> *"When men defile the Sisters*
> *When men defile the land*
> *When men invade to plunder*
> *They must pay Casmaran!"*

When the straw effigies were soaking with gasoline, Abigail threw the empty jerry can away and lit a wood match.

Then she dropped it.

The moment the fire caught, the straw arms and legs of the figures jerked and flailed, the straw bodies bobbing in a macabre dance, as if they had been cursed with a moment of life, cursed with life just long enough for it to be snuffed out. Then, flaring in a purple orchid of igniting gasoline, the flames engulfed the straw men, and Cassie pulled the others away from the shower of sparks.

"*Men, Men, Men* . . ." Abigail chanted, rubbing the spot between her legs, and the seniors in the branches joined in:

> *"Men, Men, Men,*
> *Their time will not return again.*
> *Men, Men, Men*
> *Their time has come and been!"*

As suddenly as it had flared, the flaming straw died, the effigies reduced to charred, smoking husks. For an instant, in the orange afterglow, Cassie could make out her cabinmates gaping upward, the last flicker of the fire trapped in their eyes. When the seniors repeated the chant, her friends joined in. Even Cassie found her lips moving:

> *"Men, Men, Men!*
> *Their time will not return again.*
> *Men, Men, Men!*
> *The Sisterhood will win!"*

The embers faded, and the vengeful voice softened to a soothing whisper. "Be anointed now in their ashes. Be welcomed into the fold!"

From high up in the tree a flurry of soot descended on Cassie and the others. They coughed as they inhaled it. Like black snow, it tainted their hair with its foul smell, stained their clothes, smarted their eyes with cinders.

> *"The ice men died*
> *But be forewarned*
> *Their spirits live!*
> *Each night they watch*
> *Each night they wait*
> *To seek revenge!"*

The flashlights in the tree switched off.

> *"Be quick! Be wise!*
> *Escape!"*

Shrieking, the girls of Lakeside took off through the woods.

But Cassie didn't move. Anger held her there, her body rigid, staring up at the tree. Abigail had made a promise—perhaps an unspoken one, but a promise nevertheless—that something important would happen tonight, that Consecration would somehow help her understand why her mother had loved Casmaran so. But *this* . . . it had all been a sick, sadistic game, designed to arouse hatred. A hatred she couldn't even put into words, and yet which she couldn't rid herself of, like the ashes that permeated her hair, the ashes that tainted her mouth with the taste of an unknown evil.

The stampede of the escaping Lakeside campers dwindled in the distance. Abigail and the other seniors —had they fled, too? Or were they still up in the tree, watching her?

Don't panic, she told herself. *Don't give Abigail and her friends the satisfaction of seeing you freak out.* She walked slowly away from the tree, trying to find the path back, but her thoughts tripped her up, slowed her pace, drew her down uncharted paths of their own.

She passed through a cleft between two massive boulders, and looked up. Two hulking figures were standing above. Watching her.

Men.

For a moment she stared at them, her heart pounding in her chest like two fists banging on a locked door. *The ice men?*

No more thinking. No time to think.

Run.

But as she plunged into the thicket she couldn't stifle her thoughts . . . *Why can't you turn off your mind?* The sharp rhythm of her feet pounding against the earth struck a tempo of hard questions, and like the footfalls of the figures running in pursuit, the words thudded in her mind with a heavy tread.

Ice man . . . Burning man . . .

The sea had swirled in glacial flames.

Ice and Fire.

The Chill could scorch and freeze at once, afflict with jungle-sweat and arctic cold.

Ice man . . . Burning man . . .

Cassie's mind leaped the outer bounds of her memory, to the *Pandora*, when she was four years old, to the kerosene-slick sea wild with flame . . . To the Burning Man, who had seemed to want her more desperately than he had wanted to survive the inferno.

Ice and Fire.

The Burning Man who had wanted her—only her—
who had reached out to snatch her from her mother's
arms.

*Why did he want me then? Why do the ice men want
me now?*

She pushed through the undergrowth where brambles
tore at her sweatshirt, and scrambled over sharp rocks
that mauled her knees, until she stumbled at last onto
the trail. *Keep running.* She swore at herself for having
given up dancing. Her muscles ached and her breath
came in gasps. But still she ran, past Iris, past Robin.
(The ice men don't want them . . . They want me!) She
dashed ahead until she lost sight of her friends, gulping
air into lungs that burned from smoke and ashes.

Ice Man . . . Burning Man . . .

Feet pounded on the earth behind her. Gaining.

At last, the shimmer of the lake through the trees, the
watery expanse frozen under a faint moon into a sheet
of ice. She plunged out onto the lawn.

The other girls burst out of the forest behind her,
Robin and Chelsea . . . finally Iris. The moment they
emerged from the shadows and saw their faces smeared
with ashes like chimney-sweeps, their hair wild and
gray, their panic dissolved into hysterical laughter. They
collapsed into the soft grass, clutching their sides.
Cassie stared at them numbly.

"What a trip!" Robin shouted.

Chelsea tugged at her hair. "What a *disaster*!"

"The worst!" Iris giggled, covering her mouth with
her hand.

"Just wait till next summer." Chelsea slammed her
fist into her hand. "When *we're* seniors, we'll conse-
crate the little nerds in Lakeside so they'll never forget
it!"

"Look!"

The laughter trailed off. A hulking figure loomed in
silhouette at the edge of the forest, and Cassie tensed to
run.

But as the form moved slowly onto the lawn, the girls

started laughing again. It was Jo, with Melanie riding piggyback on her shoulders, baring her teeth and rolling her eyes up until only the whites showed: "The ice man's gonna get ya!" she shouted. "The ice man's gonna get ya!"

But Cassie wasn't laughing. She was the only one who wasn't laughing. *Ice man . . . Burning Man . . .* She had no intention of telling the others—they would only tease her if she told them. And yet she felt an uneasy certainty that her pursuers were still lurking in the forest, watching her, like the cold eye of the moon gazing at her through the pines.

Chapter 12

~~~~~

They were dancing side by side, but Cassie knew it wasn't a duet. It was a duel. She and Abigail were performing to the same music, but on different edges of it, the dark and the light, like the two sides of the dance pavilion where they circled each other, one submerged in the pine shadows, the other shimmering in the sunshine reflected off the lake. And the audience––the girls from Lakeside, the seniors, and Sarah––watched with silent fascination, the way they might have watched a tightrope walker performing without a net, Cassie thought, fearful, yet waiting for the fatal fall. Strange, she had felt so tense the moment Sarah had touched the needle to the record of *Swan Lake* and the audience had hushed. But now that she was moving across the smooth oak floor, her body swept up in the tempo, she forgot the stress, possessed by a calm that only came when she danced.

In her two weeks at Casmaran, she had grown in self-confidence and strength, and her body was lean and taut again, her mind swept free of the old cobwebs. She had dismissed the "ice men" as just another of the seniors' pranks. Abigail had barely spoken to her since the night of Consecration, and she wondered whether the senior was avoiding her because she knew they would be competing today. Cassie had been thinking of nothing but this moment. And dreading it.

Abigail danced wildly, as if overcome by a seizure, her arms and legs flailing out as she spun across the floor, her dark hair flying. Her body was so limber, it seemed that she could contort it, twist it any way she wished, that whatever her mind willed, her body could achieve. And she seemed to take a savage pleasure in that.

Why did Abigail dance so fiercely? Cassie wondered. I don't have anything against her. What has she got against me? If only Abigail knew my reason for wanting to win . . . If only she knew about my mother, and about how important it was that I dance the solo for her . . . Abigail couldn't have a reason for winning as important as that.

But Abigail danced as if she *did* have a reason, as if she were daring Cassie to try and beat her. And it was that defiance that troubled Cassie, as if there were something crucial at stake, something vital that had to do with power and control, and forces she might never understand. Something terribly urgent, as dark as Consecration . . . and as disturbing as Miss Grace's kiss.

Abigail . . . Cassie was too swept up in the dance to watch her now, but she could feel the wind of the senior's movement, glimpse the blur of her body out of the corner of her eye. Abigail seemed to spin out the shadows like a spider weaving a web, shadows that shrouded the rafters and lingered in the corners of the pagoda. And as Cassie whirled across the floor, it seemed as though Abigail had woven those shadows to entrap her.

The flickering spider-shadows and the hot, shimmering air . . . Cassie felt as though she were being pursued, and as the tempo of the dancing rushed faster and faster, she realized that there was a strategy to Abigail's movement.

She's forcing me towards the edge.

Cassie had avoided looking down over the side of the pavilion into the lake, uncertain how it would affect her. Now she had no choice: she saw the water slapping the pilings of the dance pavilion, water thickened with algae to a sickly green. Water that threatened great depth, a spawning place for the Chill.

The phobia had been Cassie's secret, one she had kept from her friends at Lakeside, a secret she had even tried to keep from herself. And yet Abigail was edging her over to the splintered wood molding, all that stood between the dance floor and the water. Abigail's body spun, a malicious blur, dominating the center of the dance floor, so that Cassie had no choice but to move towards the brink.

She knows about the Chill. (How could she know?) Abigail knows, and she's using it against me.

But just when Cassie expected to feel the cold shooting through her, she felt a rush of confidence instead, and leaned over the water to taunt her murky reflection. For one moment it seemed as if she were standing still, that the pavilion, the audience, even the lake were spinning around *her*, that she was the center, the way her mother had made her feel at the center when she had danced for her in the studio at Cliff's Edge. Her mother had applauded her then, and as the music ended with the fading of strings, the girls were applauding her now.

The pavilion stopped spinning and Cassie stared out at the lake, half-expecting the wind from her dance to have sent ripples to the far shore. Even before Sarah announced it, she knew she had won—not just the lead in the dance, but something much more important.

"You were terrific!"

The girls from Lakeside crowded around her, Iris and Robin and even Chelsea showering her with congratulations. She hugged each of them, then pulled away. Abigail was walking across the dance floor to shake her hand, but the look in her eyes turned that gesture into a hostile act.

"Congratulations."

"You were great," Cassie said, forcing a smile.

"But *you* won." Abigail's fingernails cut into Cassie's palm as they shook hands, and Cassie pulled her hand away. When Abigail turned back to join the other seniors, Cassie was left with the vague impression that winning would cost more than if she had lost, that she had started a journey that might lead to a terrible destination.

"Let's split," Robin said, and Cassie followed her down the steps of the dance pavilion, trying to salvage what was left of the victory and take it with her.

She stopped. "Wait . . . my ballet shoes."

"Get them later." Iris shot a telling glance back at the dance pavilion and Cassie understood: everyone had left except Abigail and her friends.

"To hell with her." Cassie started defiantly back up the steps. Robin followed, and reluctantly Iris tagged along. Cassie hoped she had left the ballet shoes near the top of the steps, so she would be able to grab them and head back to camp before Abigail saw her. No such luck.

"You wouldn't by any chance be looking for these?" Abigail was dangling the shoes over the lake. Perched on the edge of the dance pavilion, the seniors laughed, reflections of their bodies distorted in the green water.

"Give them here." Cassie reached for the shoes, but Abigail pulled them away and held them farther out over the water. "Give them here or I'll . . ."

Abigail smirked. "You'll what?"

Cassie stepped forward and shoved Abigail, pushing her over the edge. Abigail fell off the stage but . . . there was no splash . . . no moment when she plunged beneath the murky surface.

Abigail fell off the edge into midair and . . .

Abigail's body, which must have weighed a hundred pounds, fell terribly slowly, like an astronaut in outer space, a specter in a dream.

Impossible. It was the word that Cassie and Robin and Iris would have wanted to say, had they been able to speak. But all Robin could do was lick her upper lip, while Iris crossed herself in a panicky reflex. Cassie shook her head to rid her mind of what she saw.

Impossible.

Abigail fell off the edge of the dance pavilion, fell ten feet and then . . .

The moment of impact, the instant when Abigail should have plunged into the water, drenched and humiliated . . .

It never came.

When the tip of Abigail's foot touched the surface of the lake, she rebounded off of it, up into the air and back onto the floor of the dance pavilion, as if her body had been repelled from the water by a force more potent than gravity.

It's just another one of the seniors' tricks . . . It's got to be a trick.

Cassie wanted to laugh, to pretend she knew how it was done, but her lips were numb. It would take time to recover from the shock of what she had seen, but they weren't giving her time. One by one, each of the other seniors repeated it—the busty blonde, Tris, the redhead nicknamed Buns, and the other—jumping off the stage, touching the water with one foot, then rebounding off of it back to their places. It was like a bizarre dance, Cassie thought, a dance that violated important rules that no one should break, an unnatural dance that she could never learn, that she would never *want* to learn, because it was somehow evil. Like those crazed men in India (what were they called?) who walked over hot coals without feeling pain. What powers did anyone have, she wondered, to defy the laws of gravity?

"Something wrong?" Abigail was grinning at the shock on Cassie's face. "Look, it's no big deal." She pointed towards the water. "There's an old piling, a post just underneath the surface. There used to be a loading dock there. We jump down onto the post, and hop back up . . . that's all."

Cassie nodded, angry at herself for letting so simple a trick rattle her.

"You try it," Abigail taunted. "Try it, and I'll give your shoes back. You're much better on your feet than I am—at least Sarah thinks so. If *I* can do it, it should be no sweat for you." Cassie hesitated. "Unless you're afraid of getting a little wet."

"Of course not." *How could she know?* Cassie held her voice steady, but her feet refused to step to the edge.

Abigail dipped Cassie's shoes toward the water. "These things stink. I'm not going to hold them here all day." Cassie reached out for them again, but Abigail jerked them away.

My mother bought them for me . . .

The thought allowed her to marshal her anger, gave her the strength to overcome the stirrings of nausea brought on by the stagnant smell of the water. She squinted into the lake, but the way the sunlight shimmered off the murky surface it was hard to see the underwater piling that Abigail had pointed to. "Do it," Abigail said, "before your stinking shoes get the washing they deserve."

"Go to hell." Cassie stepped up to the edge. Her reflection in the water stared back at her, like a specter hovering just beneath the surface, waiting to strike. She wavered, trying to get up the nerve.

She was so close to the edge, it didn't take much of a shove to send her flying into the air. One of them pushed her, and . . .

No time to panic. Reach out with your feet for the

piling. Bend your knees, jump up off of it the way they did.

But Cassie's feet knifed into the water and she sank in over her head.

For a moment, beneath the surface, choking on the brackish water, she opened her eyes just long enough to see that there *was* no piling. Abigail and the seniors . . . *They lied to me!* But if they had lied, then how could they . . . ? They had rebounded off of the water, she'd seen them.

Cassie sank into the stagnant shadows, and though she thrashed her arms and kicked her feet in panic, she started to black out, spiraling downward in a cold pirouette, as helpless as a clockwork ballerina on a music box. The waves pulled her beneath the dance pavilion, where rusty nails and barbed fishhooks bristled from the pilings.

I want my mother.

Cassie felt her body drenched with water as foul as kerosene, jerking like the straw men on Consecration night the moment they had burst into flame. *The Burning Man* . . . She remembered him, too, the way her panic to escape had made her thrash and choke in the vortex of the sinking *Pandora*. Her eyes sealed shut, but she could feel tendrils of seaweed clutching at her body, like the Burning Man reaching for her, entangling her legs as she kicked and fought and struggled against him.

Arms grabbed her, pulled her back up to the surface, more suddenly, she thought, more brutally than her mother's arms. The laughter of the seniors rang in her ears like the shouts of the dying on the *Pandora*. At last, her mouth opened wide, in a scream for breath.

Chapter 13

~~~

"I mean really, Cass. The water was only six feet deep." Robin eased Cassie down on her bunk and began towel-drying her hair. "But what else is new? You always had a flair for melodrama." She sniffed Cassie's hair and stuck her finger down her throat, pretending to puke, a pantomime usually guaranteed to get a rise out of Cassie. Not this time. Cassie's eyes were darting around the room, as though to ferret out fresh dangers. In the light reflected off the lake, the shadows in the cabin were the same undulating green as the depths beneath the dance pavilion.

At least the cabin was empty, except for the two of them—and Iris, who was squatting on the floor, rummaging frantically through the books she had dumped out of her trunk. The other girls from Lakeside wouldn't see her like this, Cassie thought. But what if the reason they weren't here was because the seniors were telling them what had happened? She could imagine Chelsea, Melanie and Jo hooting with laughter as Abigail described her sobbing, her face smeared with slime when Robin had dragged her out of the water. "Thanks for fishing me out," she said, taking the towel from Robin.

"Sure." Robin tilted her head to one side, the way she always did when she was trying to figure Cassie out. "You look like hell."

"Thanks." Cassie snuck a look at her reflection in the window. Robin was right: her face was gray, her hair hopeless, and the terror showed in her eyes. On the inside, she had lost it, too; the good feelings she had gathered at camp had spilled out in the murky water and been washed away. She wrapped a blanket around her so that Robin wouldn't see that she was shivering. "Did you get my shoes?"

Robin tossed them into her lap. "Anyway, you beat Abigail where it counts. She can't dance worth shit."

"Sure." Cassie pressed the soft pink leather between her fingers. The victory didn't matter to her anymore. The Chill was all that was real, the Chill that filled her mouth with the taste of brackish water and humiliation.

"Surface tension!" Iris lifted a dog-eared paperback entitled *Amazing Facts of Science* and waved it at them.

"What?"

"It was surface tension. That had to be how they did it, how the seniors could *bounce* off the water like that. It has to do with molecular resistance and . . ."

"Iris, for Chrissake." Robin rolled her eyes. "We know you're here on scholarship. You don't have to keep trying to prove it."

Iris folded the page down to mark the place, closed the book and tossed it back into the footlocker. She left the cabin, murmuring something about K.P.

"Iris always tries too hard," Robin said. "I mean, anything she could come up with out of one of those dumb books would have to sound lame."

"I really blew it." Cassie tried to laugh. *Abigail and her friends saw me freak out*. "Thanks again for . . ."

"Just stick with me, sweetheart." Robin faked a Bogie accent, then switched to her regular voice. "Hey, your teeth are chattering.'' She helped Cassie into her sleeping bag, the way Cassie used to zip her in when they had camped in back of Cliff's Edge on summer nights. Then Robin stood up with an impatient toss of her head. ''Your dad told me to take care of you, but this is ridiculous.''

Robin didn't like being cast in the role of protector, Cassie knew. She much preferred it when Cassie was in control, the way she had been on Nantucket, leaving Robin free to be the dizzy blonde. Those had always been the rules for their friendship, and maybe it was too late to try to change them now. ''I'm fine,'' she said, as if to prove that the old rules still held.

''You'll live.'' Robin gave her an affectionate punch on the arm, then backed towards the door: ''I'll be at the stables, feeding the horses. They need me more than you do.''

The screen door banged shut behind Robin, and Cassie closed her eyes, slowed her breathing until it came as regularly as the water lapping against the pilings beneath the cabin. Her body was trembling, her muscles tense from that one terrible moment when she had known she was over the edge, a dead weight falling—the moment when she had known exactly what was about to happen, yet could do nothing to stop it.

But worse than the fall, worse than the shock of the plunge into the cold water and the helpless thrashing for breath, had been the sight of the other girls who did *not* sink, Abigail and her friends, who were somehow beyond the rules . . . or in league with them.

Cassie's stomach rumbled with the stagnant water she had swallowed. The faint smell of rot, of rust and tangled seaweed from that underwater moment was more intense than a memory. It seemed to be filtering up through the floorboards, and she breathed through her mouth to avoid it. Her hands felt cold against her cheeks, a stranger's hands.

She opened her eyes and looked over the edge of the bunk at the floor. Had it always been like that? Green algae was filtering up through the cracks between the boards, as if it would seep into the room and creep up the legs of the bunk bed and . . .

Come off it. You freaked out because they pushed you in. You made an ass of yourself. Now forget it.

The red, blue and yellow signal flags along the wall hung limp in the still air. Because her mother had forbidden her to sail, Cassie had never learned the nautical code, but she wondered if somehow the flags might be spelling out a warning.

The sleeping bag was suddenly stifling. She unzipped it and climbed out. The Chill was creeping over her again, she could feel it, and to fight back, she tried to use a secret her mother had taught her to battle stage fright before a performance: *focus on something concrete . . . anything . . . The curtains, the floor. Focus on something real to make the panic dissolve like smoke.*

But the floor smelling of algae, the rafters with their sharp steel hooks, the signal flags with their secret warning . . . none of them could do it for her. They seemed too much like Abigail's tricks, disturbing her with a threat she couldn't put into words.

Cassie slipped into a pair of white shorts and a Casmaran T-shirt. She had to get out of here, alone, to get away from the lake, and . . .

Out on the lawn, the girls from Lakeside were playing softball. Melanie was pitching, and the bases were loaded. If they spotted her, Cassie was sure they would make her come over and take Melanie's place. She turned her back on them and ran towards the woods.

The trail followed the shore of the lake until it forked in two. The senior cabin was barely visible up the steep path that led to the left, and she hurried down the one to her right. Okay, she admitted, she was afraid. But why? So the seniors were bitches—so what? Were they any worse than the ninth grade girls at the Windward Country Day School in Washington—the girls who had placed obscene phone calls to the spinster headmistress, and taken a pig fetus from Biology and left it for the school nurse with a note saying it was an aborted baby?

But when she reached the dance pavilion, the reassurances no longer worked. There was something different about the mischief of the seniors at Casmaran, something that was . . . She peered down into the lake. There was no hint of a submerged piling there, not even a shadow.

How had Abigail done it? Another malicious prank, it had to be. But there were starting to be too many of them, and they were getting harder to explain. Her mouth still tasted of stagnant water, and she plucked a blade of grass to chew. She took the trail that led away from the lake and plunged into the deep forest.

The sharp, bristling evergreens with the coffin scent she remembered from the night of Consecration, seemed to have receded, leaving silver birches, and poplars, and aspens dappled with sunlight. The ground which had seemed so thorny, so unyielding that night was now scattered with thousands of tiny blossoms, buttercups and daisies in thick knots poking up through the bed of pine needles. Their fragrance made it hard to believe that she could have ever been frightened here. There was an innocence about this place, like the forest in an Early American painting she'd seen once, where a lion and a lamb lay side by side, a place where you could never lose your way. Nantucket had no forests like this, she thought. On the island, the trees were stunted, twisted by the fury of gales from the sea.

Today for the first time (how could she have missed them before?) she noticed charming little touches: a miniature stone bridge that arched a brook, a handrail of rope and logs where the trail steepened, a stone bench where a weary hiker might rest. It was as if the trails had been designed for prim Victorian ladies to walk without sullying their petticoats. Had the precautions been Miss Grace's doing, Cassie wondered, when the old lady still had all her marbles? Better not to think about Miss Grace, she decided. Better not to think about Abigail, *or* the lake, *or* Miss Grace.

She took a shortcut, pulling herself up a gully, then followed the trail as it switchbacked down the side of a ravine.

The tree. She stopped the moment she lay eyes on it, as if all along it had been her destination. The oak seemed different from the other trees in the forest, different from the sharp-edged pines and the fragile poplars. The oak's branches seemed to grasp the sky, giving form and meaning to it. She wished she could be as unshakable, as rooted in eternal certainties, as its thick, gnarled limbs. The ancient tree looked exactly the same as when her mother had come here, she imagined. In its vast life span, what were the years that separated their two visits to Casmaran?

She knelt down on one of its roots that buckled the earth, and realized that what she had at first thought was merely the pattern of the bark, were initials that had been carved into it—hundreds, so many it looked as though the trunk had been raked by claws. She ran the palm of her hand across the grooved and pitted surface, as if to read a message in Braille.

Then her hand stopped, her finger tracing two familiar letters that seemed to have been cut more deeply into the wood than the others: *A.C.*

She leaned back against the trunk, into the enfolding embrace of the gnarled roots, and looked up at the branches, so enormous they blocked out the sky, remembering the game she had played with her mother: *The first patch of blue you see through the leaves, you get one wish—wish for adventure, or wish for love.* Her mother must have wished for love, Cassie thought, and her wish had come true, until it had been cruelly cut short. She looked up into the branches, searching for the sky behind the leaves.

But she never found a patch of blue. Her eyes were drawn to two charred nooses, frayed strands of black-

ened rope that hung from the branch above her. From
Consecration night, she thought. The wind stirred and
the charred nooses moved, swayed like the pendulums
of clocks in a dream.

And there was a sound. It wasn't the groan of the
ropes against the bough, or the wind rustling the leaves.
The sound came from the top of the ravine. Footsteps
crashing through brush.

Cassie froze, her back pressed against the trunk of the
oak. If it was Abigail and the seniors . . .

*Did they follow me here? Will they drag me back to
the lake and throw me in?*

The footsteps echoed heavily on the trail, too heavily,
she judged, to belong to the girls.

The ice men?

She didn't intend to find out. She considered dashing
back up the trail towards camp, but to get there would
mean exposing herself to whoever was approaching.
The footsteps were coming closer. Whoever it was, she
was sure they were coming for her.

Impulsively, she bolted away from the protection of
the tree and scrambled up the opposite side of the
ravine, ignoring a sign: OFF LIMITS. Grasping roots
that pierced the crusty earth, she pulled herself up the
sheer face. One root gave way, and she grabbed
another, clawing up a few more feet.

No time to glance over her shoulder; no time to see
who was following her. The sandstone wall of the cliff
was crumbling underfoot, her tennis shoes slipping on
shards of flint, her hands clinging to red clots of earth.
Below her, the footsteps had reached the hanging tree,
and were rustling the thick carpet of leaves.

She gripped another root that twisted out of the cliff
wall, as coarse and black as the charred nooses dangling
from the tree. One final lunge and she collapsed on top
of the cliff, her body pressed against the mossy ledge,
gasping for breath.

Don't raise your head.

She crawled away from the brink, towards a dense

thicket of brambles, and only when she reached it, when she was certain she couldn't be seen from below, did she stand up slowly.

The climb up the face of the cliff had somehow been a climb through time as well, for the wall of brambles here stifled the sunlight, bringing her to the brink of nightfall. This forest had no lacy green leaves, no pastel flowers, just thorns and a gray moss that seemed to soak up what little light filtered down through the branches. Here, beyond the "Off Limits" sign, there were no neatly tended trails, no trails at all. She tested the ground with the tip of her tennis shoe. Even the soil was different: sharp blocks of obsidian sparkled in the black earth. Hadn't Sarah told them that the lake had once been a volcanic crater? Cassie wondered whether this ridge were somehow closer to the source of that first eruption, closer to some smoldering lava pit.

Tendrils of poison ivy snaked over the ground, their scarlet-tipped leaves like tiny arrowheads dipped in blood. Ancient . . . it felt ancient in this forest, as if prehistoric creatures that were extinct everywhere else might still be hunting here. She stopped and studied the sole of her foot. A thorn an inch long had pierced her tennis shoe and pricked the skin of her heel. She removed it carefully and took a few more steps. There was no smooth carpet of leaves as there had been below, just the lichen, and the thorn branches bristling like barbed wire, clawing at her ankles.

She headed towards a glimmer of light. Was that a clearing up ahead?

One more step.

She stumbled and fell . . .

The swarthy, bearded man stood over her, his axe raised in both fists, and there was not even time to scream.

Chapter 14

Cassie flattened against the ground, staring up at him. Sweat matted the hair on his naked chest and stained the khaki shorts that hung low on his hips. His eyes gleamed wildly from above the shaggy beard, and glinting, sharp, the axe wavered in his hand.

"You scared the hell out of me!" He spoke quickly, his thick New York accent unmistakable. When he let the axe fall to his side, it nicked his ankle. "Great!" Blood trickled from the cut. "With my luck I'll probably get gangrene."

"I . . . I'm sorry." Cassie pulled herself to her knees, her legs still shaky from the jolt of adrenalin.

He stared at the blood on his fingers for a moment as if the sight were enough to turn his stomach. Then he wiped his hand on his shorts and leaned over her. "You all right?" His stubbly face was so close to hers that she could smell the whiskey on his breath.

"I'm fine." She stood up and started to back away from him.

"No . . . Wait a minute. I mean, except for a sex-crazed raccoon and a couple of rats, you're the first living thing I've seen in weeks.''

He didn't seem so threatening when he laughed, Cassie realized. Besides, he was a lot shorter than he had looked from the ground. His wiry body was anything but muscular, and he had been so clumsy with the axe . . .

"I don't think I could stand another hour alone here with all this goddamn scenic beauty. If I lay eyes on Bambi, I think I'll . . .'' He raised the axe and she backed away again. "Sorry. Just kidding. I chop a lot.'' He threw the axe onto a pile of kindling behind a rickety split-rail fence. "Of course, I don't burn any of the wood. I mean, it's summer, right? But it beats going inside and facing . . .'' He considered continuing, then evidently thought better of it, and steered the conversation in what must have been a safer direction. "I mean, look at it from my point of view. For a kid from West 89th and Columbus, this is worse than a padded cell. No soot . . . no bag ladies. Just those goddamn birds singing all the time . . . worse than Muzak. The only semi-human beings around here are at Casmaran, and they told me if I went near the place, they'd have Miss What's-her-name . . .''

"You know Miss Grace?''

"Never had the pleasure. But they said if I made a pass at her, she'd run me over with her wheelchair. So I'm stuck all alone in my charming villa . . .'' He stabbed his thumb towards the dilapidated shack behind him.

"You live in *that*?'' The cabin was a cruel parody of the cottages at camp. Instead of geraniums, the windowbox was heaped with crushed beer cans, and the paint had blistered over time to reveal the rotting plywood beneath.

"I know what you're thinking . . . What kind of a genius would rent a summer house like that? Don't ask me . . . ask my noble slumlords at Casmaran.''

"Casmaran?''

"Casmaran owns the cabin . . . the camp . . . the lake. Casmaran owns every blessed tree for fifty square miles." He eyed her Casmaran T-shirt. "I see they own you, too."

"Well, I . . ." Cassie felt the need to explain, although she wasn't sure quite what, but he cut her off with his manic patter, as if all the words that had been stored inside him for weeks were tumbling out, as if he were so thrilled to have someone to talk to that he couldn't wait to let her answer one question before asking another.

"What can I say? The place seemed like a steal when I saw the ad posted at Columbia. Two months for two hundred bucks. Who could beat it? Rustic charm, the ad said. Rustic charm? I mean, renting me this dump . . . if that wasn't anti-Semitism, I'd like to know what is."

She took a closer look at him: the prominent nose, the full, sensual lips, the dark, heavy-lidded eyes. She wondered whether blue-blooded Casmaran was afraid of him snooping around because he was a man—or because he was a Jew.

"If you hate it so much, why don't you go home?"

He sighed. "Ah, but that would be admitting defeat." Limping from his wounded ankle, he gestured for her to follow him. She hesitated, then caught up with him. There was something about him that she trusted—maybe it was that he seemed more vulnerable than she was.

The rusty screen door stuck and he kicked it open. "I like to think of this as my condo. No gold-plated plumbing . . . no plumbing, period. Just hot and cold running angst."

The cabin was a shambles. The glass panes in one of the two tiny windows had been replaced with wadded-up newspaper, leaving the room so dark that Cassie could barely make out its furnishings: a mattress on the floor in the corner, pillows and blankets heaped on it as if someone had thrown a fit; crumpled sheets of paper and broken pencils cluttering a plywood board spread across two sawhorses. The smell of sweat and whiskey mingled with a singed-hair scent that Cassie had smelled in Robin's bedroom—marijuana.

He gestured grandiosely around the room: "Was he a latter-day hippie, scorning civilization, living off the land?" he intoned. "The Hershey Bar wrappers and empty cans of Chef Boyardee spaghetti told her nothing could be further from the truth. A fugitive from the law? He seemed too overjoyed to see her. No, despite generations of guilt, the only known felonies he had committed were against himself." He daubed at the blood on his ankle with a towel. "Self-inflicted wounds are my specialty." He tossed the towel into a rusty bucket that served as a sink.

On one wall steel panels were aglow with red and green lights. "What's that?" Cassie asked.

"The death ray. Ming the Merciless will turn it on before your amazed eyes." He flipped a switch and another bank of lights flashed on. "Watch as he turns the rich kids at Casmaran into Puerto Ricans with only one pair of designer jeans apiece."

She laughed. "Anything but that."

He sat down on the stool facing the console and slid out a double keyboard that reminded her of an electric organ. She stepped closer. "My secret weapon . . ." He twisted a dial and an electronic hum echoed off the walls of the cabin. Then he fingered a few chords on the keys, adjusting a row of knobs until the sound had the timbre of violins.

"Ming the Merciless—merciless most of all with himself, mind you—a full-fledged, but mediocre, professor at Columbia . . ." He turned another knob, raising the pitch of the violins until they reminded her of Hawaiian strings. "And then one day the poor devil heads for a tropical paradise in the Maine woods . . ." With a flick of a knob on the console, they were back to the violins. "Lo and behold, he realizes that any damage by the

death-ray to his moral fiber has been totally self-
generated and richly deserved . . .'' He leaned over to
push another switch and the music shrilled to an ironic
fanfare of trumpets: "Voilà . . . Creative sterility . . .
artistic impotence. And a rotten lay.''

Cassie wondered whether he was drunk, or stoned.
Maybe he was just lonely. Watching her father after her
mother's death, she had learned it was sometimes hard
to tell the difference. Whether he was drunk or not, she
decided that the reason he was acting this way was
because the only way he could tell the truth was to make
a joke of it.

"Are you some kind of composer?'' she asked.

"Painfully accurate, your choice of words: *some kind
of composer*. I've been trying to figure out *what* kind
for the past ten years.'' The sarcasm, the self-deprecat-
ing humor—it reminded Cassie of the jokes her father
had made about the failure of his investigation. Maybe
that was why she wasn't smiling. He picked up on it:
"Sorry, I'll turn off the spigot of self-pity.'' Almost
apologetically he switched off the bank of red lights.
"The truth, since you asked, is that I schlepped all this
chozzerai—it's technically called a Moog electronic
synthesizer—up from New York. The woods, the lake,
they were supposed to perform some sort of miracle.
Ever hear of Lourdes?'' Cassie nodded. "Then you
know the bit: Throw away the crutches. But sometimes,
there are just too goddamn *many* crutches.''

Cassie could see the sadness etched around his eyes,
and switched the subject: "Have you done any
records?''

"Sure, ten years ago. RCA was hot to sign me.
Deutsche Grammophon . . . It's called the 'early
bloomer syndrome.' You know, the wunderkind who—
how do they put it?—'peaks too soon.' '' He extended
his hand to her. "Jake Lazarus.''

"I'm sure I've heard of you,'' she lied as she shook
his hand.

"It's not exactly a household word. Even when I was twenty-five, even when they called me the next Aaron Copland, it wasn't."

"There's nothing so hot about having your name be a household word."

"Let me guess." He studied her face. "Cabot? Lowell?" She shook her head, laughing. He clapped a hand to his mouth in mock amazement: "Oh, my God, you're not a *Kennedy*?"

"Broyles."

"No kidding? As in Senator Clayburn?"

"As in Cassie."

His smile faded. "Cassie . . . the thing with your mother. I'm sorry. Jesus, it must have been horrible for you."

She said nothing. There had been too many such expressions of sympathy, and they had stopped meaning anything months ago. She nodded at the synthesizer. "Play me something you wrote . . ."

"Are you sure?" He studied her, as if trying to judge her sincerity.

"Please?"

"Why not?" he sighed. "Somebody has to have the rare opportunity to be the first to hear my 'work in progress.' "

"I'm sure it's great."

He pulled an eight-track tape from a stack of them and threaded it on a Nagra tape recorder above the Moog. "Electronic music is actually a composite. You make as many tracks as you want: different sounds, rhythms. Mix them together on a master. Then you add new sounds on the keyboard, live, to give it spontaneity. Kind of like a duet with yourself."

He switched the tape recorder to "playback" and his fingers started to fly over the keys. Harsh sounds reverberated from a pair of speakers, the notes jarring, clashing with the electronic bleeps and grating chords on the tape. The discordant notes sounded cold, metallic, as devoid of emotion as if they'd been generated by a computer, and Cassie squirmed. When the tape finally ran out and he raised his hands from the keyboard, he took a deep breath. "Well . . . ?"

Cassie forced a smile. "It was very . . . interesting."

As he cut the power and the electronic hum faded, his own energy seemed to ebb, too. He slumped forward and stared at his hands. "Was it that bad?"

"All I meant was," she backpedaled, "well, you couldn't exactly *dance* to it."

"What the hell has dancing got to do with it?"

Cassie shrank back from his outburst. "I don't know. I just guess I like music I can dance to."

He stared at her a moment, then his voice softened. "You're right. It would be a real pain in the ass to have to dance to *that*." He picked up the butt of a cigarette in an ashtray and lit up. "Let's face it. It's even hard to *listen* to it."

"But I mean, there are some very interesting sounds . . . Unusual . . . really."

"Making 'unusual' sounds is a far cry from making music. You know what the fucking music critic of the *Times* said about the last piece I was able to get an audience to sit through? *'A study in cacophony . . . an affront to the auditory nerve endings . . .'* You throw the bad reviews away . . . burn them. But those are the ones you remember. Word for fucking word. Funny . . ." For the first time since she had met him, the humor was gone from his voice. "Christ, I compose, mix it . . . shmeckle until I think it's perfect. Then when I play it back, I wonder if God hadn't intended us to stick to making music with our lips and our hands." Brutally he pushed the two keyboards back into the console, then removed the reel from the tape deck and paused, as if he were debating whether to throw the tape in the trash. "Anyway, I don't know what possessed me to ask *your* opinion." His voice took on an insulting, defensive edge. "I mean, what the hell do you know?"

"You're right," she said. "What *do* I know?" She hoped it would make him feel better, but she could see from the hurt on his face that he cared terribly about what she thought.

He stood up and tried to drain a final swig from a beer on the console. The can was empty, and he mashed it with his fist, then hurled it towards a carton filled with garbage. It missed and clattered across the floor. He gestured to the darkening sky outside. "Aren't they going to send out the bloodhounds if you don't get back soon?" He was pouting, like a little boy, she thought. Or a self-centered artist.

"It must take a lot of dedication to come up here for the summer alone . . . just to work." He didn't answer. Maybe he didn't believe her admiration was genuine. Her mother would have respected Jake, she thought. Her mother had had great respect for artists, maybe because she had been a failed one herself.

She stepped to the door, but hesitated, wanting to comfort Jake, the way she had wanted to comfort her father when he had been wallowing in the same kind of self-pity. And she was tempted to touch him, in a way she had never touched her father. But she stepped out onto the rickety porch instead. Through a latticework of trees at the far side of the clearing, she saw the lake. Her feelings were intense, but out of focus, like the campfire at Casmaran on the opposite shore that shimmered on the water, like a sudden flaring of *scorpaena*. Without another word, she jumped down from the porch, and ran towards the woods.

Jake . . . It had been a delicious fear, the clumsy goodbye, the compulsion to reach out to him . . . to kiss him? . . . that she had fought to conceal. It made her giddy with an excitement that she hadn't felt since the night she had kissed Todd, what seemed years ago.

When she found herself enmeshed in the bramble thicket, it struck her that she should have asked Jake to walk her back. She started to turn towards the cabin, but stopped. She didn't want to take the risk that he would refuse her. Besides, it seemed terribly important that he not see her as a little girl. She smiled as she broke into a run. Jake's music was the *worst*. He was smelly and sweaty and hairy and *Jewish*, and certainly drunk, and most likely all washed up, too . . . Maybe he was even crazy. She hoped to God that she'd see him again.

And then she saw the procession of torches coming towards her through the woods.

Chapter 15

The torches flared through the thorn branches, tip-ping the tiny spines with barbs of flame, as the procession snaked towards her. Abigail led the seniors, and though their firebrands must have been heavy, they held them high as they marched with an eerie silence through the woods. Cassie could smell the torches—rags dipped in kerosene—and the smell brought back the straw men, and the way the fire had breathed them to life the moment before they burned.

What were those bitches going to set on fire tonight? she wondered. Or whom?

She hid behind a boulder at the edge of the trail, pressed her body so tightly against it that she felt the coarse texture of the lichen on her cheek.

They were close enough to her that she could see that Abigail and the other seniors had painted their faces a ghostly white. She was certain they would see her too, that she would be trapped in the flare of their torches. She held her breath.

And yet they didn't see her. They looked right through her as they neared, passing only yards away. Their eyes seemed drugged, glinting darkly in the torchlight like thorns.

She felt instinctively that they weren't hunting for her, but that awareness didn't set her mind at ease. Wherever they were heading in their strange trance—whatever their goal—she sensed she would feel the aftershock.

Once the torches dissolved into the forest, night trapped her in its web. She groped her way down the gully, towards the trail that led back to camp. When she emerged on the playing field, she glanced over her shoulder: the torches had not followed her.

Or maybe they had. The stars seemed to burn as brightly as the torches, a confused procession across the sky. Instead of heading directly to the campfire by the beach in the distance, Cassie doubled back through Lakeside, so that Sarah and the others would think that she had been there all afternoon.

When she reached the campfire, a wind from the lake was fanning the blaze, so that the campers were forced to retreat back from the first row of split-log benches facing the firepit, to escape the flames that leapt out at them. On the second row of benches, Sarah was strumming a guitar and singing "Tom Dooley." The campers joined in, boisterously offkey. Sarah had a pleasant, lilting voice, Cassie thought. She sang as effortlessly as she danced. When Sarah winked at her, Cassie started over to tell her about Jake.

But something held her back. It wasn't that Sarah might bawl her out for going off-limits. It was the other girls. She could imagine what their teasing would be like if they overheard. She glanced around the campfire: Chelsea was giggling, Melanie and Jo toasting marshmallows and stuffing them into graham-cracker sandwiches with squares of Hershey Bar. If they found out where she'd been . . .

She edged to the far end of the bench, and sat down between Robin and Iris.

"Where were you?" Iris asked. Cassie didn't answer. Instead, she popped two marshmallows from the cellophane bag into her mouth, realizing that she had missed dinner. "We needed you. They were going to *drown* him."

"Drown *who*?" Cassie glanced uneasily towards the fire as a blazing log spat out a shower of hot coals and collapsed into ashes.

"Him." Iris opened the front of her jacket to reveal a white kitten curled against her T-shirt. "The cook's cat . . . that big black Manx that's always prowling around . . . She went into labor right in the middle of dinner. I mean, it was gross . . . She would give this kind of shriek, and then a kitten would come popping out. She would barely have time to lick it off before another was born, and then another and another." Cassie stroked the kitten's head. "There were seven of them, each one pure black," Iris continued, "And then this one." The white kitten opened its mouth to mew, but no sound came out. "The mother cat wouldn't lick this one off like the others . . . wouldn't let it near her milk. It was like she didn't want it to live. That's why they decided to drown it."

"Who's they?" Cassie knew the answer, of course. They had very nearly drowned *her* today. She took the kitten from Iris and pressed its tiny body against hers. She could feel its heartbeat against her chest, as fragile as a butterfly's beating wings.

" 'Put it out of its misery,' Abigail said. Can you imagine? And the seniors were all hot to go along with her. So before they came back, I grabbed him."

"*You?*" Cassie was surprised at Iris' boldness.

"I didn't have any choice." There was pride in Iris' voice. "Robin wasn't any help. She's been totally out of it . . ."

Cassie realized that Robin hadn't spoken a word, and

turned to her. "What's up?"

"I needed you," Robin said. There was an accusing edge to the past tense, as if she felt that Cassie had abandoned her.

"Tell me . . ." Robin didn't answer. "Here." Cassie held the kitten out to her. "Whatever it is, he'll make you feel better."

Robin leaned closer to take the kitten. Even in the ruddy glow of the flames, she looked terribly pale. She cradled the kitten as gently, it seemed, as she wished someone would cradle her.

"Come on . . . what's wrong?" Cassie asked again. No answer. Just a look of acceptance on Robin's face, as if she were somehow taking pride in what was causing her pain. "You're not going to tell me?"

"Not this time." A strange smile crossed Robin's lips.

"I don't get it." This was the way things were supposed to be, wasn't it? The way Robin had wanted it. Robin the dependent one, Cassie the rescuer. Only Robin wasn't playing by the rules. "Look, if you're sick, Robin, I'll take you back to the cabin."

But Robin's eyes had focused on something in the forest, something emerging onto the lawn. The torches.

Above Sarah's voice singing "Swing Low, Sweet Chariot," a chant drifted towards the campfire.

> *"Who will it be tonight?*
> *Whose turn will it be?*
> *Who will be the lucky one?*
> *The Spinning holds the key."*

"The spinning." There was a quaver in Chelsea's voice.

"Spinning?"

"Jesus, Cassie." Chelsea rolled her eyes and smoothed out the wrinkles in her satin Dodgers jacket. "Don't you know anything?"

> *"Who will it be tonight?*
> *Whose turn will it be?*
> *Who will be the lucky one?*
> *The Spinning holds the key."*

Sarah stopped strumming the guitar, and the voices of the girls around the campfire faded. The marshmallows that they had been roasting were suddenly forgotten, left to char among the coals. The seniors glided through the dark towards them, their eyes reduced to hollows in their chalk-white faces, their heads seeming to hover, disembodied in the air.

Cassie stood up. She wasn't going to take another one of Abigail's sadistic games, and she intended to tell Sarah so. But Sarah and the other counselors had left, distant silhouettes heading up the lawn towards the lodge.

Cassie grabbed Robin's arm. "Let's get you to the infirmary."

"You can't split," Jo said.

"Why the hell not?"

Chelsea shot out a manicured hand to stop them: "Everybody stays. Everybody *has* to."

"Screw it. Robin's sick." But Cassie could feel the hot breath of the torches on her neck.

> *"Who will it be tonight?*
> *Whose turn will it be?*
> *Who will be the lucky one?*
> *The Spinning holds the key."*

The seniors planted their torches in the sand, then joined hands to surround the girls from Lakeside, circling faster and faster around them. The Spinning, Cassie thought. Whatever it was, she didn't want to be there when it ended.

Melanie was licking her lips nervously; Jo's eyes were wide; and Chelsea was digging the purple points of her nails into her neck. The way the seniors moved *was* hypnotic, Cassie thought, their bodies a blur, backlit by the torches. It seemed as though the only ones who refused to yield were the three newcomers to camp this year, the three misfits: herself, Robin and Iris. Robin was hugging the kitten close to her, as if to protect it from the chanting. Iris was crossing herself, again and again, as if the movement were a nervous tic. But Cassie could feel her eyes drawn to the ring of seniors circling them.

Don't look into Abigail's eyes, she thought. But how could she avoid them? In the blur of movement, it seemed that Abigail's eyes were everywhere, surrounding her, glazed eyes that made Cassie think Abigail was drugged. But as Abigail led the others whirling in the dance, Cassie sensed that her ecstasy came from something much more potent than drugs, and much harder to explain.

Circling . . . circling . . . the seniors' dance spawned a wind that fanned the dying campfire to a roar. And still they spun faster, their white faces dissolving into rows of grinning teeth in the firelight, their feet pounding a strident tempo in the sand. Cassie glanced down and noticed one of the marshmallow sticks poking into the fire an arm's length away. The marshmallow had burned away, leaving a pointed tip that the fire had heated into a red-hot poker. *Grab it,* she thought . . . *Use it to force your way out of the circle before they can stop you* . . . But as she leaned down for the stick, it was already too late. Because the seniors had stopped.

"The Spinning holds they key."

Stretching out their arms until they extended over the flames, they turned, their fingers like the pointers of compasses stabbing north.

Pointing at one of the girls from Lakeside, and Cassie refused to accept it, refused to accept the name the seniors spoke as one.

"Robin."

Robin pressed a hand to her stomach, as if the mention of her name had made her sickness worse.

"Robin . . . Robin . . . Robin . . ." The seniors

chanted, *"Robin . . . Robin . . . Robin,"* as though the syllables were an incantation with its own magical powers. Slowly, Abigail raised her palms upward, beckoning for Robin to stand.

"Stay here," Cassie whispered. "They can't make you . . ."

Robin's voice was distant. "I have to."

"Don't be dumb!"

"I . . . I . . . *want* to."

"Are you out of your mind?" But in her calm, Robin seemed anything but that. It was Cassie whose voice cracked, Cassie who seemed to be ranting. "Come on . . . You don't have to go with them . . ."

"Fuck off! I'm sick of you telling me what to do!" Robin let the kitten slip from her hands. Though it rolled so close to the fire the flames singed its fur, Robin made no move to help.

Cassie snatched it up. "Robin!" That cold, hard look—it was something Cassie had never seen in her friend before. "Robin, *please* . . ."

Smiling her most-popular-girl-at-camp smile, Abigail held out a pendant on a thin silver chain. Cassie strained to see the bauble that flashed in the firelight, but before she could make it out, Abigail had slipped the chain around Robin's neck, and the pendant disappeared down her sweatshirt. From the jealous stares of her cabinmates, Cassie guessed that any of them would have gladly taken Robin's place.

Abigail reached out for Robin's hand, and as if someone had thrown on fresh kindling, the bonfire leapt higher, shooting sparks into the sky. Defying the heat, Abigail led Robin towards the firepit, where wind-blown flames lashed out at them in blades of orange and yellow and red. Cassie wanted to pull Robin away, but she couldn't get near her—the heat was too intense.

"Robin, don't . . ."

As Abigail slipped an arm around her and pulled her close, Robin didn't resist. They stood belly to belly in the scorching heat, Abigail pressing her hips against her.

Then Robin closed her eyes and opened her mouth. Abigail plunged her tongue inside.

The brackish taste of Miss Grace's tongue welled up in Cassie's throat, as if it had been coiled there since the first night of camp. The old woman's nameless hunger —she wondered if that was what possessed Abigail tonight.

I can't let them do this to her. But Cassie knew no one was making Robin do anything, that she was doing it because she wanted to.

The other seniors embraced Robin in turn, pressing their bodies against hers one by one, caressing her breasts in the firelight. And she opened her mouth to accept their kisses.

Then she looked back at Cassie with a defiant smile. Abigail picked up her torch, and as Robin followed her, the night seemed darker to Cassie than before.

One by one the girls from Lakeside stood up, slowly, seemingly disappointed that their turn had not come, and headed back towards the cabin. Cassie lingered on the beach, watching the seniors' procession as it snaked into the forest.

She's gone. She left you, like your mother.

On the eastern horizon, a campfire crouched on a distant hilltop far beyond the lake, orange, feline, like a tiger eyeing its prey. Why hadn't she noticed it before? Had its flames been smoldering since dusk? Or had they flared suddenly, like lava spewing from a volcano? It was impossible for Cassie to say. But she sensed that the torches were moving towards it.

And that she would never see Robin again.

Chapter 16

~~~

Jake crumpled up the pieces of composition paper and threw them, one by one, into the fire, waiting as breathlessly for them to explode into flame as if they were hand grenades. "Pay attention. This is as close as I intend to come to suicide tonight." The toad perched on the Moog didn't condescend to reply. It just stared at Jake, its throat throbbing, the membranes over its eyes glazed in boredom. "One funny thing about me," Jake said. "Desperation makes most people shut up. It only makes me run off at the mouth."

The cabin was stifling. The tin roof absorbed the heat of the day and left the room roasting after dark. He had stripped off his cut-offs, and stood naked before the fireplace. It crossed his mind that he must have looked like someone indulging in an ancient, secret rite. "Don't get me wrong, I've tried the real thing before. No leaps from tall buildings . . . no bullets in the brain, of course. Just valium. Mucho valium. I took them like M&M's, all at once. But I was chickenshit. I knew Barbara had heard the crazies in my voice on the phone . . . that she'd come home early that day . . . and that there'd be plenty of time for the stomach pump. Christ, you're married ten years and your wife knows what you're thinking before you do." He scanned the notations on another sheet of composition paper, then crumpled it into a ball and threw it into the flames after the others. "This kind of suicide takes more guts. A lot more."

The toad puffed out its throat. "Okay, so you're not impressed. You know something, you web-footed son-of-a-bitch? You're lousy in bed. The nights here have been the worst, thanks to you. But tonight's a lot easier. Because it's my last night here. I mean, who needs it?" He ran the tip of his finger along the toad's warty back. "Sorry, but I have to admit it. The only reason I'm indulging in a one-sided conversation with an amphibian is because it's easier to look into your beady eyes than those." He glanced nervously at the tiny red lights on the synthesizer that had been staring him down for hours.

Flicking a dial on the console, he played a few chords on the keyboard, the strident notes resounding in the cramped room. Then he took a drag on his joint and winced. "I don't know which is staler, my grass or my music." The electronic hum of the synthesizer annoyed him and he mashed a button. The red eyes of the Moog died stubbornly.

Satisfied to have killed it, he took another long drag on the joint, his eyes smarting from the acrid smoke. Grass made him paranoid, he knew, and yet he puffed on it anyway. "Just because you're paranoid," he mused, "doesn't mean they're really not all out to get you." But who needed enemies? he thought. As long as he had himself.

Grudgingly, Jake lay the joint stub on the console and turned to the tapes, the one he had played for Cassie, and those that he had laboriously mixed together to make it. One by one he let the transparent plastic reels unspool their shiny brown tape into the fire. The acetate strips flared brightly, and the poisonous smell of burning plastic filled the room. Then the fire went out.

"A flash in the pan," Jake mused. "Like all my work . . . like my life. A moment of brilliance, followed by . . . Damn kid. It was all her fault." He turned to the toad. "A thirteen-year-old teenybopper shoots me down, and I cave in?" He shook his head. "No, it was just a matter of timing. If she hadn't wandered in out of the woods, I would have been able to kid myself for three more weeks . . . maybe four. Until I got back to the Big Apple and played it for someone who would have been a lot less polite. At least she let me down easy . . ."

He took a final hit from the joint stub. It burnt his lips and mixed sourly with the taste of Wild Turkey, but instead of bringing the numbness he wanted, the two intoxicants canceled each other out, and forced him back to reality. "Okay, so the nature-boy bit was a disaster. No snappy tunes came out of the Wurlitzer." He sighed. "So I guess it's back to New York." He said the word as though it was Siberia. The end of the line. For going back meant admitting to himself that he didn't have it anymore, admitting that it was gone.

He threw a battered canvas suitcase on the mattress and flipped open the latches. A photograph of his wife stuck out of the side pocket. It was Barbara's favorite picture of herself, taken at the Metropolitan when she was restoring the gold leaf on an illuminated letter of a medieval Book of Kells with a tiny paintbrush and a magnifying glass. She had given him the picture to take with him, but he hadn't put it up. He wouldn't have been able to stand her supremely competent gaze, judging him.

Reluctantly, his eyes returned to her face. The intelligent brunette with the impudent smile would have seemed striking to him, had not ten years of marriage dulled the edge. She had become an expert at preserving antiquities as a curator at the Met, but their marriage felt so old, so stale, it was like one of those fragile artifacts she handled with such caution—breathe on it and it might crumble to dust.

"Her patience is her best quality," he said to the toad. "She must have learned it restoring all those rotting manuscripts. God knows, she's patient enough with me . . ." *When I can't get it up in bed*, he should have added. But he didn't have the heart to tell even the toad that. "I wonder what she'll say when I show up on her doorstep three weeks early, and tell her I couldn't get it up with my music either?"

The toad shot out its tongue to pick off a fly from the rim of a beer can on the console, but the fly darted away. Jake managed a wan smile. "Looks like I'm not the only one who can't get it up."

He wedged the photograph back into the pocket of the suitcase. "Maybe I'll walk in and find her in the arms of another man. A clean-cut Gentile instead of a nervous Jew. No, she's too damned faithful. Besides, the other curators in that mausoleum are too light on their feet to get turned on by her." He threw some T-shirts into the suitcase. "Face it, what you're afraid to admit is that if your wife were making it with another man, you wouldn't give a damn. You don't have any more passion left for her than you have for your music. Even that kid from Casmaran could see that."

The toad's eyes were drooping. "You look just like my old shrink." The amphibian's eyes sealed shut. "I get the message: my fifty minutes are up." Jake lay down on the mattress, the unwashed sheets gritty against his bare back. "When I pull out tomorrow, I'll leave the Moog . . . all the other crap here. It's yours, Horatio, for services rendered. Maybe you can lay eggs in it or something . . ." He looked up at the cobwebbed rafters. "I should make it back to the city in time for a little borscht at the Carnegie Deli, with a healthy dollop of sour cream. And my first hot pastrami in a month. Now that, my friend, could arouse a spark of passion even in me."

Impossible to sleep. The only effect of the booze and dope had been to turn Jake's stomach. An owl screeched as it circled over the cabin, hunting for rats. Even the rats were different up here, he thought, more devious, more elusive than the variety that made themselves at home in his Upper West Side apartment.

The room was suffocatingly hot, and reeked of burnt plastic. He stood up unsteadily, slipped on his cut-offs and pushed open the screen door. Outside on the porch he took a deep breath: the air smelled of pines, but the perfume bored him. Without the asbestos particles, the soot, the carbon monoxide he was used to, the night wind was too thin to revive him. At least in New York, he reminded himself, there was always enough human misery to distract him from his own.

He looked up into the sky. All right, so for once in his life he could actually see stars. But they mocked him, like the lights of his Moog, rendered him puny and insignificant.

The Milky Way, the chirping cicadas, the rustling pine branches, the wind moaning, rippling across the lake . . . He didn't understand them. They were much more baffling, much more ominous to him than the sirens and saxophones of Manhattan.

God, he would do anything to be able to write music again. *Real* music. When he was young, creative, he mused, he had thought the problem had been whether or not to sell out. But now that he had hit rock bottom, now that he was ready—even eager—to sell his soul, he had come to the grim conclusion that nobody was interested in buying.

The fire on the hilltop across the lake, so far away that it looked like a yellow moon that had collided with the trees . . . he didn't understand that, either. The only fire he had seen here before was the nightly campfire at Casmaran, on the opposite shore. But this one had to be a good hour's trek into the forest, in the middle of nowhere. The fire, a fierce and hungry orange, must be enormous.

It reminded him of the Burning Man.

He hadn't thought of the Burning Man for months,

maybe years, but he had dreamt of him often enough. It had been little more than a bad joke at first, a spot of black humor. In the sixties, he had been the youngest composer to have a piece performed at Lincoln Center. His moment of glory had been turned into disaster by the critics, and adding to the debacle, was the protester who had chosen that evening to set himself on fire on the plaza in front of Alice Tully Hall. The corpse had never been identified—nor the cause for which he gave his life. But Felix Cruller, the most perverse of the critics, had made the most of it in the *Times*, suggesting that the self-immolation of Jake's career had been just as sudden and complete. The photo of the Burning Man had wound up next to the review, as though it were an illustration, and something had driven Jake to save it, the kneeling man engulfed in flames, as though it were a picture of himself the night he had died.

Staring at the fire burning on the distant hill, Jake wondered how it must have felt, that decisive moment when the man had set himself on fire. It had been a creative decision, he decided, and like all creative decisions, irreversible. One which for boldness, he knew he could never rival. The distant bonfire shot orange streaks into the sky, and he felt a strange certainty that it must have been the color of the fire when it had consumed the man, as though flames took on a fiercer hue when they devoured something alive. The wind rose in his ears, and he wondered if that was how the roar of the flames had sounded to the Burning Man, the last music he had ever heard, like the beating of wings.

The sudden wind bore another sound . . . a sound that didn't come from nature. Its sharper edge pricked Jake's consciousness, like the shards of flint in the dirt of the clearing that caught the light of the moon.

At first he thought it was only the alcohol or the grass that had transformed the mournful sigh of the wind into *this*. Yet, as his ears filtered out the enveloping evening wind to grasp the eerie strains, he knew that it wasn't a figment of his weary imagination.

Music. Neither harmony nor cacophony, but the fusion of violently clashing notes and rhythms from deep in the night. Melodic? No, he couldn't call it that. But hypnotic . . . haunting. Terrifying, as passion, overheard, can be. Was it a celebration? A lament? He tried to use his musical skills to classify the sounds, to analyze the components, but the alien scale, the primitive rhythms, didn't yield to reason.

Then why did he respond so intensely to it? It touched a part of him that he thought had died long ago, the part that could respond to music, not as technique or craft, but as pure emotion. It aroused the child in him, the spark of wonder that he thought he had lost.

He tried to distinguish the individual instruments that melded so seamlessly: strings, plucked with feverish fingers, but with a timbre like no violin or guitar he had ever heard; a reed horn with a somber, ominous tone; a drum, pounding as insistently as a heartbeat. And . . . *voices*? They seemed to be filtered, not only through distance, but also through time, echoing across hundreds, perhaps even thousands of years, like a buried memory from a lost civilization. Sounds which for their purity, their power, were more intense and vivid than any music today. He knew he would never be able to imitate them on his electronic synthesizer, for all its ten thousand transistors.

Jake hurried inside and brought out his Nagra, threading on a tape and walking towards the edge of the clearing. He clamped on his earphones and aimed the Sennheiser microphone in the direction of the sounds, stepping lightly on the earth, as if afraid his footsteps might scare them away. But in only a few minutes, the music faded with the dying wind. He strained forward with the microphone to catch the final notes, and then they was gone, lost in the breeze taunting the pine boughs.

Something inside of him still vibrated to the music, and the resonance tempted him to reach deep into himself, tempted him to unearth melodies of his own. They had been elusive, those forest rhythms, but they had lingered long enough to spark a feeling, astonishing and a little bit terrifying—that he still might have something left to say in his music. All of a sudden Jake knew he wasn't going to leave tomorrow.

He guessed that it was the most important decision of his life.

Chapter 17

Robin was dead. It was crazy to think that, of course, paranoid, Cassie knew that. But it didn't make her any less certain. Back at the cabin the night before, when she had waited up to ask Sarah where they had taken Robin, Sarah had just smiled and said, "*It's a camp tradition. They do it when they need one of the younger girls . . .*"

Cassie had lain awake in her bunk all night, watching the moon dissolve into the lake, thinking *they need one of the younger girls for what*? And when dawn came and still Robin hadn't come back, Cassie had started to rock, rocking with the rhythm of her mother's lullabies, the drowsy pace of her heartbeat. It hadn't put her to sleep.

Now, as she stumbled down the trail along with the others on the morning hike, she tried to remember Robin, to picture her face in her mind. It was as hard as it had been to picture her mother's face after that day at Woods Hole.

"Death Caps . . . Destroying Angels . . . Spring Amanitas . . . My God, have you ever seen so many poisonous mushrooms?'' Iris scribbled the names of the species in a spiral notebook as she picked her way among them, the fleshy fungi clinging to rotting logs in their path.

Sarah was ahead, up the trail, in the next stand of pines. She hadn't taken them to this part of the forest before, Cassie realized. Why were they suddenly hiking through an area where everything was so dangerous? Cassie kicked at a clump of Destroying Angels, grinding them to a yellow pulp under her heel as she passed. Death Caps pushed up through cracks in the lichened rocks, and as she stepped on them, they made a sighing noise, the scent of sour milk rising to her nostrils. She was desperate to talk to someone about what had happened last night, but Iris was hopeless.

''I mean, I've seen poison oak and poison ivy before.'' Iris slipped her finger into the notebook to keep her place. ''But can you believe it? *Brain Gyrometra*.'' She poked a tiny mottled green fungus on a tree stump with her pencil. ''Its cap looks just like a human forebrain, see? There must be hundreds of them, thousands . . . enough to wipe out the entire summer population of Maine.''

There was something poisonous about this place, Cassie brooded, the camp, the lake, the woods. There had to be, to take her friend from her. Robin only came here to keep you company, Cassie thought. Were you really the one at fault? You should have held onto Robin, just like you should have held onto your mother . . .

The others had hiked far ahead, and Cassie didn't have the energy to catch up with them. She slumped down on a tree stump, and Iris joined her.

''Do you realize that ninety percent of all the people who die from eating poisonous mushrooms in the U.S. die from those in the Amanita family?'' Cassie didn't answer. ''Look, if you're not interested . . .''

''I'm not.'' *Why don't you just shut up*? Cassie wanted to say to the girl with the long-winded scientific explanations that never explained anything. Why did she always have to try to impress you with how much she knew? Since Robin had gone, Iris had stuck close to her, the way those mushrooms stuck to the logs, Cassie thought. As if she had inherited her friendship from Robin. Cassie resented it. She didn't want the other girls to lump her in with the weirdo from South Boston.

Iris held up a pink flower that poked up between the toadstools. "This is windflower. It likes to live among the poisonous fungi. In the Middle Ages, they used to brew tea from its leaves to induce menstruation." She crushed the petals between her fingers and threw them to the ground.

God, I need Robin. Robin had always been able to tell her when her anxieties were full of it. How could Iris put her fears to rest? Cassie thought, Iris, who blew things out of proportion.

"This forest . . . It's positively lethal! Maybe we could get it in the *Guinness Book of World Records* or something." Iris edged between two clumps of red-tipped poison oak. "It must be the soil . . ." She laughed nervously and dug her toe into the black volcanic dirt. "Something decaying here that makes this weird stuff grow . . ." She took a few more steps and froze.

Cassie bumped into her. "What is it now? *The Mushroom That Ate Cleveland*?"

Iris pointed towards a clump of blackberry bushes. "God . . . He's got a gun!" She ran up the trail, towards Sarah.

Cassie peered cautiously into the bushes. When she saw who it was, she broke into a smile. Jake. The "gun" he held was a shotgun microphone—she'd seen TV crews using them at her father's speeches. In her eagerness to reach him, she crashed through the bushes.

A flock of blue birds exploded from a tree.

"Jesus Christ!" He pulled off his headphones. "You scared the goddamn meadowlarks away."

"*Those weren't meadowlarks.*" It was Sarah, with

Iris and the other girls at her side. "They're bluejays. And they sound like hell."

The birds fluttered back to roost in another tree, and broke into a hoarse, grating cackle. Sarah's eyes met Jake's and both of them laughed. They stood there, looking at each other without talking, Cassie noticed, the way two people do when they have never seen each other before but want to know each other. Cassie could have killed them both.

"I guess my experience with wildlife never got much past Central Park." It annoyed Cassie the way the moment he laid eyes on Sarah he turned on the charm. He was staring at Sarah's body and Cassie could see why: with the light falling behind her, Sarah's breasts were clearly visible through the flimsy cloth of her Indian blouse.

Sarah gave a toss of her head and her blonde hair shimmered. "So what's your excuse?"

"Excuse?"

"You're trespassing on camp property."

"Shame on me." He smiled. "I was just, you know, recording some sounds to put into this piece I'm working on . . ."

"Piece?"

"Electronic music. I'm a composer. I thought some bird song . . . *real* birds . . . might work well in the thing I'm putting together." He gestured towards the tin roof of his cabin, visible through the trees. "Want to come by and hear it? We could have a beer . . ."

The sonofabitch. He didn't offer me a thing. Cassie glanced around her at the other girls: Melanie, Chelsea, Jo, even Iris . . . They were eating it up, gaping as if they'd never seen a man before. She bit her lip. *If they realize you're jealous . . .*

"You know you're not supposed to go any further than the edge of the clearing," Sarah said, but she was smiling.

"I've got criminal tendencies."

Sarah had come here deliberately today—there was

no question in Cassie's mind now—just to meet him. How could she have been so stupid not to see it coming?

"Well, now that you know where I am," he said to Sarah, "drop in any time . . . while the kiddies are taking a nap." He took all the campers in at a glance, and Cassie could see that he hardly recognized her. *You were dumb to think anything else.*

Sarah toyed with the whistle around her neck. "It's against the rules, of course."

"I think I'm going to puke," Cassie whispered to Iris, then turned abruptly and headed back towards camp.

God, it hurt to walk out like that, Cassie thought. It wouldn't have been so bad if she'd had Robin to confide in, but without her, she felt totally alone. She stumbled as she took a shortcut through the woods. She hated herself for her adolescent awkwardness, her little-girl body . . . hated herself for having a crush on Jake, even though he obviously didn't know she was alive.

Iris caught up with her. "I suppose they'll probably copulate," she said, with as much distaste as she had described the poisonous mushrooms.

"The word," Cassie murmured icily, "is *fuck*. Well, let them." Iris nodded. At least she had *her* fooled, Cassie thought.

They clambered into a creek bed. After weeks of hot, dry days, the brook had dwindled to a trickle, and they had to pick their way around muddy pools that smelled of rot, where yellow jackets swarmed.

And then Cassie saw her on the trail.

At first all she could see was Robin's face smiling through the trees. She was leading the seniors on horseback behind her, down the dry creekbed, a rocky trail impossibly steep for horses, Cassie thought.

She's okay. She's never looked better. Cassie ran towards her.

And then, as they emerged from the trees, Cassie saw that Robin was whipping her horse's flanks with a thorn branch to force it over the sharp rocks.

"What are you *doing*?" Cassie had meant to sound

calm, but her voice rose shrilly. It only seemed to make Robin beat the horse more mercilessly, until the welts on its flanks bled, staining its black coat. Under the hail of blows, the horse took a few more steps down the sheer slope. Then a boulder gave way beneath its hooves and it groaned in pain, its muzzle flecked with foam.

"Robin, are you crazy?" Robin had loved animals. People don't change like that, Cassie thought. They don't change overnight, so drastically, so cruelly . . . But Robin was beating the horse again, the barbed switch wet with blood. "Stop!" Cassie grabbed her arm, but Robin took a swipe at her with the crop.

"Get out of my way, cunt!" The other seniors caught up with Robin, their horses raising a cloud of dust, and Cassie stared up through it at her friend, trying to make some sense of her transformation. Her face hadn't changed. Robin still had the same pixie nose and curly blonde hair. But she held her body differently, her shoulders thrust back, her spine stiff. Her body . . . that was what had changed. What could they have done to her last night?

The seniors riding bareback behind Robin were clad in bikinis, defying the forest's brambles and poison oak to flaunt their bodies. And Robin's breasts . . . her hips . . . they seemed to have developed overnight, her bathing suit suddenly two sizes too small for her.

Robin tried to force the horse past her. "Get out of my way, Cassie. I don't need to put up with your bullshit anymore."

Abigail reined her horse up beside Robin's. "Looks like that Jew's got Cassie creaming in her pants."

"Too bad," Robin laughed. "He's got the hots for Sarah."

"Go to hell!"

How did they know? Cassie thought. *How could they?*

"Look at her," Robin smirked. "She's going to come just thinking about him."

"She'd like to suck his cock," Abigail said.

"Maybe she already has!"

Cassie lunged for Robin and dragged her off the horse. Robin lashed out with the thorn branch, swinging it so hard that it flew from her grasp into the dirt. Suddenly the furry that had been bottled up inside Cassie for weeks erupted, and she shoved Robin into the creekbed, driving her fist into her belly. Before she could twist Robin's arm behind her, Robin tripped her, and they rolled into a muddy pool.

Maybe their friendship had always been a sham, Cassie thought as her rage took hold. Maybe they had always been enemies . . . competing over Todd . . . locked in a breakneck race over who would get to be a woman first. Well, the race was over. Robin had won, and that was reason enough to fight back.

No more thinking.

It felt good, this chance to escape her thoughts in the fury of the moment, as completely as she lost herself in her dancing.

Then it hurt. Robin fought with a ferocity Cassie had never seen in her before, and it was all she could do to defend herself.

Rolling on the ground, Cassie grappled for a hammerlock on her friend, and was amazed by what she found. She had thought she knew Robin's body as well as she knew her own. They had played together, wrestled and showered and skinny-dipped together since they could walk. But Robin's body . . . It wasn't Robin's body anymore. Robin's baby-fat was gone, replaced by solid muscle. Whenever they had fought as kids, Cassie had won—she was in good shape from dancing, while Robin, so self-indulgent, so flabby, got winded easily, or just gave up. But now Robin was the one with the strength. And even more incredibly, she was the one with the will. Robin seemed to have the same visceral hatred for Cassie that Abigail had shown at the dance pavilion. But why?

Cassie lay, dazed and breathless, in the mud, but

Robin wasn't even breathing hard. She scrambled to her feet and jumped on top of Cassie, knocking the breath out of her. She pressed a knee to her chest, pinning her arms and thighs, but with a sharp elbow to her ribs, Cassie loosened Robin's grip long enough to rip her bikini top open. In response, Robin grabbed Cassie's throat, and rocked back and forth on top of her. Cassie struggled to free her arms, but couldn't. She tried to suck in a breath, but Robin's fingers shut off her windpipe.

No more air. Cassie's mouth was wide open, but she couldn't seize one more breath. She was getting dizzy. The ground started to slip away from under her. Before she could black out, she shaped a word: "*Please.*"

Robin tightened her grip on Cassie's throat and began to rock frantically astride her chest. Cassie realized with horror that Robin was approaching orgasm.

In a final, desperate lunge born of disgust, Cassie wrenched a hand from under Robin's legs and clawed at her breasts.

The growth under Robin's left arm . . . a fleshy polyp . . . It wasn't there yesterday when we took a shower together . . .

Cassie tore at the tiny appendage with her nails.

"Bitch!" Robin shrieked. Whimpering with pain, she shot her hand under her arm and staggered off of Cassie. Abigail ran over to help her back onto her horse.

Without a word, the seniors rode off up the creek bed, leaving Cassie sprawled in the mud gasping for breath.

"I don't believe it!" Iris crossed herself and jumped down to help Cassie. "What did you *do* to her?"

"I . . . I don't know." Cassie grabbed Iris' outstretched hand and pulled herself weakly to her feet. Her body ached and her neck was raw and red where Robin had choked her.

"You won!" Iris steadied her arm.

Cassie shook her head. Robin had died, the Robin she

had known. Murdered suddenly, swiftly, in one night.

It was not until they neared the camp that she was aware of the moistness of her fingers. No matter how fiercely her mind resisted, she remembered: when she had scratched at the tiny protrusion under Robin's left arm, a white liquid had spurted out, as sour-smelling as the milky poison in the Death Caps. She wiped her hand on her T-shirt, but the stickiness wouldn't go away. She sensed that it foretold something terrible, as terrible as if Robin had throttled the life out of her in the dust.

Chapter 18

"A nipple," Cassie said.

"*Sure . . .*"

"It was a nipple under her arm. A third nipple."

Iris said nothing in reply, and it was too dark for Cassie to read her expression. In the windowless twilight of the cement-block shower house, green algae grew in a slippery mural across the walls. Iris had wanted to give the kitten in the box under her bed a saucer of milk, but Cassie had insisted they come here first, to wash off the mud and sweat of the fight . . . and the liquid from that nipple on her fingers.

The algae smell in the shower house reminded Cassie of the forest, and she wondered whether poisonous things grew here, too. She pulled off her towel and turned on the water, scalding hot. "Aren't you going to tell me I'm crazy?"

"No . . ." Iris hugged her towel around her as though to avoid facing her emaciated body. "I've got this big medical encyclopedia at home. Some of the pictures are really gross, but there's this one of a woman with three nipples. It's some kind of inherited genetic thing, like freckles, or hemophilia. Hideous maybe, but no big deal."

The explanation didn't soothe Cassie any more than the hot water that stung her skinned knees and bruised arms. "But . . . Robin didn't have it before. I know she didn't."

Iris hung her towel on a hook and stepped into the shower cautiously, as if she feared she might drown in the spray. "She always had it. It's something you're born with. It doesn't just grow overnight."

"Robin was my best friend. I would have noticed."

"My mom had six toes on one foot and I never noticed until last year."

"That's *your* problem."

"Besides, it's not a *real* third breast." Iris shied away from a centipede crawling across the wet cement floor. "It's just a . . . growth . . . like a benign tumor, or a wart or something."

Cassie started to mention the milky liquid that had spurted out of it, but stopped. She didn't want to remind herself. Scrubbing her body obsessively, she avoided washing under her left arm, as though afraid that a third nipple might have appeared there too.

"She's a freak," Cassie said, more loudly than she needed to, hoping to silence the voices in her mind. *There must have always been something wrong with her . . . something hidden, like that ugly growth under her arm you never noticed before.*

Iris turned off the shower with a nervous yank of her arm, and darted over to the lockers, the reflex, Cassie thought, of someone used to being teased about her pigeon-breasted body. Cassie lingered under the spray long enough to convince herself that no amount of soap and scalding water would ease her tension. By the time she reached the lockers, she had expected Iris to be fully clothed, in her usual eagerness to conceal her body. But Iris was naked, standing frozen in front of her open locker.

"What's wrong?"

"I got it . . . Cassie, I finally got it!"

Iris turned around, holding up her panties. My mother lied to me, Cassie thought. There was nothing beautiful about this moment of becoming a woman. Even in her worst fantasies, Cassie had never imagined that there would be so much blood. "We'd better get you back to the cabin," she whispered, hoping she had hidden her disgust.

Iris let the panties drop to the floor, dazed, and Cassie wrapped a towel around her. "I got it," Iris repeated as she walked unsteadily towards the door.

"You feel okay?"

"I don't know . . . I'm so nervous . . . What should I do?"

Cassie stopped and looked at her: "Didn't your mom tell you about it? I mean, what it would be like?"

Iris shook her head. "She doesn't like to talk about things like that."

"Oh, great!"

"But I read about it. I mean, that medical encyclopedia has this whole chapter on it, with illustrations." When they reached the porch of their cabin, Iris put a hand up to cover her eyes. "I guess it didn't say how I would feel."

"It won't be so bad . . ."

"No, Cassie, you don't understand." She wiped her eyes. "I'm *happy*. I mean, I guess I never really thought . . . I never really believed it would happen to me. I've always felt so different from everyone else. But now . . ." She didn't have to finish. Cassie read the look in Iris' eyes: *Now, maybe they'll accept me.*

Cassie squirmed. Iris was staring at her as if Cassie were the needy one. "Wow! I didn't realize you *hadn't* yet. I'm sorry . . ."

"Forget it," Cassie said quickly.

"You'll get yours . . . soon," Iris said, and Cassie knew she must have sensed the envy in her voice. "I mean, if I can get *mine* . . ."

"I said, forget it."

The cabin was deserted, and at the sight of the empty bunks, Iris slouched down on hers, seemingly disappointed that she couldn't announce the news to the others.

Cassie rummaged in her footlocker. "Here . . ."

"What?"

Cassie held up a tampon. "I brought a box along. Wishful thinking, I guess."

"You've got to be kidding. No way am I going to stick that thing inside me!" Iris lay back on her bunk. "When you get cramps, you're supposed to put your feet up. That's what the book said. Losing all that blood . . . it can make you weak." She glanced up at the crucifix on the wall and crossed herself, as if grateful a prayer had been answered. "Wait till I write my mom . . ." She leaned up on an elbow and for the first time since Cassie had known her, Iris smiled: "No . . . I don't think I *will* tell her."

Then Iris seemed to forget Cassie was there, lost in her private bedtime ritual: lifting the top sheet just enough to slip in one leg at a time, plumping the pillow, then wriggling down until only the top of her head poked up above the blanket.

"*No . . .!*"

Like a marionette jerked up by the strings, Iris pulled her legs up quickly and kicked back the covers.

Something at the foot of the bed riveted her, something that had been hidden beneath the sheets.

"The blood," she whispered. "*The blood!*"

Cassie stared at the contorted form that stained the sheets at the foot of Iris' bed. Blood from its slit throat matted its fur. The kitten.

"*The blood . . .!*"

The blood in Iris' panties . . . It had not been her own. Cassie knew where it had come from and who had put it there. Iris broke into sobs and huddled in a corner of the bunk, her chest heaving, and Cassie slipped an arm around her. "It's all right . . ." she whispered.

"Everything's going to be okay." But she didn't like the way her voice rang hollowly off the raftered ceiling, in the still air.

The ground resisted as they dug into it, stubborn and unyielding, as rock-hard as the headstones poking up from the thistles and weeds. It seemed impossible that the ice cutters long ago could have carved deep enough into this flinty soil, when the ground was frozen, to plant the dead here. The effort it took to dig the small hole drenched Iris and Cassie in sweat, but the surrounding gravestones somehow drove them to work with heightened urgency. Not until they had finished hacking at the earth, chipping away at it with their trowels as though it were a block of ice, did they stop to catch their breaths.

Iris brushed away pebbles from the shallow grave. "The worst thing that ever happened to me before this," she said, "was last year at school. I was a lab assistant in Biology. You know, the kid with the highest grades gets to feed the lab animals, clean their cages . . ." Cassie pretended to listen as she stared into the sky: gray clouds were rolling in from the horizon, the same gray as the granite slabs around them. "The job was okay, I guess," Iris continued, "until the end of the year. Just before school was about to let out for the summer, Sister Garth—she's the nun who was the bio teacher—she told me she was going to some retreat for the summer and wouldn't be able to come in and feed the lab rats, so . . ." Iris took a deep breath. "So she had me fill up this twenty-gallon aquarium with water. Then she gave me a pair of rubber gloves and told me to . . ."

Cassie looked at her blankly. "What?"

"Drown them." Iris glanced into the grave. "She made it sound so practical, even merciful. But I wouldn't do it."

"What did she do?"

"She put on the rubber gloves herself . . ."

"Jesus . . ."

"I mean, what could I say? She was the teacher. The first rat didn't put up a fight. It took her only about two minutes to kill it. But the others . . . God, after the first one, she couldn't even catch the others! I couldn't believe it . . . Here was this room with a crucifix on the wall, and this nun is running around trying to drown a bunch of rats!" She tried a nervous laugh and failed, then wiped obsessively at the dried blood on her fingers.

"When my mother died, there was hardly any blood at all," Cassie said. "Just one tiny red spot . . ." She touched her forehead. "Like a Hindu holy mark."

A dark speck bobbed along the sawtooth horizon of pines, barely visible against the approaching clouds. Cassie watched it dip below the trees, then shoot up into the sky again, flying closer.

"What I could never figure out," Iris murmured, "was how they knew. The rats, I mean. Rats are only dumb animals, right? But I swear, Cassie, every one of them knew what was about to happen to them . . . They *knew*." She sighed. "That was the worst part."

Cassie watched the black speck soaring in the sky, watched it until she could see what it was—the wings spread like dark blades, the hooked beak, the talons. A bird of prey. And the awareness swooped down on her with such suddenness that she blurted it out: "My mother knew. The look on her face when she fell over the side of the dock . . . It was as if she had . . ."

"What?"

Cassie faced Iris. "As if she had *expected* it. As if she knew all along she was going to . . . die."

As if to avoid intruding on Cassie's thoughts, Iris knelt down and nestled the kitten's body in its shoebox coffin, into the grave. "The ancient Egyptians," she said, "I read somewhere that they used to bury all kinds of stuff in the pyramids. And cats . . . they believed cats were sacred. They used to mummify them, to sleep beside their dead masters."

Cassie looked down at the cardboard box, remembering how perfect her mother had looked in her coffin of split pine. And yet something had been wrong then . . . something that only struck her now: her mother's hands, folded on her chest . . . Her mother's hands . . .

The ring . . . the silver ring in the shape of a hand that her mother had always worn . . . the ring Cassie had hated. It hadn't been on her mother's finger. Could it have slipped off in the fall from the scaffolding, the plunge into the water? Not likely. It had been too tight for her mother to remove, even using all her strength. Too tight for a mortician to remove without cutting off her finger.

Someone had taken it. But how?

And why?

It must have been there. You just must not have seen it, like you didn't notice the nipple under Robin's arm.

Cassie helped Iris shovel dirt over the shoebox, trying to bury the unruly wisp of a memory that kept her mother's funeral from being neatly tucked away in her mind.

Leave mother's coffin shut, she told herself. *Don't pry it open, or you'll never be able to close it again.*

Cassie was surprised with herself. Instead of ridiculing Iris as she fashioned a crude cross of twigs and planted it on top of the grave, she was actually helping her. There was not a single stone cross among the slabs tumbled around them; maybe that was what compelled Cassie to do it. She looked up into the sky. The bird of prey was gone, leaving the gray clouds to merge together into a shroud.

Iris patted the mound of dirt and stood up, brushing off her knees. She tugged at the crucifix around her neck and murmured a prayer. And Cassie didn't tease her. Somehow, the thought of the missing ring, the final terrible knowledge in her mother's eyes . . . She threw a handful of earth on the grave, the pebbles thudding dully as they fell, and when Iris picked some daisies

from among the weeds of the graveyard, Cassie helped
her spread them over the dirt.

If Cassie had looked over her shoulder as she and Iris
threaded their way back among the toppled headstones
in the graveyard, she would have seen the creature that
was watching them, silently, shrewdly. The black Manx,
the mother cat, staring at them with demon-yellow eyes.
Biding her time. Waiting for the gust of wind that
knocked over the fragile cross of twigs.

If Cassie had looked back, she would have seen the
mother cat creep silently towards the freshly dug grave
and rake her claws across the dirt. Slowly. Patiently.
Until the corpse of the kitten was unearthed.

If Cassie had been watching, she would have seen the
Manx seize the kitten's blood-matted body in her jaws,
and drag it into the woods.

But Cassie saw nothing. For she had turned away
from the tombstones, as if expecting to read her own
name on one of them. The foreboding, the certainty of
doom—she knew now how those rats had felt. How her
mother must have felt.

Iris had been right. Knowing was the worst part.

Chapter 19

~~~

"But you've *got* to!"

"Honey, I'm sorry. I'm really sorry."

From where she stood at the phone in the corner of the lodge, Cassie could hear the laughter outside, see the sudden tight embraces in the sunlight as daughters ran into their mothers' arms.

"There's nothing I can do."

"But you promised." She heard herself whining like a little girl, and she didn't try to hide it. She had been waiting for her father since dawn. "You've got to come . . ."

"Christ, what a terrible connection . . ." Clay's voice was fading in and out, but when the static ebbed for a brief moment, she could hear the excitement in it. "Sweetheart, I know how much you wanted me to come . . . I couldn't wait to see you dance. But what can I say? This is the one thing on earth that could possibly keep me away."

The stuffed animal heads were staring at her from the

walls, as if they knew the reason she needed him, as if they knew it had absolutely nothing to do with the dancing now. She wanted to tell him that it was much more urgent than that, but it was also much harder to talk about, and it left her fumbling for words. "Why can't you? Why can't you come?"

A pause, then, "They think they've found your mother's murderer."

She could say nothing, but turned her eyes away from the mothers and daughters embracing on the lawn.

"I think it's finally over, Cassie. The Director is handling it personally, flying out to see to the indictment today. Apparently some kind of extremist group . . . in California. The Director said I could come along. They've got the suspect in custody, Cassie."

"But you said you'd come and . . ."

"I owe her this, Cassie. I owe it to myself. And to you. But most of all for Ann. You see that, don't you?"

But Cassie couldn't see. She couldn't forgive him for this. Not ever.

She's dead and I'm alive. She doesn't need you anymore but I need you. Right now.

He was waiting for a response from her, she knew, a few words to diminish his guilt. But other words were stirring inside her, forming on her lips: "Dad . . ."

The static was getting worse.

"Dad!"

Was he speaking to her? Was he still there?

"Cassie?"

And then the line went dead.

Cassie flinched, and rattled the phone hook, but it did no good. The receiver felt terribly heavy as she slid it back on its hook. The stuffed animal heads glaring down at her—they reminded her of things dead but not buried. She rushed outside.

The breeze was blowing in mounting gusts, flapping a sign between the two firs sheltering the main lodge: "Welcome—Daughters of Casmaran." Crepe paper streamers fluttered in the breeze off the lake, writing frantic shadow-messages on the lawn. Mothers and daughters gathered around the punchbowl to the sound of laughter. The wind whipped Cassie's hair in her face, blinding her, roaring in her ears like the ocean of static that had drowned her father.

"For a second, Jake, I thought you'd hung up on me." Barbara's voice faded in and out. The phone had gone dead for thirty seconds, and then clicked mysteriously back to life.

"What can I say? This is the middle of nowhere. The phone lines up here are fucked."

"Then maybe that's why I didn't hear you right a minute ago when you said you didn't want me to come."

He hesitated. "I'm too busy."

"*Jake* . . ." Even over the bad connection of the pay phone, even over the clang of the cash register and the country-and-western drone of the jukebox at Murdock's General Store, Jake could hear his wife sigh. "But you said it was going badly. Maybe I could help."

"Everything's changed. It's okay now."

Barbara's voice was cautious. "*Are you sure?*"

The dusty room felt stifling hot all of a sudden, even though the Copenhagen Chewing Tobacco thermometer on the wall read only seventy-five. "I'm fine," he managed.

"You don't sound fine."

Damn, she knew him well. He wiped the sweat from his brow and glanced at the grizzled grocer behind the tarnished cash register. Murdock was staring back at him warily, as if suspecting his only customer was planning to rob the place.

Jake tried to think. He hadn't slept for . . . how long? Thirty-six hours? Sleep had been impossible since he'd heard the music. The music in the woods had been like some strange upper that had kept his heart racing, made booze or grass superfluous. Barbara's silence was heavy with suspicion. He could picture her tugging on her long brown hair, biting on a nail, trying not to let her fear get the better of her.

"You haven't met someone, have you? I mean, we're not dealing with a midlife crisis fling?"

"Come *on*, Barbara." But it feels like it, he wanted to say. The giddy, crazy excitement, the need for secrecy, and the willingness to betray the world were the same he had felt when he had first met Barbara. He had been faithful to her until now. Now he was cheating on her, having an affair, though not the way she would have imagined. The passion he felt for his music was suddenly much greater than any he had ever felt for her. The only reason he had interrupted his frenzy of work to drive all the way here and phone her was because he knew if he didn't, she would show up on his doorstep tomorrow, when he least wanted to see her.

"But I miss you . . ." She said it as if that would overrule all his objections.

"I miss you, too." He knew he was both lying to her and to himself. He cradled the receiver in the crook of his neck and leaned against the wall, scanning the old phone numbers scratched in the knotty pine, as if trying to read a script for a role he could no longer play.

He didn't miss her. He felt greedy to be left alone with the music, alone with what it had awakened in him.

"*You'll be my sweet Texas rose* . . ." The country-and-western tune on the jukebox clashed with the melodies in his mind, infuriating him.

"Well, what can I say? I'm glad it's going so well, Jake. I can't wait to hear it." Her unconvincing tone confirmed that she thought the worst, that she suspected he had worked all summer and come up with nothing. That she feared his elation came because he had chosen a simple, drastic solution, the same that he had chosen that night when they had pumped twenty-five valium out of his stomach at Bellevue.

A long pause. Finally, "When are you coming home?"

"When?" He repeated the word slowly, stalling. He hadn't thought beyond tonight, tonight when he prayed the music—the inspiration—would come again. It had to come again.

"I love you." Barbara's words were smothered in static.

Thank God the phone went dead before he had to answer her with "*I love you, too*." As he hung up the receiver, the only emotion he felt was the compulsion to return to work.

He headed towards the door, but realized that if he was going to hole up in the cabin, he would need supplies. The shelves of the general store were stocked with moldy cartons and rusty cans, as if the grocer knew his customers had nowhere else to go. In his haste, Jake didn't bother searching for the one box of Wheaties that wasn't infested with weevils, the one can of tuna that wasn't dented. Instead he began picking up things at random—cake mixes and Fritos and TV dinners, Shake 'n' Bake and Jello. When he plunked them down on the counter, Murdock eyed him suspiciously, rubbing a thumb along his unshaven cheek as cautiously as if he were testing a razor.

"Add it to my account," Jake said.

Murdock stabbed his finger and the nickel-plated cash register clanged like a slot machine hitting triple oranges. "That'll be thirty-two dollars and ninety cents. Cash."

"What is this? I've been running up a tab all summer."

"That was before I heard where you was stayin'." He shot a glance at the phone. "You're over at the lake, aren't you? The Casmaran cabin."

Jake nodded cautiously. The way Murdock was looking at him, he felt as though he were confessing to a crime.

Murdock gripped both sides of the cash register, like a preacher at a pulpit. "If you're stayin' in the Casmaran cabin, it's cash only, friend. I've had it up to here with you people."

"Really? And what kind of people is that?"

The old man's gaunt face stretched into a smirk. "New York. You're from New York, ain't you?"

So that's it, Jake thought. *He hates Jews.*

"How did you know?"

"Every summer it's the same thing. Those bleedin' hearts over at the camp rent their damn cabin to some so-called *artist* . . ." (*Read dirty Jew*, Jake thought.) "Some guy comin' up here from New York, some artsy-fartsy asshole thinks he's bein' creative out there in the woods."

Jake considered slugging him. But a glance out the window at the wall of trees beyond the porch reminded him that if he didn't buy his groceries at Murdock's Stop 'n' Shop, there'd be nowhere else for a hundred miles.

"And every summer it's the same shit," Murdock muttered. "The fella from that cabin runs up a tab as long as my arm buyin' food and booze, then takes a powder before the season's half over."

"He splits for home?"

"Who knows? That's the last I see of him. All I know is he stiffs me with the bill." Murdock picked up the three cans of tuna Jake had stacked on the counter and headed back to the shelf with them. "No credit, friend. I'm through bein' stung by Shylocks."

The way Murdock limped across the warped floor, hunched, Scrooge-like, over the three dented cans, reminded Jake of Felix Cruller, the critic from the *Times* who had savaged his last piece. Jake scooped up the groceries from the counter and walked out the door without paying. When he finished *this* piece and laid it on him, he'd blow old Cruller away.

The pickup was slow to accelerate, but once Jake got

it barreling along, he was pushing sixty. The truck's wheels crisscrossed over the white line as he forced it on with drunken excitement. The trip to the telephone had cost him valuable time, but had won him something more important: isolation. The same isolation that had once driven him crazy was now essential for his work. He would be ready for the music when it came again tonight. Waiting. And if it didn't come, he would wait for it tomorrow night and the night after that. He would be there to seize it, record it—to extract inspiration from it. To make it his own.

The pickup swerved around a corner and Jake's eyes darted from the dusty asphalt to the side of the road. Where the hell was he? The wall of evergreens gave the impression that despite his speed, he was hardly moving at all. He had lost his bearings, as if his giddy high had clouded his judgment on mundane matters, and searched frantically along the roadside for a landmark. He cursed himself for his stupidity and looked up at the sky, as if it might provide a clue to his location.

And when he looked up . . .

It shot across the sky so quickly that he wondered at first if he had seen anything at all. Maybe it was just a side-effect of his euphoria, he thought, like spots before the eyes.

But when he saw another one, he jammed on the brakes, skidding across the road onto the dirt shoulder with a screech of burning rubber.

From this distance, silhouetted against the gray of the gathering clouds, it was impossible to tell how large they were. They had no wings, but they were hurtling through the air, heading into a strong wind and seemingly unharried by it.

But if they weren't birds . . .

At first he blamed his ignorance of nature for not knowing what they were. There had to be a simple, rational explanation. But before he had a chance to sort it out, to analyze the sight, they vanished among the trees.

Magic? Since last night, when he'd heard the music, he already knew this place was magic. But the idea didn't frighten him. Right now, he needed that magic more than he had ever needed anything before.

He shoved the truck back into gear, the engine rumbling to life. As baffling as it had been, the mystery above the trees had also been strangely reassuring. A promise that the music—the music on which everything depended—would come again tonight.

Chapter 20

—————➤—————

". . . And it is a special privilege to welcome our
fellow daughters of Casmaran here today . . ."

Sarah was addressing the audience from the dance
pavilion stage, wearing a lemon-yellow Lacoste shirt
and white bermudas instead of her usual leotard and
Indian blouse, the whistle around her neck replaced by a
string of pearls. The women sat in aluminum folding
chairs facing her, their hands folded in their laps, the
summer suits in silk and linen unwrinkled even in the
muggy heat. Cassie noticed that they all wore sunglasses, though the sky had clouded over. Their eyes
were hidden, yet she felt that they were staring at her.

Why had none of the girls' fathers come today?
Cassie wondered, uneasy at the realization. The women
wore the plastic nametags that had been awaiting them
in the lodge, nametags that were for the most part un-
necessary. Their faces would have been familiar to
anyone who read a newspaper or magazine, Cassie
thought, recognizing several of them from the political
receptions and speeches that she'd attended with her
father.

"I'd like to introduce our guests," Sarah said, nodding to them one by one: ". . . Mrs. Sybil Flint, Head of the World Hunger Fund . . ." Robin's mother. The statuesque blonde in the Italian leather jacket, one of those infuriatingly cool Nordic women, had never been close with her mother, Cassie thought, even though they had been summer neighbors on Nantucket. The woman was sitting next to her daughter, and Cassie wondered whether she had noticed the change in Robin. Or perhaps mother and daughter were simply more alike now.

". . . Catherine Gorham, publisher of the Washington Herald . . ."

The prim woman in dull blue had dined at their townhouse in Georgetown more that once, and Cassie remembered being trundled out in her quilted satin bathrobe to say good night, the woman responding with a grin that came a little too readily to be genuine. She had written the obituary for Cassie's mother herself and it had appeared edged in black on the front page of the newspaper. But it struck Cassie now that her mother had once confided that she couldn't stand her.

". . . General Loren Bradshaw . . ." The mannish woman had worn civilian clothes here, of course, but the beige suit was as severe, as crisply starched as if it were a uniform. It was hard for Cassie to imagine that this lady with the ramrod-straight posture could ever have had a daughter. And yet she was holding hands with Tris, the blonde Amazon from the senior cabin. General Bradshaw was the only woman on the Joint Chiefs of Staff, Cassie thought, the only woman on the reviewing stand at Woods Hole besides herself and her mother the morning Ann . . .

The General had run like the others. She had run like hell.

"Of course, one of us is missing today," Sarah said. "One of the most respected campers ever to bunk up at Casmaran. Ann Cunningham Broyles."

There was a respectful moment of silence, and Cassie

squirmed under the pitying gaze of the audience. Bitches, hypocritical bitches. Every one of these mothers had been seniors once, she thought. Which ones had tormented her mother, the way Abigail and Robin had tormented her? Maybe as adults they had learned how to hide their sadistic selves under veils of politeness, but deep down they were still no different from their daughters at Casmaran. If they were the "lifelong friends" her mother had meant in the letter, then why had none of them come to the funeral?

Cassie picked out Abigail in the audience. She had never imagined her as having a mother. And when Sarah rattled off the name of Abigail's mother, everything suddenly made even less sense than before.

". . . Margot Burgess . . . Director of the FBI . . ."

The gray silk dress adorned with a single jade teardrop on a gold chain, the close-cropped gray coiffure, sensible while still feminine . . . Cassie refused to believe that she could be Abigail's mother, refused to believe that someone entrusted with upholding law and order could have a child so evil.

But then a thought sliced across Cassie's mind and she forgot all about Abigail: *What is Margot Burgess doing here?*

Her father had said that the FBI Director was leaving immediately for California, and that he was going along. Had he just been lying so he wouldn't have to come?

But there was another possibility, one that was even more disturbing. What if Margot Burgess had lied to him? What if she had sent him out to the West Coast on a wild goose chase, while she came here? Cassie didn't understand, and yet she read a threat in Margot Burgess' presence, a threat that was too intense to grasp head-on, like trying to stare directly into the sun.

The women were blending together into a faceless crowd before Cassie's eyes, like the generals and admirals at Woods Hole, obeying a reverent silence like the one before her mother had climbed the scaffolding.

"Today we're honored with a special guest," Sarah said. The audience murmured enthusiastically. "A guest who hasn't blessed us with her presence for many years . . ." Sarah nodded to Cassie. "But first, some special entertainment."

Cassie felt naked in her leotard. It was suddenly as if she were about to perform for the same audience she had performed for at Woods Hole when she had taken the bottle of champagne. The breeze off the lake stung like an ocean wind. As she started up the steps to the dance pavilion, the stairs creaked, like those leading to the scaffolding that had faced the submarine. Why did she feel so certain that once she stepped out onto this wind-whipped platform something equally unexpected and horrible would happen?

Someone put on *Swan Lake*, the overture rich with violins.

Everybody's watching.

As Cassie wavered on the edge of the stage, expectant applause rippled through the audience. Although intended to encourage her, she knew, it had the opposite effect. It sounded too much like the applause of the crowd at Woods Hole, the moment the champagne had exploded against the steel hull.

She stared back at the women watching her from behind sunglasses that reflected the glare of the sky with a metallic gaze. *She must be seriously disturbed*, she was sure they were thinking. *Not surprising, after all she's been through . . .*

To hell with them. They can't make me dance.

The last thing Cassie wanted to do was lose herself in the music. She should be thinking now, making sense of things that didn't make sense, trying to put the pieces of this unsettling puzzle together.

And then she saw someone watching her, someone in the woods on the opposite side of the dance pavilion from the audience, where the forest formed a green velvet backdrop. Jake had pulled his pickup to a stop on the dirt road and leaned out of the open widow. He was smiling at her.

Jake. It was almost like having her father there to watch.

Dance. Show him how good you are. Show him how you can make the music come alive.

She was only dimly aware of how she reached the center of the stage, and yet when she moved across the smooth wood floor, the music *did* take hold, like the wind that was blowing ever more strongly off the lake.

She spun gracefully towards the water, then circled back in a series of *jetés*, stealing a glance at Jake in the woods. As she danced she could feel the tension easing from her body, and for a moment it was as if her mother were dancing with her, as if the events that had tainted Casmaran had never happened. The music had brought her under its spell, and she glanced back at the audience, certain it had captured them, too.

But they weren't paying attention; they weren't even looking up at the stage. They had twisted around in their seats, craning their necks to stare behind them. The record ended, but there was no applause, for the audience was standing in respectful silence as Abigail pushed a wheelchair towards them, with a passenger, small and frail.

Miss Grace.

Cassie's eyes darted back to the woods. A cloud of dust hovered where Jake's truck had been.

The old lady was close enough that Cassie could see the harlequin sunglasses that hung crookedly on her beak of a nose. She was swathed in a winding sheet of gauzy scarves, as if to protect her shriveled skin from the fresh air and sunlight.

An awed hush settled over the group as Abigail wheeled Miss Grace's chair closer. It struck Cassie as strange that the women who had gathered here, each so powerful in her own right, should be so humble, so submissive, before this senile invalid. She suspected that it was for this audience with Miss Grace—and not to see their daughters—that they had traveled all this way. And Miss Grace . . . What had compelled her today to leave the shadows where she had taken refuge for so many years, and venture into the harsh noon light?

Abigail turned the wheelchair around at the base of the stairs to the dance pavilion so that Miss Grace faced the women, and sat down on the grass at her feet. Miss Grace's lips parted, as red with lipstick as an open wound, and words crept out, so faint that Cassie held her breath to hear.

"My, how gratifying it is to see so many of my girls here today . . ." The old woman's voice cracked, as if she longed to shed tears but could only summon their parched memory. "I call you my 'girls' of course, because I don't just see you as daughters of Casmaran. I see you as *my* daughters." She tried to laugh away her emotion, the strength in her voice building. "I want to thank all of you for your generous contributions to our construction fund. The new arts and crafts cottage will further nurture the creativity that we so cherish here, and the basketball court that should be completed well before next season, will foster Casmaran's high ideals of sportsmanship . . ."

She cleared her throat, as though her next words would hold momentous importance. "All of us were campers at Casmaran once. We traveled up the path from the junior cabins through Lakeside, and went through the Spinning to join the seniors on Hilltop. We learned what demands the Sisterhood places on us. And we must be especially mindful of them now. For this is the year of years; the generation of which it is written . . ." Puzzled, Cassie studied the women in the audience, hoping to find the meaning of Miss Grace's sermon on their faces. But their look of reverence told her nothing.

Miss Grace's voice was sibilant through her false teeth: "I have consecrated my life to Casmaran. So have you . . ." With what seemed enormous physical effort, she tilted her head to face the seniors as they moved from their mothers to sit next to Abigail in the grass at her feet. "This will be your last summer at Casmaran as campers, so this will be our time to say adieu." Cassie could see that the girls' eyes were wet with tears, as first Abigail, and then the others stood up and walked forward to take Miss Grace's limp hand and press it gently between theirs. And when it was Robin's turn, from where she stood on the stage of the dance pavilion, Cassie saw the glint of something silver under Miss Grace's lace glove.

It looked like . . . It was only a wild guess . . . How could she be sure?

You've got to see.

As the last senior returned to her seat, Cassie descended the steps from the dance pavilion and a murmur of disapproval from the audience made her quicken her pace. As she stepped in front of the wheelchair she could see the dark suggestion of eyes beneath the tinted lenses of Miss Grace's sunglasses. Eyes that seemed to be looking at her differently than they had in the cottage. Was it fear Cassie saw in them? She reached out for Miss Grace's hand.

"Don't!" The old lady shook her head and tried to squirm away, but her paralysis made that impossible. Cassie grabbed the cold fingers.

And squeezed.

The sharp silver ring on Miss Grace's hand cut through the lace to pierce Cassie's palm, and the blood that moistened her hand told her that there would be a new scar to intertwine with the two already there, a scar that was proof of what her mind still refused to accept: her mother had worn that ring, and it had been stolen after her murder.

Cassie dropped the old lady's hand into her lap and broke into a run. Over her shoulder, she caught a glimpse of the campers and their mothers in their prim designer clothes. Not one of them moved to stop her, but she could feel their eyes on her. And when she reached the manicured lawn, she kept right on going, past the cabins, past the main lodge, and through the graveyard. Despite her headlong pace towards the forest, she read two words that had been chiseled in granite. *"Choose death."*

Her mother's ring. *Impossible*. Plunging into the shadowy isolation of the trees, Cassie's anxiety mushroomed. The chiffon sash around the waist of her leotard snagged on a holly bush and she tore it off, forcing herself up a steep slope, running to escape the growing awareness. But it clung to her, like the foxtails that pierced the skin on her ankles with their barbs.

Miss Grace? How did she get the ring?

Doubts chattered in her mind like the magpies in the branches overhead. She moved quickly, hoping her speed would somehow accelerate her thoughts.

But mother loved Casmaran . . . she said so in the letter . . .

Miss Grace has her ring.

When at last she stepped from the thicket into the clearing, the slate-gray sky admitted as little sunlight as the forest's web of thorn branches. For a moment it was a relief to be free of the cackling birds high in the treetops, that had followed her here. But the sudden stillness was even more disturbing.

Maybe he's gone home. Back to New York.

The steps groaned loudly in the silence as she climbed onto the porch of the cabin.

"Jake?"

The flapping of wings as a hawk merged with the sky.

"Jake?"

She banged on the door. No answer. She tried the rusty door handle, but it was locked, and she stood on tiptoe to peer through the smudged windows. The room was a study in black and white: crude wood furniture, papers crumpled everywhere, the Moog dark and dead. A swarm of flies buzzing over greasy dishes offered the only trace of movement. She strained to see if Jake was stretched out on the mattress on the floor, but the sun suddenly pierced the clouds, turning the grimy window into a mirror.

A mirror that reflected a stranger standing behind her. In one swift second, her eyes took in the sheathed hunting knife, the knee-high boots, the windbreaker camouflaged the same green as the forest. If he was a hunter, she knew who was his prey.

Part Three

THE GLORY HAND

Chapter 21

~~~~~

For a moment, Cassie could not tear her eyes from him.

His face was sallow, an oddly emaciated face for so muscular a body, she thought, as if the arteries above his neck had atrophied so that blood didn't pump into his head at all. Slicked-down black hair molded his skull like feathers. He lunged towards her.

She sidestepped him and jumped off of the porch, running towards the back of the cabin. But in a blur of movement another hunter's-green jacket rounded the corner, another set of arms reached out to grab her. She bolted towards the lake.

It was a dozen yards to the shore. She waded into the stand of cattails that thrust from the mud, heading towards a sandbar that extended into the water. A mistake. She stood out in silhouette against the glare of the water, and they spotted her. As the men ran towards her, Cassie scanned the shore: a dilapidated tin-roofed shack twenty yards to the left tilted up from the mud, like the rotting hull of a boat that had run aground. She tripped over a rock beneath the surface and fell, then crawled . . . splashed . . . towards it.

There was no door on the side of the shack that faced her, only a rusted metal flap, some kind of trapdoor —large enough for a dog, or a child, perhaps. But not a man. It resisted shrilly as she wrenched it open. Heavy footsteps crunched onto the pebbles of the beach. She hoisted herself up and squeezed into the opening.

The door clanked shut behind her, shutting off all light, and she teetered, groping in the darkness for a handhold. She reached out . . . clutched at thin air.

She was falling into a void, hurtling down a chute of corrugated tin in a bruising, battering descent.

She landed on her back, hard, the impact knocking the breath out of her, and when she opened her eyes it was as dark as if her lids were still closed.

Am I dead?

No, she was still breathing. She pressed a hand to her pounding heart.

The interior of the shack seemed enormous in the dark—it had been dug out to extend far beneath the water level of the lake, she realized. Her fall had been cushioned by the damp, spongy floor, and she raked her fingers across it: sawdust, impregnated with rot. Its smell was enough to turn her stomach, but it had saved her life.

She tried to pull herself to her feet, but pain shot through her leg from her ankle to her thigh. Her fingers moved down to touch the rusty cutting edge of . . . a scythe? A saw? The heavy blade pressed down on her right ankle, clamping it as tightly as a bear trap. She tried to lift the blade off, but it had been imbedded by the years into the floor, and there was no way to pull her leg out from beneath it.

A scream of hinges and the door to the chute above yawned wide. A face blocked the opening, backlit by the gray sky.

She tried to scramble out of the sudden square of light

it threw on the sawdust, but the blade bit into her ankle, holding her prisoner.

"*Cassie*?" The gruff voice echoed hollowly down the metal chute.

How does he know my name?

"*Cassie*?" The echo, breathless and angry from the chase.

"*Is the little bitch in there?*" Another head forced the first out of the way, blocking out the patch of sky and plunging her back into shadow.

"*No way.*"

"*Shit!*" The silhouettes bobbed in the opening for a moment, and then were gone, leaving a square of sky.

In the dusty shaft of light, Cassie could see more clearly. The walls of the shack were sheathed in metal that glowed dully, like the walls of a crypt. The moldy sawdust, the metal chute, the floor far below the water level of the lake . . . this had to be one of the abandoned sheds that Sarah had mentioned, where the ice cutters had stored blocks of ice until spring. No wonder she was shivering. She wondered whether the morgue at Woods Hole where they had taken her mother's body had been as cold as this.

And then she heard something stirring in the sawdust, the sound of claws scratching, teeth gnawing. Rats, scurrying in the shadows, bloated rats with thick, healthy coats of fur. She stretched until her leg ached, straining to see what had brought them here.

The fragments that the rodents gnawed were too decayed to be recognizable. Time had swathed them with layer upon layer of cobwebs, but the rats had ripped at the translucent shrouds to reveal yellowed manuscripts and wooden carvings, and what looked like paintings in murky oils. Cassie wondered if these things had once been precious—even sacred.

I've got to get out of here.

Sweat drenched her face, stung her lips. She strained against the metal blade until she felt the filmy moistness of blood. The rats stopped gnawing on the artifacts. They must have smelled the blood, she thought, for they began to skitter closer to her.

"Help me!" she screamed as she struggled to lift the metal blade. Again and again she called out, until her voice was hoarse, but the rats began scratching at her legs with their claws, pricking her skin with their needle-sharp teeth. She struggled to squirm away, but the pain from her ankle held her prisoner. When she threw a handful of sawdust at them, the moldy wood particles invaded her nose and mouth, and she began to cough. The noise lured more rats out of the shadows.

Until another sharp sound from the far side of the shack made them freeze.

A scimitar of light slashed up to the ceiling as a door behind her creaked open on rusty hinges, blinding her with daylight.

"*Hey!*" A man's voice.

They waited for me. They knew I was here all along.

She flattened into the sawdust.

Too late. The man had seen her.

"*What the hell are you doing in here?*"

"Jake . . ."

"I was recording . . . Jesus, I heard screams . . ." He clattered down a wooden ramp, sending the rats darting back into the shadows. Then he set down the tape recorder slung over his shoulder and strained to lift the blade. When she was able to roll free, they both saw the blood that stained the sawdust.

"Are you okay?"

"I . . . I don't know . . ." Cassie grabbed his arm and pulled herself up, setting her weight cautiously on the wounded ankle.

"You could have killed yourself in here. What the hell were you trying to prove?" He wiped the blood from her leg with a handkerchief, and she didn't flinch. "You're lucky it's not broken."

Cassie took one deep breath, then broke down in sobs. "These men . . . they were chasing me. Jake, they were going to *get* me . . ." She wanted to stop, to control the hysteria in her voice, but the words poured out against her will: "There were two of them . . . They knew my name. They were going to *kill* me!"

"I didn't see any men."

He means he doesn't believe you. But he's got to. Her mind reeled back, stumbling over the strange, inexplicable things that had happened since she'd come to Casmaran. "The girls at camp . . . Abigail bounced off the lake, and then they took Robin away . . . and now she's just like them. She's got this . . . this *tit* under her arm . . . And then they killed the kitten and put the blood . . ."

"Hey, take it easy."

She hated his condescending tone. But when he slipped his arm around her, she allowed him to hold her close to him. "You've got to believe me . . ." Her words trailed off into sobs, and he didn't let her go. "I'm not crazy."

"Of course you're not."

"Why do they want to hurt me? Why do they want to *kill* me?"

"Nobody wants to hurt you." His embrace loosened suddenly.

"Jake, listen to me . . ."

"Wait . . ." He had noticed the crumbling artifacts in the sawdust and let go of her, kneeling down for a closer look.

"Jake . . ." He began sorting through the filthy debris as if he had forgotten she was there. His face took on a look she hadn't seen in him before—intense, haunted—as if he were the one on the edge of hysteria. Cassie watched as he rummaged among old picture frames from which the rats had already stripped the canvas. Slowly he lifted out a painting which had survived its ordeal in the ice house better than the others.

It struck Cassie that perhaps the rats had spared this one because even they found the images repulsive: fading, ethereal figures of naked women in murky greens and browns, their flesh cadaverous, their limbs contorted, dancing in ecstasy. Some of the women played musical instruments—a primitive harp, a strange violin, the twisted horn of a ram—while others coupled obscenely with dogs and goats. And in one corner of the unfinished canvas was a strange candelabrum that caught her eye. Its five candles looked like a hand, with each fingertip ablaze. Somehow it evoked the pointed, silver fingers of her mother's ring.

The image, at once alien and oddly familiar, forced her to say the sentence aloud for the first time: "Miss Grace has my mother's ring."

But Jake didn't hear her. He was leaning the canvas against the rusty blade, handling it as gently as if it were a masterpiece, studying it with fascination. Without tearing his eyes away from the contorted figures, the bizarre musical instruments, he murmured, "You'll be okay, Cassie. It was probably just too soon to leave home . . . after what happened to your mother . . . It probably would have been better if you had stayed with your father this summer."

Sensible, Cassie thought. Sensible bullshit. He was just saying it to get rid of her. It was as if his sudden infatuation with the obscene painting meant that he, too, was betraying her.

She started up the ramp, out of the shack, the pain in her leg beginning to ease. But before she left, she stole one look back over her shoulder. Jake was gazing at the painting with feverish intensity, his head tilted slightly to one side, as if he were listening to the music those strange instruments in the picture were playing. As if their music had captured him.

Chapter 22

~~~~~~

Something stupid. Barbara was certain Jake was
about to do something incredibly dumb. But then, she
thought, wasn't calling it that really just a lie, a way of
denying the truth? She feared Jake was going to kill
himself.

For hours, all the way from Bangor airport, the forest
had been telling her it had been a mistake to let him
come here alone. In the gray overcast of late afternoon,
the wilderness seemed hostile and unyielding, so much
less "civilized" than the forests on Long Island where
she had grown up. In a strange way, the brooding shadows, the twisted alleys of mossy tree trunks, reminded
her more of the back streets of New York City, where
Jake had been raised, than it did of the manicured
woods of her native Great Neck.

Save him.

Maybe that was why she had become a curator of art
in the first place: a need to rescue fragile things after
everyone else had given up on them. At thirteen, her
parents' marriage had fallen apart, as threadbare as the

Bayeux tapestry. And in the ten years after that, her mother and father had died, each slowly, each painfully, of cancer. "Beyond saving," the doctors had said. After that, she had devoted herself to preserving things fashioned of gilt or parchment or silver vermeil, because in her life the things that had really mattered had all been beyond her power to save.

And Jake. She had married him after that disastrous concert at Lincoln Center. Perhaps, she suspected, her purpose had been to save him too. When he had tried to kill himself with an overdose five years ago, she hadn't ascribed it to his failure as an artist, but to her failure as a wife. Today, the danger had become more urgent than gradual decay. The threat was sudden. Immediate.

Save him.

She rechecked the scrap of paper where she'd scrawled the directions to the cabin, and turned off the main highway onto a narrow side road, the asphalt pocked with holes. Accelerator foot to the floor, she forced the rented Chevette ahead: 55 . . . 65 . . . 70. Reckless, she thought. Definitely not her style. She was usually more cautious and methodical than most men— certainly more than Jake. Her cool-headedness had assured her steady, deliberate rise through the pecking order at the Met. Today's rush of female intuition took her by surprise, but she listened to it.

Save him.

On a hairpin curve, a steel sign riddled with bullet holes from some amateur hunter spelled out DANGER. Outside her window, she glimpsed a shattered railing where a car had gone over the brink.

When she had talked to Jake on the phone, she had read the danger signs. The edge of hysteria in his voice —she was sure it masked despair. The last time she had heard him so euphoric had been the night they had called her from Bellevue Emergency.

The road shifted from gravel to dirt, and dead-ended at a lake. Even the long, dreary ride hadn't prepared her for his cabin: the rusty tin roof, the rotting wood of the walls—it was little more than a hovel. Enough to push any dyed-in-the-wool New Yorker off the deep end, she thought. She parked her car beside the pickup.

Switching off the ignition, she felt her eagerness to see him replaced by a sudden attack of doubt. She studied her haggard face in the rearview mirror as if it were a medieval artifact too far gone to be worth saving. Strands of auburn hair plastered her forehead in the muggy heat that persisted into dusk. Usually she played down her natural beauty, using little makeup, as if her lustrous dark eyes and long lashes, if enhanced, would interfere with the impression of shrewd competence she wanted to convey. But on the plane from New York today she had put on more makeup than usual, telling herself that it was because Jake hadn't seen a woman in nearly two months, that he deserved it, but really, she knew, out of her own insecurity. After the sweaty drive, her mascara and eye shadow were smudged, giving her a wild, confused look. It would have to do.

Her high heels sank into the dust of the clearing as she stepped from the car. There had been no time to change from her silk shirtwaist dress; she had taken a taxi directly from the museum to La Guardia for the flight to Bangor. She hefted a shopping bag out of the trunk and carried it up the rickety steps to the porch.

Standing there, with the shopping bag in one arm, she impulsively pulled out the two silver barettes that held her hair austerely back from her face, and let it fall around her shoulders, the way she knew Jake liked it. When she knocked on the door, it opened to her touch.

The cabin was dark and she groped for the cord of the bare bulb overhead. The mess appalled her. So this was what happened when she wasn't there to pick up after him. She put down the shopping bags and set to work, straightening the chairs at the plywood table, throwing crumpled papers into the carton that passed as a trash bin. It was only after she had folded a filthy sweatshirt and laid it on the unmade bed that she realized the reason she was cleaning so compulsively. She was looking for something. By the mattress she spotted his shaving kit, and hastily zipped it open. She had been right. A plastic jar of valium was inside. Still full, thank God. She slipped it into her purse.

"What the hell are you doing?"

He was standing in the doorway, his tape recorder slung over his shoulder. She stepped forward and kissed him, but his lips were cold, unresponsive, and he gripped her arms so tightly that it hurt. She had expected him to be unshaven and unwashed, of course. What surprised her was his sullen strength, a strength hinting at a violence she had never seen in him before.

"You shouldn't have come," he said. "I told you not to come."

"I did come, and I should have." She wanted to slap him, to send him back outside to make a second entrance and start all over again. "The way you sounded on the phone . . . Jake, you sounded . . . weird." She hugged his sweaty body. "Phew," she laughed. "Doesn't this place have a shower?"

He squirmed out of her arms and walked over to slide the tape recorder on top of the Moog. "I told you. I haven't had time. I've been working around the clock."

"Don't get me wrong." She ran a hand along his bearded cheek. "You stink. But that doesn't mean I don't like it." Something was wrong. His body was tense, his eyes avoiding hers, and he turned his head so that her next kiss glanced off his cheek.

She sat down on the mattress in the corner. Maybe that was it, she thought. As much as anything, he had come here to escape the trouble he'd been having in bed, and now she was walking in as though she suddenly expected him to perform. "Look, tonight we don't have to . . . I mean, I'm wiped out from the trip. All I want to do is collapse."

He ignored her, carrying in a painting about three feet square that he had leaned in the doorway. She walked over and studied it with a professional eye. The dancers were hard to make out in the shadows, as if the murky oils absorbed what little light there was. "Something to cheer up the place?" She laughed. "No, I know. You're switching careers—that's what you've been keeping from me."

He shook his head. "One of the artists who stayed here before : . . He must have painted it."

"Before I met you, when I was in grad school, I did some art therapy. I ran this project at the Bridgewater Institution for the Criminally Insane." She hesitated, then decided to make a joke of it. "This kind of reminds me of some of the stuff I saw." Her smile faded. "The uneven brushstroke, the distorted perspective, the morbid choice of colors . . . Not to mention the subject matter. The whole thing's pretty sick, don't you think?"

Jake didn't answer, absorbed by the painting, and she ran a thumbnail along the edge, revealing a pastel layer of paint beneath the thick overlay of sickly greens and grays. "I'd say the artist went through some kind of transformation. It's almost as if at first he had a light, even a euphoric concept. Then a darker, more bizarre vision took hold . . ." She stopped: Didn't Jake see she was talking about him? "Jake, we've been married for ten years. Tell me what's wrong."

"I told you, Barbara . . ." His voice sounded distant, more distant than when he had been talking to her on the telephone hundreds of miles away. "Nothing's wrong . . ."

She sighed and handed him the shopping bag. "I thought you'd sell your soul for this." She pulled out a pastrami sandwich wrapped in tin foil. "I didn't have time to run over to the Carnegie Deli, but I did my best."

As she cleared the table to make way for the pint containers of cole slaw and potato salad, she rambled on, talking about the VIP opening at the museum, about Otto, the medieval-instrument curator whose office was next to hers, and his latest esoteric acquisition. When she found herself gossiping about the neighbors down the hall, with Jake still barely responding, she stopped.

"All right, you made your point. You're pissed off that I came. But I'm here." She glanced back at him, expecting him to be devouring the sandwich, surprised to see that he'd left it untouched on the table. Turning his back to her, he had begun cleaning the recording heads of the Nagra with a tiny brush. The cicadas outside the cabin had started up, and the sound seemed to speed his work.

"Jake, come home with me."

"No."

"Then I'm staying."

"Out of the question."

"Jesus Christ! Last month you were afraid to come up here without me. Now you're trying to get rid of me. What the hell's going on?"

When he had finished threading a fresh tape onto the tape recorder, he turned to her, his anger gone, replaced by a strange serenity. "I don't expect you to understand."

"Try me."

"I've been doing incredible work up here in the past few days, Barbara. Incredible."

"What kind of work?"

"I've found something here . . . something wonderful."

She eyed him suspiciously. "Like what?"

"Music . . ."

"Music?"

"Coming from the forest at night . . ."

"*Right.*"

"Barbara, after dark I hear these weird instruments. I don't know what they are, or where they're coming from, but they give me something, a spark I can use in my own work, the spark I've been missing."

She gestured at the stub of a joint in the ashtray. "What kind of grass have you been smoking?"

"And there are voices . . . I've heard voices, Barbara, singing."

"Jake, this place isn't good for you. Come back to New York with me."

"I can't. The music that comes from out there . . . I need it."

"The music's in your head."

"It's *not*! It's out *there*!" He shot a finger towards the door. Then his eyes locked with hers. "You don't believe me, do you? Christ, I shouldn't have expected you to understand. How could you?"

"Help me understand." She glanced at the tapes scattered on top of the Moog. "Play me what you've done." She waited, watched him weighing the decision. For years it had been a ritual with them—she'd beg him to let her hear his work-in-progress and he would resist at first. But he had always given in, grateful for her support.

"No," he said. She reached for a tape, but he snatched it away. *"I said no!"*

"All right." She backed off, confused. She had learned to deal with Jake's self-hatred, but not this . . . obsession.

"I want you to go now, Barbara." He took her arm and opened the door for her. For a moment, she thought that his look was one of pleading, that this time he needed her to leave as much as he once might have needed her to stay. Her eyes were brimming with tears as she felt his lips brush against her cheek. Without returning the kiss, she ran from the porch towards the car.

In the three steps it took her to cross the clearing, the cicadas surged louder. Switching on the ignition, she glanced back towards the cabin, hoping he had changed his mind, hoping that he had run out onto the porch to call her back. But he was busy connecting the microphone cable to the Nagra. She gunned the Chevette up the dirt driveway, the evergreens a blur through her tears.

When she lost sight of the cabin in the rearview mirror, she pulled the tape from the folds of her skirt. "7/30," yesterday's date, was written across it. She wondered how long it would take Jake to realize she'd stolen it.

Listening to Jake's music on the tape . . . Barbara was convinced it would be the only way to understand what was going on inside of him. As she nosed the car onto State 340 to Bangor, she hoped to God that the tape wasn't blank.

Chapter 23

The two girls embraced in the light of the campfire on the beach. Cassie watched them from where she stood, concealed on the edge of the forest: Abigail, kissing one of the girls from Lakeside, the younger girl's face hidden as Abigail embraced her, and plunged her tongue into her mouth.

Their torches planted in the sand, the seniors surrounded the girls from Lakeside, who watched the ritual with the same obedient silence that they had watched Miss Grace. You chose the right time to be away at the ice house, Cassie thought. At least you escaped the Spinning. But who had they chosen? Against the fire's glare it was impossible to recognize which of Cassie's bunkmates Abigail embraced.

And then Abigail withdrew her lips, and Cassie recognized the frail girl in her arms. *"Iris."* Cassie barely mouthed the name, but in the silence, it carried so far that the girls at the campfire turned towards her. She stepped out from the trees, onto the sand.

"Cassie!" Iris' usually somber eyes shone with a radiance Cassie hadn't seen in them before. "I can't believe it. They picked *me*!"

"You don't have to go." Cassie tried to remain calm. "You don't have to, Iris."

"We only ask once," Abigail said to Iris. "That is, if we ask at all."

"They can't make you go, Iris." Cassie's voice had a dull ring.

"But don't you see?" Iris reached out to Cassie with both hands, in a sweeping, self-confident gesture. "No one's *making* me do anything. I mean, they really *want* me!"

Cassie understood enough to know that it would be pointless to argue with her. It was clear what Iris was feeling: *My whole life I've wanted to belong somewhere. I can't pass up the chance now.*

But *Iris*? The girl the seniors had tormented more than any of the others? Why Iris? "It's bullshit," Cassie said. "You know they don't give a shit about you."

Robin stepped closer to Iris. "You're just jealous."

"You wish we'd chosen you," Abigail laughed.

"Iris . . . please . . . don't . . ." Cassie could hear herself begging, and she realized that she must look like Iris had looked when she had arrived at camp, small and scared and strangely old.

Abigail held a silver pendant out to Iris, the chain dangling from her fist. "It's yours."

Instead of taking it, Iris clutched the crucifix around her neck and squeezed it, the way she squeezed it when she was afraid. She understands, Cassie thought—Iris knows I was speaking the truth. She must be holding the crucifix so tightly to summon her strength.

Then, with a violent twist of her wrist, Iris snapped the thin gold chain and threw the crucifix into the fire. The flames leapt higher, and Cassie backed away from the heat. There had never been a prayer of stopping Iris, she could see that. What Abigail offered, Iris needed too desperately to refuse.

Slowly Abigail opened her fist and held out the silver

pendant, like a prize. Iris slipped the necklace over her head, and in the glimmer of the firelight, Cassie saw it.

To shut it out of her mind, she turned and ran. But her labored breathing, the pounding of her feet on the sand, could not block out the awareness: A tiny silver hand dangled around Iris' neck, a silver hand with sharp, pointed fingers, like the hand on her mother's ring. Glinting in the light from the fire, the sharp fingers had seemed tipped with claws of flame.

The screen door banged shut behind her as Cassie ran into her cabin, and she glanced over at the bunk: Iris' footlocker was gone, her mattress stripped of its sleeping bag and pillow. They had left only one of Iris' belongings behind—the crucifix on the wall. The way it hung there, gray in the shadows, it reminded Cassie of the mounted animal heads in the dining hall, something that had once been alive, now dead.

And then she saw something else, on the floor under the bed: a Kotex wrapper. So it had finally happened—the change Iris had been both dreading and eagerly awaiting. Suddenly it struck Cassie—that was why the seniors had chosen her tonight.

And Robin?

The first night of the Spinning, when they had picked Robin, hadn't Robin been sick? Hadn't she seemed to take pride in some secret pain? Cassie tried to recall if that pride had been on Iris' face tonight.

When you become a woman. That's when they want you. That's when they get you.

Waves were lapping at the pilings beneath the cabin, and Cassie remembered the riptides off of Nantucket, the way the waves had a pull of their own that nothing could stop. She wondered if the tide that had taken Robin's body, and Iris', would take hers too.

Stop thinking.

Her arms and legs ached from the day's punishment: the tumble down the chute into the ice house, and the weight of the rusty blade. Her mind ached like her muscles, with a gnawing pain that she doubted would ever heal.

She lay back on her bunk and when she closed her eyes she saw her mother, the frightened girl in the photo on Miss Grace's wall. Had Ann Cunningham become a woman at Casmaran, too? Had her soul undergone the transformation that was even more drastic than the one that had seized hold of her body?

She became one of them, and she wanted you to become one of them, too.

Impossible.

Borne on the wind, music filtered into the cabin from somewhere in the forest, and Cassie was certain that she knew its source. The Spinning, reaching its secret climax.

You've got to find out what they do there. What they did to your mother. What they want to do to Iris.

Stop them.

Laughter outside the cabin window. Cassie jumped down from her bunk and looked through the dusty windowpane. The campfire had burned to embers, and her bunkmates were coming across the beach towards the cabin. Without taking time to pull her jeans on over her leotard, she slipped into tennis shoes, and eased open the door. Crouching low, she darted down the ramp and across the lawn, around the back of the lodge. As she picked her way among the headstones in the graveyard, the moon diseased the lake in its glow, transforming the trees, the grass, her body, into marble.

The music. It drifted out of the forest to meet Cassie like a swamp mist. Usually, with a dancer's love of movement, she let music sweep her along. But not tonight. Her legs defied the rhythm, deliberately ran against it, the way she might have avoided wading across a river with a treacherous current. Cautiously, she followed the music up the slope towards the seniors' cottage.

The windows of the white clapboard cabin were dark, and the embers of the firepit where Abigail and the others had begun their procession for the Spinning smoldered greenish-blue. More like ice than fire, Cassie thought. The ashes smelled strange . . . foul . . . and among them were remains of something charred. Cassie wondered what Abigail and Robin and their friends had fed to the fire before they had abandoned it.

The music called to her much more clearly here, as if it were beamed directly towards this hill, and she plunged into the forest, towards its source. The music came in waves, like the chanting of the cicadas, taunting her, luring her down one trail, only to weaken again in volume, as if it were coming from another direction entirely. The music was like a cunning, breathing thing, she thought, deliberately deceiving her, leading her through a maze of paths to conceal its lair. And in the game of hide and seek, she found herself being led into a part of the forest where she had not been.

In her haste, she lost her balance. Her heels slipped off the edge of the trail and she tumbled down a rocky slope. When she hit bottom, she stood up and wiped the dirt and pebbles from her hands. She listened. The music was playing a cruel joke. It sounded farther away now than it had from the porch of her cabin.

She turned slowly to get her bearings. The moon had slid out from behind the clouds to reveal a gigantic silhouette looming in the darkness. The Hanging Tree? She approached it slowly . . . Wasn't it in the opposite direction from the trail she had just taken?

It can't be.

The thick trunk with gnarled roots that buckled the earth . . . The canopy of leaves . . . She reached out to run her fingers across its scarred bark, to touch, for a moment, the initials her mother had carved there.

But instead of feeling wood under her fingertips, she touched an arm, an arm reaching out from behind the tree trunk, clawing suddenly out of the dark to grab her. She staggered backward, and her mind skidded wildly: the ice men? The ice men again?

Runpleaserun . . .

Now that she needed it, the steely moon abandoned her, smothered by the clouds as though a dark hand had concealed its face. Groping blindly, she stumbled head-on into . . .

Another man.

Powerful arms reached out to clutch her, and as she tried to fight free, the moon knifed out again: the sunken cheeks, the beaklike nose, the slicked-down black hair molding his skull, like the feathers of a bird of prey . . . The man from the ice house. The man she had escaped once.

But not this time. He slid a flashlight beam down her body, the circle of light descending in a slow, lascivious caress.

"No!" The word came out in a groan, an admission of defeat, for she knew she couldn't fight free of his grip.

"Let her go."

The man who had emerged from behind the Hanging Tree was walking towards her, his face still in shadow, his footfalls heavy on the pine needles. Even before he turned his flashlight on his face, the smell of stale sweat and Old Spice told her who it was. The crewcut . . . the small, ferret eyes. The square jaw massacring a wad of gum.

"Runt?"

Seconds after that shocked moment of recognition, everything would change more drastically, more horribly, than any of the three of them standing beside the Hanging Tree could have imagined. Soon Runt would realize that he didn't really have everything under control at all. But up until then, Wayne N. Runtledge and his partner, Len Ryan, had had things pretty much their own way, ever since Senator Clayburn Broyles had sent the two of them into the Casmaran Woods to make sure that no kidnappers or assassins—and certainly no reporters—interrupted the tranquility of his daughter's

summer at camp. It would have been a lot easier, Runt
had argued, without the secrecy. But the Senator had
given his word to Cassie that she could go to camp
without her least favorite chaperone. And like any
dedicated politician, Runt judged, Broyles felt the need
to preserve appearances, even while breaking a promise.

It had been a royal pain, camping out in the woods,
forced to live off of freeze-dried stew, with so much
meat-on-the-hoof walking around, just asking for it.
They could have bagged God knows how many good-
sized bucks, except that a single blast from Runt's
Walther would have blown their cover. Still, in its own
way, it beat being assigned to a limo detail in Washington: one hand on their binoculars, the other on their
dicks, watching the teenyboppers at Casmaran changing
into and out of their bikini undies. (The counselors
weren't so bad, either.) No, Runt had to admit, there
were worse ways to spend the summer than getting paid
a hundred bucks a day to jerk off.

Of course, if it had been up to him, instead of the
Service, he wouldn't have chosen Len Ryan as a partner. The Russian-made Kytusha rocket whose explosion
had remodeled Len's face at Khe Sanh had scarred his
personality as well, making him as surly at noon as he
was when Runt shook him awake for the graveyard
watch at three A.M. But Len had earned his keep. He'd
been the one who'd found the double lid of Colombian
Gold hidden in the knothole of that enormous oak tree,
the private stash of some brown-thighed camper, no
doubt. A couple of hits of that stuff after taps played at
Casmaran, and he and Len had slept like babies.

But Runt had kept the grass away from Len tonight.
There would be no more dope for awhile—not after the
way the Broyles kid had been acting the last few days.
Their job had been a piece of cake when she had stayed
where she was supposed to, dancing around in her
leotard, or showering with her skinny friend in the
bathhouse where the peepholes revealed a good shot of

beaver. But since Cassie had begun wandering off alone in the woods, they'd had to tighten up. Sneaking over to that shack on the other side of the lake—had the silly bitch gone into heat, or what? Runt couldn't figure out what the hell she saw in the Jew living there—any guy who could make up crap like that and call it music had to be a faggot.

But what if they *were* fucking their brains out? Runt had instructions to protect the Senator's kid from bodily harm. He wasn't sure if that included protecting her cherry, but he wasn't about to wait and find out. What would the Senator do if after letting his wife get knocked off, Runt let his daughter get knocked *up*? No, after losing Cassie in broad daylight near the Jew's cabin today, Runt and Len had kept their hands off the stash—and their dicks—on the chance that she'd try something again tonight.

This time they'd caught her. And now that they'd blown their cover anyway, Runt wanted to hurt her, just a little. He just wanted to see the shock on her face when she realized he had been there all along. Shock . . . and okay, yes, maybe a little fear, too.

The kid *was* shocked, her mouth hanging open, her eyes wide. She had turned as white as the moon that crept, like a ghost, through the clouds.

But Runt's satisfaction died quickly, the moment it dawned that it wasn't him Cassie feared. It wasn't even Len who had scared her shitless. She was staring right past them . . . *through* them . . . at something behind their backs.

Cassie gasped, helpless, like a fish hurled out of water. The wet cloth that had been clamped over her nose and mouth (it reeked of cleaning fluid? alcohol?) smothered her face, burned her eyes, blocked off her air. She gagged from the fumes, kicked and flailed with her arms and legs. But it was no use fighting it . . . she was sinking into a stupor. And as her mind began to falter, it muffled the sounds of the struggle that engulfed her.

The forest shuddered—something crashed to the ground, something enormous, as if the giant oak had been felled in a single stroke. She realized, too late, that it was the sound of her own body falling to earth.

Runt heard Cassie whimpering.

Some-fucking-one's grabbed the kid right out from under me.

But who? Where was the son-of-a-bitch? At least after all this waiting he deserved the chance to kick the shit out of someone. But he couldn't see a thing. "Len!" He called out blindly. The only reply was a groan from his partner that told him he would be facing the enemy alone.

I'll kill the motherfucker!

Runt spun around, but his reflexes were slower than they'd been in the swamps of Khe Sanh fifteen years ago, and Christ, the dope they'd been smoking up here must have been *killer shit*. He could hardly *move*.

Grab the gun. An instinctive reflex of hand to holster. *Go for it.*

Why can't you grab the fucking gun?

Runt had felt no incision, no blade. But his hand was gone. In the pitch dark he could feel his life's blood pumping out onto the ground from his stump of a wrist, like a black stream of piss.

Where the fuck's my hand?

The sudden loss of blood . . . the sudden loss of pints of blood . . . It made him light-headed, giddy, the way no Colombian Gold ever could.

Please.

please don't hurt me anymore . . .

He was only dimly aware of hurtling into the air, of crashing skyward through the branches of the Hanging Tree. He didn't hear the impact of his body, the crunch of bone against wood. He heard voices. Women's voices, laughing with the scorn of whores.

Their laughter. It was even worse than what they had done to him.

What was so funny?

What was so goddamn funny?

It was the last, feeble thought that drained through Runt's mind, before his brain switched off for good.

Chapter 24

~~~~~~~

Even before the rumble of Barbara's Chevette had
faded away down the dirt driveway, Jake had heard the
music rising, born at the moment the sun had died. He
had rushed into the forest after it, into a darkness that
had come as suddenly as the slamming of a door.

The music . . . though the melody was the same as the
night before, it had an even greater hold over him.
When he passed within the shadow of the Hanging Tree,
he had no reason to know what terrible upheaval had
just taken place there. The blood on the ground was hidden by the night, and besides, his eyes were as good as
closed, his ears attuned to the subtle shifts in the music's
volume, that he hoped would guide him down the right
trail.

Follow it.

Groping through the forest under the cobwebbed
moon, he discovered a faint path that penetrated the
brambles, and hurried down it, crushing Death Angels
underfoot.

The music . . . he felt like a hunter in pursuit of a

feline beast, an animal at once beautiful and deadly. (Deadly because it was beautiful? Or beautiful because it was deadly?) He felt like a hunter who might at any moment become the prey. Thorns pricked at his hands, his arms, and he wondered whether the wall of brambles had been planted there to stave off intruders. He plunged into them, as if they were proof of the music's power, proof that there had to be something precious beyond them, to be so jealously guarded.

A glow from far down the trail, a glow too intense, too yellow to be moonlight. The yellow of a neon sign on Forty-second Street, a color both exquisite and seductive because it was corrupt. It was just beyond a tall stand of pines . . . a few dozen yards . . .

Instead of quickening his pace, he stopped. Two eyes stared at him, luminous and cold, like embers of the moon.

An animal, hackles raised, nostrils flared, a wolf as black as if it had been carved out of the night sky, stood squarely in the cleft between two boulders, blocking his path. Two eyes, silver and unblinking. For a moment, Jake felt as if he were looking down the barrels of two guns.

It bared its fangs and the chatter of the cicadas died. A guttural growl. And echoing it, the music took on an undertone of menace. But the darkening of the melody only increased Jake's fascination with it. He felt as though he were standing on the brink of a widening gorge, riveted by the chasm.

Does the beast hear the music? he wondered. Were its ears picking up levels, depths of sound he didn't know existed? Without taking his eyes from the animal, he bent down slowly and picked up a fallen tree branch. A snarl was welling in his throat—like the wolf's, he thought—part of a rage, a primal fury he had never felt before.

You need the music. You need it too badly to let anything stop you. He took a step forward. *Break open its skull . . .*

He drew back the club to strike, but the animal reared onto its hind legs and tore the branch out of his hand with its jaws. Crouching low, it tensed its haunches, ready to go for Jake's throat. But suddenly the posture of the wolf changed. Its hackles lowered, and its tail wilted between its legs, its growl reduced to a whimper. Meekly, it scuttled into the shadows as a woman emerged, clad in white, from among the trees.

Moonlight etched her face in a silver silhouette, a face he knew. She held out her hands to him. The music in the distance seemed to change its tone, the note of menace softening to something approaching tenderness. He didn't move—he couldn't—for fear the vision before him would prove as elusive as the music.

Sarah didn't say a word. She glided towards him, and when she was within his reach, so close he could smell the jasmine she had woven into her hair, she pulled off her gauzy shift. She was looking at him as if she were expecting something from him, as if there were something he had—something inside him—that she had to possess. And a numbing certainty washed over him: she would be disappointed.

Questions formed in his throat, rose to his mouth, but she stopped them with a cool finger on his lips. Her eyes were fierce and wild, as fierce as the wolf's eyes had been. Yet somehow the ferocity lured him closer.

Why did she want *him*?

She pulled him against her, and he felt his body begin to respond. There were questions to ask her, but . . . (*Don't talk, you'll lose it if you talk.*) She was like the music in the forest that overwhelmed him without his understanding.

Suddenly he didn't care why she wanted him. He felt her flesh against his, a fine layer of down giving her skin a softness that his wife's never had. Her muscles were taut, yet supple, as Barbara's had never been. And then Barbara was forgotten, irrelevant, as Sarah pulled him gently to the ground.

He pressed his face into her hair and inhaled a perfume sweet-laden with night-blooming jasmine, the scent of tropical flowers that he was certain had never grown in the forests of Maine. And he wanted her.

What if you can't?

His mind flinched from the old fear, the humiliating failures with his wife. Then Sarah ran her fingers over his body, and he felt a new strength. When her body enfolded his, it was as if he were possessing the music, a composer merging with his symphony.

Wait.

Now that he was as close to the music as he was to her lips, a note rang false . . .

Something's terribly wrong.

Something's (Block it out. Block out the thought) wrong.

The faintest tinge of suspicion was enough to weaken him.

Don't lose it.

His fingers brushed something under her arm . . . something that shouldn't have been there.

Its touch repelled him, and he opened his eyes to see it—a fleshy protrusion under her left arm, the size of the first joint of his index finger. A sticky liquid oozed from it onto his hand.

Hadn't Cassie said . . . ?

Cassie's friend had one.

Then he remembered the painting he'd exhumed from the ice house. The crazed women dancing . . . didn't they have those fleshy polyps under their arms too, a small detail defined by the painter with exaggerated precision, as though it were somehow terribly important? He pried himself away from her, fought to his feet.

She doesn't give a damn about you . . . She's trying to keep you from the music . . . Preying on your weakness . . . because she knows you are weak.

He glanced down the trail, but the glow had died. The music had ended. He turned and ran back towards the cabin.

As he did, he shot a look over his shoulder. In his humiliation, his rage, he was sure his sight was deceiving him: Sarah's eyes had merged with the eyes of the wolf, her body with its body, as if she and the beast were two halves of a single, cunning thing. He turned away and ran. But when he glimpsed his cabin through the trees at last, he realized that he hadn't escaped. Because he knew he would go back there. He might be weak . . . he might be a coward. But tomorrow night, tomorrow night even Sarah would not be able to stop him.

Chapter 25

~~~~

Someone was following her, she was sure of it. Barbara glanced furtively behind her at the sea of faces on Fifth Avenue. All of them were stalking her, the entire rush-hour horde.

You're paranoid, she repeated to herself several times, with a New Yorker's contempt for timidity. *It's only the heat breathing down your neck.* At 8:30 in the morning the sun had yet to bore through the grimy haze, but it was already so humid that her blouse clung to her body.

The tape . . . the tape made you paranoid.

She clutched her Panasonic tape recorder by its shoulder strap, and glanced through the clear plastic lid to make sure that the tape was still threaded onto it. *You've got to play the tape for Otto. But if you do, he'll say you're crazy . . .*

As the light changed, she barely had the strength to cross the street, and the thought shot through her mind that she might be too weak to make it to the Met. Had she eaten dinner? Had she eaten anything last night?

The cup of black coffee she had gulped down before leaving her apartment felt like acid in her empty stomach, threatening her with nausea.

No, it wasn't the coffee. It was the rising sense of chaos that nauseated her. She had fought against chaos, the curator's enemy, at the Met all these years, and now it was overwhelming her, spinning everything out of control. The chaos of uncertainty and doubt, the chaos of the unknown.

Because the tape she had stolen from Jake's cabin hadn't been blank. On the surface it had been a barrage of electronic sounds, like Jake's earlier works. But with a disturbing difference. This time it was fused with a primal, primitive revel, a blending of instruments and voices she couldn't identify. It was clearly his most brilliant composition. But when she had heard it, when she had closed her eyes and listened to it over and over in their apartment until dawn, a single image had filled her mind: the painting Jake had brought into the cabin with him. The fierce, wild strokes of green and gray, the distorted figures with their sinister energy—the music on the tape had that same cutting edge of madness. And the music's violence revealed a part of Jake she hadn't known existed. She read it as a cry for help.

The massive bronze doors of the Met were locked—the museum would not open for another hour—so she hurried through the employees' entrance. A gray-haired guard eyed her tape recorder, made a note of it, and pushed the button of the turnstyle to let her in. "Didn't see you yesterday, Mrs. Lazarus . . ."

"I was sick."

"First day you took off all year."

Barbara didn't reply. Her obsession with her work seemed irrelevant now. Preserving dried parchment and beaten gold meant nothing. She was out to save a life.

A spindly black janitor in the elevator grinned at Barbara as the doors slid open. He was about to push the button for her office floor when she stabbed it first.

He noticed that her hand was trembling. "You okay?"

She tried to smile back. "Do I look that bad?" She knew she must, after staying up all night listening to the tape. She couldn't even remember if she'd combed her hair this morning.

The elevator doors slid open to reveal the music from a sepulchral woodwind. She strode quickly down the corridor towards it. Bach . . . He was no doubt playing it by heart. Bach . . . A bad sign. If it had been Debussy or Chopin, it would have meant he was receiving visitors. But no one who had experienced his wrath dared interrupt Otto Kunstler when he was playing Bach. She pushed open the frosted glass door stenciled *Curator—European Musical Instruments* without knocking.

"Otto?"

The portly old man sitting behind a cluttered desk winced when he saw her, but didn't stop blowing into what looked like an ancient recorder with elephantiasis. Six feet long, it was carved from walnut and adorned with flowers and cupids in mother-of-pearl. The melody he coaxed from it had a stately timbre.

"Otto . . . I've got to play something for you."

He shut his eyes and pressed on with the fugue, his thick silver beard glistening with drops of spit. She clamped a lid on her impatience and waited until the piece finally ended.

"Otto . . ."

"Shame on you, Barbara." His harsh Viennese accent made him sound hoarse. He removed a handkerchief from the pocket of his coat, mopped the perspiration from his bald head with it, and patted his lips. "Can't you leave a man to fondle his woodwinds in peace?"

"I needed to speak with the world's leading expert on musical instruments. Where else could I go?"

"Flattery, Barbara, shameless flattery. Is that how a young lady rises so quickly through the ranks in this incorruptible institution?" He wiped his lips again, this time, she guessed, to hide his smile.

"Otto, please . . ." He licked the reed, and teased her with another, more sprightly cantata. "Otto, it's terribly important."

He spat out the mouthpiece. "My hearing . . . Every day, the doctor tells me, it grows weaker." He tapped the hearing aid on his left ear. "My days with my harem are numbered, Barbara." He riffled through the pages of the Met instrument catalogue on his desk. "Before it's too late, I intend to feast on all their sounds. Every last one of them. So spare me the interruptions. Is that too much for an old man to ask?"

She slid the tape recorder onto the table beside him. "Please . . . listen to this."

He caressed the instrument in his hands. "With this cornucopia of sound at my bidding, must you inflict on me an abomination that comes from transistors and tape?"

"Yes."

He eyed the tape recorder suspiciously. "By your husband, I presume. The electronic *wunderkind*?"

Barbara considered cutting his sarcasm short, then thought better of it. "Yes, it's Jake's. And you've got to listen."

"Got to? I have a hundred different kinds of bagpipes entrusted to me, my dear, harps that King David himself might have played. I have Louis Armstrong's trumpet and Paganini's Stradivarius. Why, when the time comes for Gabriel to blow his horn, he'll have to come here to get it on loan! Otto Kunstler does not *have* to listen to anything!"

"Please . . ."

He tilted his head to the sound of her voice, and as if reading the urgency in its timbre, let out a long sigh of defeat. "Very well." He closed his eyes and folded his arms, tapping his thumbs impatiently against his chest.

She punched the playback button on the tape recorder. Beneath an electronic barrage of bleeps and screeches hovered a faint hint of . . . what? Strings? A horn? Even after having listened to it a dozen times, Barbara couldn't be sure. But this time she tried not to concentrate. Each time she had listened, it had taken a tighter hold over her, as if with each playing, one more instrument joined the cacophony, one more shrill voice captured her in the feverish chorus. She secretly hoped that Otto would shrug the piece off with his usual sarcasm.

At first, in jest, he pretended to turn off his hearing aid. But then he stopped, leaned closer. It surprised her that after trying so hard to get Otto's attention, his sudden, intense fascination with the music did not please her. He was no longer slouching in the chair, but sat rigidly, like a doctor who had noticed a telltale shadow on an X-ray. He pursed his lips precisely, his brow straining, his face starting to redden, as if he were playing a perverse musical instrument that refused to yield a single note. When the tape ended, he opened his eyes in a hurry, as if he did not want to face the images flickering across his closed eyelids. ''Where did you get that?''

''I told you . . . It's Jake's.''

''No, no . . .'' he waved his hand impatiently. ''Not that electronic junk. I know he made *that* up. The sounds underneath . . . the counterpoint. Where did he record the source music?''

''I don't know. I mean, he's been in Maine all summer. In a cabin out in the middle of nowhere. Otto, that's the part I don't understand. He said he recorded it up there.''

''In the woods?'' Without another word, Otto pushed himself away from the desk, revealing a sizable paunch. He took the tape recorder from her and rewound the tape with surprising deftness.

''I mean . . . I don't understand,'' she said. ''What could *make* music like that?''

''What indeed?'' He clicked the tape out of the machine. ''Come.''

Otto had a limp, but perhaps to prove his stubborn-

ness he did not use a cane. Even so, it was all Barbara
could do to keep up with him as he hurried down the
corridor. At the end of the hall, he unlocked a frosted-
glass door and flipped on the lights to a soundproof
studio. Folding chairs and music stands were arranged
for a string quartet, and a small glassed-in recording
booth in the corner was banked with tape decks and
TEAC consoles. He took her inside the booth and
threaded on the tape.

"What are you going to do?" She eyed the powerful
36-inch speakers uneasily, not sure whether she could
bear hearing the music magnified to its full strength.

"The doctor has his microscope," he said. "I have
this. There are eight separate tracks on Jake's tape, each
of which he recorded one at a time. Here I can scan each
of them separately." He flipped a switch and the full
composition blared from the speakers. "All that electronic gibberish . . . I'm going to filter it out, get at the
source music. Let's try the first track."

He turned a knob, and as the tape glided under the
magnetic head, Barbara heard a series of wheezes and
bleeps. She recognized them as the percussive sounds
Jake created electronically to underscore his pieces.
"Not this . . ." He grimaced, switching quickly to track
two: harsh, brassy electronic sounds. "Nor this . . ."

The next track Otto diagnosed as "natural sounds"—
waves lapping, wind through trees—sounds which, he
explained scornfully, it had become fashionable for
modern composers to lift directly from nature, rather
than evoking them in their music, as the earlier, great
composers had done.

When he turned the knob and brought up the volume
on the fourth track, she heard an intermittent cawing.
"Crows?"

"Bluejays," he corrected her.

He proceeded to the next track, and cocked his head
to one side. "Ah . . ." The wild undercurrent throbbed
over the speakers, free of the electronic overlay Jake
had added. As Otto adjusted the tone, Barbara felt the

urge to back away, to flee the recording booth. The notes phased in and out as if they had been recorded across a great distance, surging, slashing like knives. A dozen or more shrill voices meshed with the unknown instruments, building to a crescendo, as though the music were somehow the recording of a violent crime.

The tape clicked off. At first neither of them spoke. Then Otto began his question slowly, as if to avoid any possibility of her misunderstanding. "You said Jake was in Maine?" She nodded. "Where . . . ? Why . . . ?"

"He's staying in this cabin he rented a few hours north of Bangor . . . near a lake. He went up there to work. He felt the city just wasn't doing it for him anymore. He needed some new . . ."

"Inspiration?" Again, the sarcasm. But something else had entered Otto's tone. Was it a note of concern?

"I couldn't leave work to go with him, but I was supposed to visit him this weekend. Then he called yesterday and told me not to come. He sounded so strange on the phone . . . it frightened me. I caught the next plane, rented a car in Bangor and drove like hell. When I got there all he could talk about was this music he'd been hearing, music from the forest . . . at night. At first I didn't believe him. I thought he'd gone off the deep end. But I mean . . ." She glanced uneasily at the tape. "He didn't imagine that."

"I'm afraid he didn't." Otto gave his beard a vicious tug and winced from the self-inflicted pain. Then he took her arm and led her hastily towards the door. He almost shoved her into the staff elevator, then stabbed the button for the second sub-basement. On the ride down in the padded cubicle, he avoided her eyes and ignored her questions, staring at the glowing numbers that flickered past as if reading an ominous message.

When the doors slid open, they picked their way down a narrow corridor, a darkened labyrinth of spinets and harpsichords, bass violas and tubas and tympani, some on display in glass cases, others shrouded in canvas drapes like corpses in a morgue. Odd, she thought, that in this Fort Knox of the world's most magnificent musical treasures, the only sound was the insectlike hum of the humidifiers.

He flicked a combination lock to a vault marked *Musical Instruments, Occidental*. When the massive steel fire-door clicked open, he turned on the fluorescent lights. She followed him inside, past storage cabinets which housed gilt harps and ivory-inlaid flutes, until at last he unlocked a glass case with a key from his pocket. Delicately, he removed a horn that had been hollowed from a single ivory tusk, carved with a geometric pattern of skulls. When he took a deep breath and blew, it emitted a mournful moan.

"That's on the tape," Barbara murmured. The heavy timbre of the instrument lingered in the air.

"An oliphant," Otto said, holding it up to the light. "Carved in North Africa. Made its way to Italy with the Phoenicians, until it reached the court of King Philip IV of Spain. It was never played by the court musicians, however, for it usually had a . . . symbolic significance." He replaced it hastily in its case, as though glad to be locking it away. Then he looked at her. "Musical instruments are like women, Barbara. Sometimes the most beautiful must be approached with caution." Without explaining what he meant, he removed what looked like a hand-carved lute of mahogany inlaid with ebony from a bell-shaped leather case. He plucked the strings, tuning it, then reached back into the case for a horsehair bow. When he drew the bow across the strings the sound was muted, as if decades, perhaps even centuries of silence, had dulled its tone. But Barbara recognized the plaintive resonance from the tape.

"What is it?"

"A gamba, predecessor of symphonic instruments like the cello, and less refined ones, like the guitar. It hasn't been included in performances for two hundred years, except by musicians in medieval consort groups, or by . . ." He cleared his throat and, instead of finishing his sentence, opened another case displaying a collection of bagpipes: animal skins, withered and life-less, the largest one with a ragged fox head wrapped around the wooden tubing. "That reedy sound, that bleating on the tape," Otto said, "it was undoubtedly made by an instrument very much like this one."

"I thought bagpipes were played only in Scotland."

"On the contrary. It's a quite universal instrument . . . one that has changed little since it was first devised, centuries before Christ. During the Dark Ages, and in medieval times, it was played in remote villages throughout Europe."

"But why would anyone be playing it now?"

"How should *I* know?" he snapped, so suddenly that Barbara suspected he *did* know.

"Otto . . ." Even as she started to ask him, even as she started to plead with him to tell her, she was sorry she had come, sorry she had requested his help. Sorry, most of all, that he *would* tell her everything.

"Music has always voiced the most primitive, the most forbidden of human urges, Barbara. Passions that go deeper than words. Musical instruments were first developed, you must understand, for ancient rites, by cults sacred . . . or profane." He was trying to ease her into it gently, she thought, like someone breaking the news of a death.

I don't want to hear this.

"In my studies of ancient musical instruments, I had to learn things, Barbara, delve into secrets that some-times I wish I had never uncovered. Music, especially the most primitive . . . it can bring one to the outer reaches of the soul." His voice hushed, and she was sur-prised to hear his arrogance give way to humility. "Even if you grew up hundreds of years ago, when those in-struments on the tape were crafted, you never would have heard them played together."

"Why?"

"Because for hundreds of years, people believed that when certain instruments were played together . . ." He gestured to the separate cases. ". . . some of those we have classified here . . . It was believed that their music had an evil power."

"Then . . . who played them?"

"I suppose I would have to say," Otto murmured, "that they were played by the damned."

Barbara felt a sinking feeling in the pit of her stomach. "I don't understand . . . How could Jake have recorded that music in the middle of nowhere?"

Otto's eyes had taken on a faraway look, as if he were trying to focus them on something indistinct in the distance. "It's been so long since I read the literature . . . But in the summer—yes, that much I do remember —they gathered to play in the summer." His eyes glazed over with a melancholy she had not seen in him before, and he suddenly seemed as ancient and fragile as the instruments that surrounded him. "Three hundred years ago, it was not uncommon to hear them in the woods of Massachusetts. But after the trials in Salem . . . 1692 . . . it became too risky for them to gather for their rituals near populated areas . . ."

"Salem? What are you talking about, Otto? Witches? You don't expect me to . . ."

"What you or I think doesn't matter. What *is* important is that some *did* worship Satan . . . And some still do."

"Don't be ridiculous!"

Otto ignored her outburst. "The trials, the hangings didn't stop them. The fact is that three of those who were convicted of witchcraft in Salem were never sent to the gallows. They were set free . . . an act of clemency, or so it seemed at the time."

"What do you mean?"

"The women were pregnant. And they bore their young, a saving remnant." He raised his hand to silence the objections on her lips: "Hear me out, Barbara. I had to learn the secrets for my work. Now you had better learn them too."

He beckoned for her to follow him as he threaded his way among the instruments in the vault, to a cabinet that was as chaotic as the instrument cases had been immaculate. It was crammed floor-to-ceiling with manuscripts, sheaves of music, and books bound in peeling Morocco leather. He rummaged among them, finally pulled a book down from the top shelf and pored through its pages.

"The music . . . they played it on summer nights . . . a kind of prelude." He slammed the book shut—apparently it didn't give him what he wanted—and returned it to the shelf. He chose another, smaller book, flipping through the pages. "Each summer, the first gatherings were insignificant, dress rehearsals, really, for Lammas."

"Lammas?"

"The vernal exaltation of the Prince of Darkness."

"What you're saying . . ." Barbara was amazed at herself for taking him seriously. "If it's true . . . Otto, why?"

"The music they played on the final night, the night of Lammas, was certainly strange enough," he continued, "but the true abomination wasn't . . . well, it wasn't the music at all. It was something else, something much more monstrous. They needed an unbaptized male each year for this Grand Sabbath . . . someone who had not been anointed with holy water . . ."

Barbara's mind reeled back to the rainy April night when Jake had told her about the ad for the cabin on the music department bulletin board. "When Jake called to rent it, they asked him questions, the kind of questions . . . The way they asked him to repeat his name, he thought they were trying to find out if he was Jewish, that if they knew he was Jewish they would turn him down . . ." She stopped herself. *What if that was the very reason they chose him?*

Otto was feverishly poring through still another book, its pages a maze of what looked like astrological charts. He stopped at a page, ran his finger across a row of numbers: "The dates of the lesser Sabbaths were governed by the lunar cycle. They change every year. But Lammas . . . the night of the Grand Sabbath . . . it was always—it *is* always on the same night.

"When?"

"The night of August first."

"But . . . that's tomorrow, isn't it?"

Otto twisted the watchband on his wrist to read the tiny gold date on the dial. "No, Barbara." He shook his head. "It's not tomorrow. It's today."

His words were all but lost, for . . . *No, it was impossible* . . . the bagpipes in the glass case were beginning to moan, their skins filling with air until the membranes stretched taut. The stuffed head of the fox on one bobbed as it played, as if it were stirring back to life.

This isn't happening, Barbara told herself. *This can't be happening.* She stared around her at the instruments—the copper and brass distorted their faces into grotesques, like fun-house mirrors. She stepped back as timbrels and cymbals shivered, electric, like the warning from a hundred rattlesnakes.

"What's happening?"

"Barbara, you've got to . . ." Otto stammered in his haste, as though to answer her questions before she could ask them, while there was still time. "You've got to get Jake out of there!" Rumblings from a row of kettle drums drowned him out. Accordions and tubas groaned, coronets shrilling a raucous fanfare, quivering from the power that had seized them. The cacophony built to a crescendo until Barbara pressed her hands over her ears and Otto tore out his hearing aid. He was yelling something to her, and though she couldn't hear his words over the bedlam, she read his lips: *"Get out!"*

She staggered out of the door of the vault, past pianos where a hundred invisible fingers rippled the keys, past trumpets that invisible lips filled with air. Blaring, resounding, the instruments started to shake in their cases along the walls. A piccolo shrieked, shattering the glass, and others joined in, clattering to the floor.

Barbara overcame her panic long enough to turn back to try to get to Otto. But there was no way to reach him. An ebony grand piano had slid across the floor to block the door, trapping him inside the vault. As the music shrilled to a deafening pitch, she backed away, down the corridor.

For a fragile moment, when her back pressed against the fire exit, one note rang out above the rest—a note more piercing than flute or woodwind, a cry that she recognized as distinctly human in its pain. And when she heard it, she knew that Otto had escaped the bedlam, into silence.

She threw her body against the fire door. It yielded, and she dashed up three flights of cement stairs to the museum lobby. She burst through the milling crowd and outside into the humid air, stumbling down the broad steps of the Met towards the sidewalk. Only then did she realize that she had left the tape behind. But the tape didn't matter anymore. It had told her more than she had wanted to know.

It can't be, the precise, rational museum curator inside her protested. *Don't believe it.*

And yet she did believe. The proof was back there, in the second sub-basement of the Met.

She ran blindly into the traffic, waving frantically to hail a taxi. The honking horns that assailed her sounded like raucous trumpets heralding the onset of Lammas.

Chapter 26

For a moment, swimming back to consciousness, Cassie thought the cool hand on her forehead was her mother's. Until the voice cut through the gauzy dream, as if to remind her: *Your mother's dead.*

"Cassie?"

"Where am I?" The words were garbled by the thermometer someone had slipped into her mouth. Her eyes focused with difficulty in the gray light—the rain that trickled down the window warped the cabins beyond the lawn into crooked huts. The cubicle was crowded with chipped enamel furniture: a bedstand, a chair, a dresser. It reminded her of the viewing room at the mortuary where she had last seen her mother.

"Welcome to Germ City." Sarah's fingertips felt soothing against Cassie's skin, but the smell of Lysol and rubbing alcohol brought bile up from her stomach.

Cassie ran a hand along her arm, remembering the mud that had caked her body in the forest. Someone had cleaned her up, put her in a coarse green hospital nightgown. She was soaking wet, but not from the rain, she realized. It was fever sweat. She pressed a hand to her temple. The rain drumming on the tin roof of the infirmary magnified the throbbing in her head. "What happened?" She tried to swing her legs over the side of the cot, but the wave of dizziness forced her head back down on the pillow.

"Drink this." A teaspoon rattled in a cup. "It'll help." Sarah withdrew the thermometer from Cassie's mouth and put the ceramic rim of the cup to her lips. Cassie inhaled cinnamon and cloves, the scent replacing the nausea lingering in her throat. What looked like dried rose petals were floating in the liquid, tinging it a warm pink. "Different herbs are good for different things," Sarah said. "Mint's great for upset stomach. Camomile's for insomnia. This one's . . . well, it's good for the nerves."

Her mother had given her home-brewed tea, too, Cassie remembered, tea made from herbs she had grown at Cliff's Edge. She took a sip. The liquid was sweet on her tongue, warming her, and as Sarah promised, it calmed her, too.

"Better now?" Sarah asked.

"Thanks." Her face beaded with sweat as she finished the cup.

Sarah's fingers smoothed the strands of Cassie's damp hair from her cheek. "When you didn't show up last night for 'lights out,' I went looking for you. That storm made rivers out of the trails. I don't know where you thought you were going, running around in the woods in your leotard, but I found you lying face down in six inches of mud. You've been out cold all day. You're lucky you don't have pneumonia . . ." She checked the thermometer. "Yet."

Cassie strained to clear her head, to think back to what had happened, but her memories from last night were blurred, like the view through the rain-wet windows. It hadn't been raining last night when she had left the cabin, had it? No, the moon had snuck out from behind the clouds, shining just long enough for her to see . . .

"*Runt* . . ." The word sounded strange on Cassie's lips, false somehow, as if she were uncertain whether she had really seen him. "Something horrible happened to him."

"Something horrible almost happened to *you*."

"I went to find Iris . . . and there was . . . I mean, there were two of them—Runt, he's my father's body-guard, and this other guy, the guy who chased me into the ice house yesterday . . ." She tried to sit up, but Sarah eased her gently back down. "You don't believe me!"

"I believe you saw *men* . . . or what looked like them. But not Runt, or whatever you said his name was."

"Who were they?"

"You weren't supposed to know about them yet."

"What are you talking about?"

Sarah sighed: "I told Abigail to wait to put them up until the last day of camp." She glanced outside at the rain. "Until just before they needed them for the farewell ceremony. They'll never get those straw men lit now."

"But they weren't straw. They were real. I saw Runt, and . . ."

"Now take it easy, Cassie . . ." The concern in Sarah's voice deepened: "Let's not overdo it." She turned off the overhead light, bathing the room in shadows. "I'll go over to the lodge . . . bring you something for dinner. There's fried chicken tonight. Or something that passes for fried chicken." When Cassie closed her eyes, Sarah tucked the sheet more snugly around her, slipped on a yellow poncho, and walked out the door.

Cassie waited until Sarah dissolved into another warped, crooked shape beyond the rain-drenched window. Then she sat up slowly, her legs shaky as she dropped them over the side of the bed. But she made it to the door.

The smell of Lysol and rubbing alcohol from the infirmary faded away in the drizzle outside. In the crisp air she could detect a faint but persistent smell impregnating her hair. Sarah had cleaned away the mud, she thought, along with the wet, sticky pine needles, but not that smell. A smell that told her that last night hadn't been a nightmare. As the rain drenched her hair, the scent emerged more strongly . . . a smell from school in Washington . . . from science class . . . Chloroform.

In the downpour the forest was an angry green, like the sea off of Nantucket in a gale, Cassie thought. It was as if the New England summer had disappeared in one downpour, to be replaced by a sudden, unyielding winter. Rain-heavy branches slapped against her, and her hands tingled from the cold. She blew on them, then swept her wet hair from her eyes and pushed deeper into the woods. The fallen branches, the trail that had turned to mud, the sharp and slippery rocks . . . they were obstacles in her path. But there was a more serious obstacle—the thought that hovered in her mind: Sarah had lied.

The Hanging Tree seemed even more enormous in the glowering light. The storm clouds hung low, as though caught in its branches. But no . . . Sarah had been right. Two straw men, like those that had been burned on Consecration night, hung from ropes that dangled from the oak's boughs, the nooses creaking in the storm wind. The straw glistened, the same wet gray as the oak's bark. It was exactly as Sarah had said: no one would be able to set these figures on fire now. The straw was so wet it was starting to dissolve, to . . .

Cassie stepped closer. The arm of one of the effigies . . . the rain had soaked through. The arm was dripping blood.

Chapter 27

The doorknob felt moist and cold, as repellent to the touch as the flesh beneath the straw would have been, Cassie thought, and yet she clutched it tightly for fear she might fall. Her panic had carried her here without her realizing her destination, and she was grateful for that. If she'd known where she was running, would she have had the nerve? The rage, the rage that she had leveled at herself (*See, you're not crazy. You're not!*) . . . it would be aimed at the right person now.

Miss Grace . . . She knew everything. She had to know. Wasn't the camp hers? Wasn't she wearing her mother's ring? And everything that the old woman knew—about the letter, about what had happened here—Cassie vowed she'd get it out of her.

But she's a frail cripple, a voice inside her pleaded.

Choke the truth out of her, the rage in Cassie snapped back. *Put your hands around her throat and she'll tell you everything.* She imagined her palms clamped around the veined neck, and the intensity of her anger scared her. Then, standing there on the porch, she could feel the blind fury ebbing, leaving her weary, drained. She rested a hand uncertainly on the doorknob.

The door creaked ajar.

Water dripped from Cassie's hospital gown onto the hooked rug, which muffled her footsteps. The velvet curtains of the parlor were drawn as tight as an old woman's eyelids, and yet even in the dim light she could see that the bric-a-brac had changed: a stuffed owl and a stuffed sparrow hawk, and . . . at the base of a Tiffany lamp, it looked like the stuffed figure of a white kitten, the body mounted as if curled in sleep. Her knee bumped against a brassbound trunk, and a stuffed squirrel on top of it shivered. The grandfather clock skipped every third beat, as hesitant as her footsteps.

The wheelchair—it was facing the cold hearth. Its varnished wood back, gleaming as shiny as a coffin, was all Cassie could see, and from this angle she couldn't tell whether or not the old woman was seated in it.

"Miss Grace?" She was surprised at how polite her voice sounded, how humble.

Breathing—slow, asthmatic breathing—more regular than the ticking of the grandfather clock, told Cassie that the old woman was there. *She's sleeping.* Even though the back of the wheelchair blocked any view of her, Cassie was sure of it.

The thought emboldened her to step closer, and she edged across a threadbare oriental carpet until she could have reached out and touched the back of the wheelchair, the mustard-yellow afghan draped over its arms. Suddenly it seemed like a terrible risk to awaken her.

Steal the ring instead, Cassie convinced herself. (*Why had she taken it? And how?*) That would be revenge enough. Cassie edged closer.

Slip the ring off her finger. Then run like hell.

The floorboards groaned, and fearing that another step would give her away, she stretched out her arm, her muscles straining. *Better to stay behind the wheelchair, so that if the old lady wakes up, she won't see you.* It meant groping blindly under the afghan.

Which hand? Cassie ran her fingers across her own palm, to remember the handshake at the dance pavilion on Visiting Day, when the ring had pierced her skin.

Her left hand. Pull it off her ring finger and . . .

Cassie forced her hand under the blanket. Something was wrong. The hand she felt under the afghan wasn't withered, with swollen, arthritic knuckles. The skin was soft, smooth. And before she could realize that it wasn't wearing the ring, the hand seized hers.

With a screech of steel spokes, the chair spun to face her.

"Looking for something, Cassie?"

"Iris . . . ?" The frail girl had wrapped Miss Grace's shawl over her faded T-shirt. And the arrogant smile on her face was Abigail's. She didn't let go of Cassie's hand, and her grip—Iris' grip that had always been so flaccid and weak was . . .

You're crushing my hand.

"Looking for the ring, Cassie?"

"Give it to me!"

"I don't have it."

"It belonged to my mother. I want it."

"Cassie, I haven't the foggiest idea where it is." Iris' voice was so calm, Cassie thought. How could weak, little Iris suddenly be so strong, so confident? "You really missed something last night, Cassie," Iris sighed. "I'm not kidding. It was incredible. But you'll see . . . tonight."

"The hell I will!" Cassie tried to wrench her hand from Iris' grasp, but she didn't have to. Iris let go.

"Look, Cassie, we were wrong about the seniors. They're not so bad, really they're not."

"Don't touch me . . ."

"They like *you*, Cassie. You may not believe that, but they do. They've just been giving you a hard time because they wanted to see if you could take it."

Cassie was backing to the door. "I don't have to hear this bullshit . . ."

"Go ahead, leave if you want. But you'd feel a lot

better if you knew everything.''

It was the reason she had come to Miss Grace's cottage, to find the answer to all the painful riddles. And yet now that she had the chance, Cassie didn't want to hear it: "*You . . . can't . . . make . . . me . . .*"

"Come on, Cassie. Nobody's *making* you do anything. "Don't you see? It's been inside you all along. It's in your blood . . . in your genes. At Casmaran, they just help you . . . find yourself.''

"What . . .'' Cassie hesitated at the door. "What do you mean?''

"Cassie, you know me. I've always been the sensible, scientific type, right? And, well, what I did last night . . . it makes so much sense." She stopped herself, and the puzzled look on Cassie's face made her take another tack. "Okay, so I was Catholic. Maybe that made it easier for me to get '*into*' it.''

"Get 'into' what?''

"I mean, there's nothing weird about it, really. This thing is just a religion, that's all. I mean, it's a free country, isn't it? That's what they teach us at school. We're free to worship any God we choose . . . And believe me, this one is a lot better than that other one, because He accepts you for what you are. He doesn't expect you to be what you're not.'' She added in a lower voice: "They don't pick on me anymore, Cassie. I mean, I'm just one of the girls now, like Abigail or Robin or any one of the seniors. It was worth it for that. I don't have to be afraid anymore . . .''

"I'm not afraid, either.'' But Cassie's voice rang too loudly, as if she were trying to convince herself: *It's only Iris. It's just dumb little Iris sitting there.*

"Anyway, after tonight, Cassie, you'll be one of us, whether you like it or not.''

Before Cassie could ask Iris what she meant, she could feel the change creeping over her—a twinge in her belly that knotted into a cramp. A cramp that doubled her over, forced her to grasp her sides.

Oh, God.

The pain shot into her back, stabbed down into her legs, but she managed to pull open the door.

"Hey, come on, Cassie. Don't go." Iris leaned forward in the wheelchair, holding out a hand to help. "I mean, it's pouring down rain outside. You'll catch pneumonia, for God's sake. I'll make some tea and we can build a . . ."

"*The tea* . . ." Cassie said. "Sarah put something in that tea." The next cramp brought up a taste from her stomach—the cloying sweetness of dried flower petals mixed with bile. *"The tea . . ."*

Iris rolled her eyes. "I wondered how long it would take you to figure that out, Cassie. I mean, how dense can you be?"

"You told me about them on that hike . . ." Cassie murmured. "Windflowers . . . You said they could be used to bring on someone's . . ."

"So, Casmaran rushes things a little," Iris interrupted. "But it's all very organic. I mean, it would have to be, right? You know Sarah." The pains shooting through her stomach made Cassie bite her lip to stifle a groan. Iris stood up from the wheelchair. "Here, have a seat. It won't hurt so bad if you take it easy. I mean, I thought I was dying when I got them at first. But they don't last long, really. It's no big thing." She reached out and gave Cassie's arm a reassuring squeeze: "I mean, think how long you've been waiting for it."

Cassie pushed Iris' hand away and wrenched the door wide. The roar of the rain drowned out her footsteps as she descended the porch stairs painfully, one at a time.

Iris didn't try to stop her. Iris didn't have to stop her, Cassie thought. *They've taken over your body. You can't escape what's inside you.*

But your mind, they haven't got your mind yet. She tried to force her legs into a run, but her muscles refused to obey. *Once they've got your body*, she thought, *there's nothing your mind can do.* Tears ran down her face, along with the rain, tears that told her she could not run far.

She did not remember falling, but suddenly Cassie's cheek was pressed against a rock, water from the downpour trickling into her mouth. The rain felt as cold on her eyelids as two silver coins.

Mud seeped between her lips, and dimly Cassie remembered the Spinning, the way Abigail had probed her tongue between Iris' lips with that kiss of welcome. Before she passed out, Cassie knew the taste.

Chapter 28

~~~~~

As Barbara gunned the car down the highway at dusk, she felt as though she were careening on the razor's edge between day and night. The clock on the dashboard read 7:55. Until twilight sharpened into dark, she would be in neutral territory, she thought. But after night fell . . .

The New England Airlines jet had arrived late at Bangor, and she forced the rented Chevette to make up for lost time. There had been no other cars for miles, and she allowed hers to straddle the white center line, as if the road were hers alone. She searched the thicket beyond the windshield for a landmark. In the aftermath of the cloudburst, the map that had guided her on her last trip to Jake's was useless. The wind had snatched away the road signs, felled trees to conceal the turn-offs. The weathered barns, the handful of clapboard farm houses she remembered from the day before, seemed to have disappeared, as if gutted by the impending night.

Despite the suspicion that she was being followed, a

suspicion that had gnawed at her since she'd left her apartment this morning, a glance into the rearview mirror told her that there was no one behind her—just the white center line of the highway, as faint in the twilight as the trail left by a snail. Her palms were wet, the steering wheel slipping beneath them. When she glanced at the speedometer she was surprised to see she was pushing 70. She hated the way her panic had affected her, depriving her of her usual cool reason. Her eyes darted up to her face in the mirror, as if to reassure herself that with everything shifting so crazily around her, at least *she* hadn't changed. But the image was hardly reassuring. The twilight's afterglow tinged her skin the sickly green of the painting at Jake's, as though she herself were being transformed into one of the crazed harpies in the revel.

Or the condemned woman in her dream.

On the plane from New York, she had dozed fitfully, and had dreamt she was standing on a scaffold, a noose around her neck. Otto was the hangman, dressed in the severe black cloak of a Puritan at Salem. "Guilty," he had said. *"Guilty."*

When he had pushed open the trapdoor beneath her, she had swung by the rope, gasping, writhing, whispering hoarsely: "It's not true . . . I'm not guilty . . . I'm not!" But the rope had pulled tighter around her throat, choking off her words.

Until the plane had shuddered through a downdraft and awakened her.

The tires of the Chevette skidded around a rain-slick curve and she twisted the wheel, forcing the car—and her mind—back on course. The winding road was a test of hand and eye, especially treacherous after the downpour which had ended just minutes before. But she couldn't focus on the road, her mind flashing towards her destination: *What, dear God, will you find?* She summoned the nerve to lower her right foot another inch, and floor the accelerator. The road seemed to be hurtling her towards the darkening sky, that was veined with lightning from the fleeing storm.

Jake. She didn't regret that she'd come. Because despite the bad times they'd been through, she still loved him. She thought ahead to the moment she would see him. She wouldn't allow either of them to talk—hadn't there always been too much talk?—she would hold him, press him in her arms, and he would understand what she meant to say. He would thank her for coming.

Wouldn't he?

What if he were furious? What if he refused to leave with her? What if . . .?

Like the doubts buffeting her, a crosswind toyed with the car, threatening to hurl it off the road.

The fuel gauge dipped towards empty. Damn the rental agency, she thought. No, it was her own fault. They had warned her, but she had been in too great a hurry to stop at the airport gas station before setting out on the desolate road. Even if she found her way to the cabin in this maze of wilderness, even if she could persuade Jake to leave with her, there might not be enough gas to make it back to Bangor.

A turnoff up ahead. A fence topped with barbed wire, a gate padlocked with a rusty chain. Her headlights picked up the letters burned into the wood sign above it: *Casmaran*. She hadn't seen that sign yesterday, which meant that tonight she had driven too far. Cursing, she skidded into a "U" turn, her tires spraying mud.

The evergreens skewered what was left of the sun, leaving a bloodstain in the western sky. She switched on her lights reluctantly, an admission of defeat. It felt as though darkness had plunged her into hostile territory and it seemed that even her high beams were powerless to pierce it, as powerless as they were to probe the dense forest that rose up on both sides of the road. And with nightfall, the same wind that brought the sweet scent of wet pines, brought something else.

The music. Hearing it through the open car window, what surprised Barbara wasn't the music's ferocity—she had expected that. What caught her off guard was the way it attracted her, enticed her. Its tempo seemed oddly in rhythm with the beating of her heart.

She rolled up the window to shut out the perfume of the pines, and the music, for fear that together they might seduce her, just as she was certain they had seduced Jake. But the music filtered through the glass, and it was growing louder. She flicked on the radio, hoping that country-and-western or punk rock would drown out the melody. But the forest music seemed to be coming over the radio too. She twisted the radio knob frantically: the haunting music was on every frequency, as if it had erased all other sound from the air.

Lightning seared the sky, and the music echoed louder, like thunder, so loud that it drowned out the engine. She hoped that the next flash of lightning would reveal the turnoff to Jake's cabin.

But the next blinding blue spark showed her something else.

At first she thought that the swarm soaring in the sky was a flock of crows. But they were too large, and they were speeding towards her too rapidly for that. One of them struck the windshield, a blur too sudden to identify, its impact imprinting a jagged spiderweb in the glass. Then the others hurtled towards her, shadowy forms coming head-on, and the car shuddered as one by one, each thudded against the windshield and was gone before she could make it out through the riddled glass.

Gone?

No, they were circling, coming back at her again.

Her foot was already pressing the accelerator to the floor, but she forced her weight down on it as though to wring out a final burst of speed. The shadowy escort darted around the car, spiraling faster and faster, whipping the wind into a deafening howl. And swept up in the slipstream, the car screeched out of control, careened end over end towards the shoulder.

Barbara's body tensed as she waited for the Chevette to hurtle to earth in an explosion of splintered glass.

But something else was happening. Something she could neither have foreseen nor defended herself against. The tires of the Chevette were easing up from the pavement, axles groaning from the stress. The car was lifting off the ground. Barbara clutched the steering wheel more tightly, denying it, denying it just as she had denied the music in the forest.

Her eyes stared out the window, unblinking: The car was skimming the treetops . . . She was looking down upon . . . cabins . . . a dock . . . a lake where in the next explosion of lightning the car was reflected like a dead moon.

And beyond, in a clearing in the depths of the forest, a bonfire raged.

The earth sped away as the car hurtled higher, forcing Barbara to shut her eyes in a sickening rush of vertigo. She was about to gag, when suddenly the nausea vanished.

The car had stopped its upward spiral in mid air and the doors rattled on their hinges. She could feel her mind sinking back into the dream: she was dangling by a noose in midair, her feet kicking wildly, unable to touch the ground, unable, she knew, ever to touch the ground again.

Then, with cruel abruptness, the law of gravity that had been so capriciously violated, was applied with rigor. (*"Guilty,"* Otto had said, *"Guilty!"*) And there was no time left for Barbara to protest her innocence.

The car shot into the lake, a cold meteor. And after the crescendo of impact, the music rose in a requiem that cast a pall over the forest. As if a second, deeper night were falling, a night from which all who heard the melody would never awaken.

Chapter 29

The Burning Man. He rose out of the sea, cloaked in flames that devoured the oil slick spewing from the gutted ship. Reaching out across space and time, the Burning Man had come, and Cassie floundered in the water as He neared, a fiery wave cresting to engulf her. But His touch was surprisingly gentle as he swept her out of the numbing cold. As gentle as her mother's. As gentle as a lover's . . .

Cassie strained for a glimpse of his face, but she was swallowed up in the watery darkness. *You must be dead . . . You must be dead to be so blind and cold and still.* But as slowly as sunrise, her eyes were opening to reveal the glow of a fire. The flames did nothing to warm her, but soaked her with sweat, so that she felt as though she were burning and drowning at the same time. And this time, the Burning Man knelt so close to her she could feel his breath.

"It's going to be okay, Cassie. You're safe now."
The roar of the ocean in Cassie's ears softened to rain

tapping on the roof of a cabin. Jake's cabin.

He sat down on the mattress where she lay. "Iris . . ." she began, but it hurt to speak and she stumbled over the words. Rain sizzled on the logs in the fireplace, and smoke seeping from it into the room made her cough. At last she managed, "Take . . . me . . . home." Her voice was small and scared as she said it, but she no longer cared whether she sounded like a child in front of him. Just so he helped her.

"I found you in the clearing," he said. "I'm getting you on the next plane out of Bangor." Before she could throw her arms around him for saying it, he stood up and walked over to the Moog. Cassie watched as he selected a tape and began threading it onto his Nagra, like a hunter loading a gun.

"What are you doing?"

He didn't answer. The storm had suddenly died, the drumming of raindrops reduced to a staccato beat, and he was listening to another sound, dimly perceptible beyond it. He tilted his head, as though the sound froze him in place, and Cassie strained to hear it too.

The music. The flames in the fireplace flared as if they were being fed by the sound. The music seemed to be fanning some flame inside Jake, too, she thought, something feverish and intense. She didn't like what it did to him, the way his muscles tensed, the way his eyes took on a haunted look.

"I've got to go . . ." He pulled a sweatshirt over his head.

"You said you were going to take me . . ."

"I will. But first I've got to find out where it comes from. I . . ."

"No!" Her voice was suddenly shrill: "You won't come back. You . . ." She tried to pull herself up from the mattress, but the cramps in her stomach forced her back down again, onto the grimy sheets. "Please . . ." She began crying softly.

"Come on, Cassie. I'll be back soon." Cassie detected impatience beneath his smile. "Look, I'm a

devout coward. As soon as I see what I need to see—
whatever it is—I'll run like hell."

"Please!"

He kissed her on the forehead. "Try to sleep. When
you wake up, I'll get us both the hell out of here." He
grabbed his Nagra and headed out the door.

"You bastard!" she shouted after him. "Bastard!"

When the door slammed shut behind him, the flames
in the fireplace flickered, dying. The room edged into
darkness, as though the storm had seeped through the
plywood, permeating it with a widening stain. The walls
groaned in a sudden gust of wind, and Cassie felt as if
the cabin were slipping towards the lake, to sink into the
depths, like the *Pandora*.

The notes echoing through the trees filled Jake with a
surge of energy, and he clawed his way through a
thicket, scrambled over granite boulders, drawn to the
source. Last night when he had set out on this same
hunt, the music had eluded him, dissolving like a mist as
he had advanced towards it. But tonight it was guiding
him.

Summoning him.

The music hung heavy in the air, like incense, and the
forest that had thwarted and threatened him suddenly
seemed welcoming. Through the soles of his feet he
could feel the soft earth throbbing to the rhythm, the
branches of the pines overhead swaying to its cadence.

The wonder of it.

A glow filtered through the trees, as though the music
were incandescent, shimmering the boughs. Sap oozed
from the bark in the heat, a molten amber that filled the
air with an intoxicating scent that drowned out the other
smells, smells less familiar, less pleasant, drifting towards him.

One final ridge of black volcanic soil, where a wall of
brambles grew, and the earth's crust rose steep. And
then he stepped into the clearing.

After the darkness of the forest, the brilliance of the

bonfire dazzled him. Its flames leapt twenty feet into the air, spewing galaxies of sparks towards the stars. In its aura, images were haloed with golden light—naked women drawing horsehair bows across the strings of instruments carved in ivory and ebony and sandalwood, blowing into animal-hide bagpipes, pounding on timbrels and blaring horns, the brass glinting in the firelight.

Their music . . . details which had eluded Jake from the distant vantage-point of his cabin stood out in bold relief: subtle cross-currents of harmony, odd syncopations, their feverish intensity, their passion, magnified. He did not bother to switch on his tape recorder. The music seemed too fragile, too ethereal, to capture on tape. Besides, there was no need. After tonight, he felt certain the music would be forever locked within him. He let the tape recorder slip to the ground, the tape unreeling in the dirt.

Cassie cried for help until she was hoarse, scratched and bit and lashed out with her fists, but there were too many of them, and they fought too fiercely. Abigail, Robin, and Iris had dragged her from Jake's cabin, forced her onto the back of a black stallion. And now that she had surrendered, too numb to resist any longer, now that she clung to his mane as they led her through the forest, she noticed they were no longer treating her like a prisoner. They looked up at her with a respect she couldn't fathom. As they led the horse into the clearing, it seemed they were escorting her like a victor, as though she had won some prize she did not understand.

You will see only what you want to see tonight, the music told Jake. *You will hear only what you want to hear.*

The yellow smoke that swirled around him smelled of incense, the holy scent of a cathedral, and the fire's arches of red and yellow and blue dazzled him like stained-glass windows, overwhelmed him with a glory that had been denied him in the vaultlike synagogues of his youth. The choir that stood at the shining altar . . . theirs wasn't the sad wailing of the old men dovening in temple, old men wailing Kaddish over the dead. Tonight, Jake felt as though he were hearing pure joy, the songs of angels, unashamed in their nakedness. He could hear fragments of the words: "*Blessed . . . sanctified . . . Master of the Universe . . .*"

The wonder of it.

He watched as Sarah took communion wafers and held them out to the girls in turn. Each closed her eyes as she took the wafer on her tongue. His mouth was dry, his lips sealed tightly shut, but he felt as if he could taste them, pure and blessed. The taste of salvation. He did not know whom they worshipped, only that he could hear a voice rising within: *Praise Him*.

Jake was blind, but Cassie could see. She smelled the sulfur fumes swirling around her, mixed with the stench of sweat, and the wafers made of excrement that the girls savored. There was no shining altar, only a block of obsidian, like a charred meteor where crude niches had been carved to hold the black candles. With a dagger, Sarah was inscribing a circle in the volcanic earth, and within the circle, at the initiates' feet, she scrawled a five-pointed star.

Sarah sprinkled salt on the earth before her, then beckoned with the dagger for a black ram to be led into the circle. With a quick slash of the blade, she slit its jugular vein, and its blood gushed out into the goblet she held beneath it. The ram fell to its knees, and she pressed the goblet to the wound until the brim overflowed with the hot red liquid.

Then Sarah lifted the goblet to the sky:

> "*Blessed among the angels*
> *The Evil One who forgives our Evil,*
> *The Sinful One who forgives our Sin,*
> *The Lustful One who sanctifies our lust with His.*"

Sarah passed the cup among those who knelt before her, Abigail and Robin and Iris and the others. They sipped from it delicately, as if not to spill a single drop, and when they had finished they murmured as one: "Anoint us."

Sarah dipped the blade into the goblet of blood: "Blessed be He, the Black Lord . . . The son of Midnight . . . The Accursed One."

"Anoint us," they chanted.

"The Vigilant, the Possessor, the Undiminished."

"Anoint us!"

Sarah pulled the dagger from the goblet and touched the blood-drenched tip to the eyes, the breasts, the lips and loins of each of the girls as they recited in unison:

"Blessed be my eyes, that I may see your path . . .
Blessed be my breasts, that I may suckle your
    young . . .
Blessed be my loins, that I may be fruitful with
    your daughters . . ."

"Accept Him as your savior," Sarah said when the last of the girls had been anointed. "There is no other."

"Praise Him!"

You will see only what you want to see . . .

"Praise . . ." Jake could taste the words, sweet on his lips, but could not yet say them. The bodies dancing in a circle around him were tinged golden in the firelight, like gilded saints. Their bodies were so lithe, so young . . . He admired their taut muscles, their skin the color of the amber oozing from the pine boughs. The music given flesh, he thought. He wanted to join them but his body seemed drugged, leaden.

You can not dance, the voice in his mind said, *but you will dance to His music in your heart. In your soul.*

Jake was blind, but Cassie could see. The oil painting

that she'd found in the ice house hadn't been the vision of a madman. It was congealing to life before her eyes, in the same lurid yellows and greens as those of the canvas. But she could see only fragments of the tableau, as if to grasp it all at once would overwhelm her.

One by one, the girls knelt to kiss Sarah on the buttocks. Then they merged into the undulating serpent of flesh, and women, older women with withered thighs and hanging dugs, joined in—mothers from Visiting Day, joining with their daughters in the revel. The "proper," the "well-born," the "right" people, Cassie thought bitterly, reduced tonight to . . . beasts? No, something else. Something worse. Bereft of her conservative silk dress, her naked breasts smeared with grease that smelled of animal entrails, was Abigail's mother, Margot Burgess, the FBI Director (the betrayer, Cassie thought); and Loren Bradshaw, the General, using one of the black candles as a wax phallus. And Robin's mother, her body writhing in the dust as a wolf lapped between her thighs. Robin leered up at Cassie from where she sat near the bonfire, nursing the black Manx at the third nipple under her arm.

Then Iris pulled Cassie from the horse and dragged her to the block of obsidian, forced her down onto it with a strength Cassie couldn't defy. The stone felt cold against her back, like a slab in a morgue, she thought vaguely, her emotions too raw to fight back. Iris placed a crucifix upside down, at Cassie's feet, then smeared it with excrement. *Pass out*, Cassie tried to command herself, but her senses were too numb even for that. *Stare up into the night sky*. But it did no good to retreat into herself, for she was waylaid by a word echoing in her mind . . . a troublesome drone, like a trapped and dying insect.

Pandorapandorapandora . . .

Suddenly she understood what power had lured her here through a labyrinth of time. She knew who the mothers and daughters of Casmaran were waiting for.

*The icy water and the oil slick burning on the sea . . .
The ferry boat groaning as it turned over to die, victims
lost in the vortex of its plunge into the deep . . . The
escape into the water that had cradled her so terribly
close to death . . .*

She had seen Him only once, but she could feel His touch in the flames of the bonfire, flames that pricked her like the pointed fingers of her mother's ring. It was as though the bonfire had been spawned on that distant night years before, aboard the *Pandora*, and had smoldered dormant over the years, waiting until tonight to reach flashpoint.

Naked and proud, Sarah was smiling down at her, a smile of welcome, even of love. "I know how you must feel, Cassie. The shock. The horror. When I was your age, when it was *my* night, I felt it, too . . . And the pain. But the pain has to be."

"You can't make me . . ." Cassie's voice locked in her throat. She didn't know what they meant to do to her. The only thing she knew for certain was that it must not happen.

"Casmaran. In the mother tongue it means 'summer's promise.' Tonight, when you join us, that promise will be fulfilled."

"I won't!"

"This is a special night, Cassie. Your night. Because you were born to be one of us."

"I could never be like you!"

"But Cassie, surely you must have realized by now. You must have guessed: your mother was one of us, too."

Cassie flinched as if she had been slapped: "You're lying!"

"I have no reason to lie to you, Cassie. Your mother came to Casmaran when she was your age, just like her mother and grandmother before her. We loved her like a sister . . . because she *was* our sister . . ."

"No!"

"She learned to worship the Dark Prince. And she knew that her daughter was destined to worship Him, too."

"That's . . . not . . . true!" (*It's all lies. It has to be.*)

"He wanted you early, Cassie, before your time. If only you knew what an honor that is . . ."

"You're out of your fucking mind!"

"He would have taken you that night aboard the ship, but Ann stopped Him. He had given her the ring because she was His favorite; He never expected that she would use its powers against Him."

Cassie remembered the scars on her mother's legs, and the limp; hidden signs of a struggle she had never understood. "I don't want to hear!" She pressed her hands to her ears, but the childhood memory that had been so out of focus, so blurred in her mind, sharpened with startling suddenness: *The last gasp for breath, then the bile of the sea forced down her throat . . . Her mother had never tasted it. While the others had been drowning around her, her mother had floated on the surface (flashes of Abigail and the seniors, rebounding off of Lake Casmaran). Cassie had floundered, drowning, but her mother had swept her out of the waves, into her arms.*

"Ann wanted you all to herself, Cassie. She loved you more than she loved His spirit. But when she denied His right to take you, that made Him want you even more. So He bided his time. Ten years are nothing to Him . . . A hundred years, a thousand years, are nothing. He waited until the year of your womanhood. This was your summer to come here, Cassie, but Ann refused you to Him again. She said it was because she loved you too much to give you up, but it wasn't love, Cassie. It was selfishness . . ."

The bonfire roared like the sea outside the window at Cliff's Edge, and Cassie remembered the gauzy curtains flailing, writing shadows like flames across the floor . . .

"*You* were there that night," Cassie whispered.

"We tried to reason with her . . ."

"She was screaming at *you!*"

As Robin and Iris held her down on the obsidian slab, a vision from that last night assaulted Cassie: her mother lying in bed, bathed in sweat in the moonlight, the open window letting in the cruel breath of the sea as it never had before . . . Her mother had been so still on the sheets that at first Cassie had thought she was . . .

"*You killed her!*" It was a cold awareness, that she realized had been lurking inside her for days, but that only now could she say aloud: "*You killed her because she wouldn't let you take me.*"

"If there had been any other way . . ."

"The letter . . . the letter I found in her purse . . ." Cassie murmured, "*You* wrote that letter!"

"How else could we have gotten you here? We did it for you, Cassie. I know you can't see that now. You can't accept it. But someday you will."

She died for me, Cassie thought. *She died to save me.* The awareness sapped her rage—sickened her with longing and guilt. It made her want to yield, to be taken by the forces that had taken her mother. To join her, if only in death.

She started to cry, and Sarah reached out to smooth a strand of hair from her eyes. "Your mother couldn't have stopped it from happening. No one could have. Because you're the thirteenth, Cassie. The final member of the coven. We are all His brides, but in your generation, you will be His favorite."

Sarah dipped the dagger into the chalice, and dripped blood from it onto Cassie's breasts, her thighs, her lips, whispering in a language that Cassie could not—that she did not *want* to—understand. She lay deathly still and the blood felt cold against her skin, like the waters off Nantucket where she had almost drowned. She closed her eyes and wished to God she *had* drowned then. At least she would have escaped Him.

"Soon you will admit Him into your body, Cassie,"

Sarah whispered. "And then you will invite him into your heart."

Naked, Sarah extended her hands to Jake as he entered from the clearing, as though she were welcoming him to her corner of the night. He could see the shadow under her arm of the third nipple that had so repelled him before, but he no longer felt the revulsion. "The Dark Prince needs the body of a man," Sarah whispered. "The body of a man who has not been contaminated with Holy Water."

And I am a Jew.

It had all been part of their plan, Jake realized that now. It was the reason they had rented him the cabin . . . the reason they had seduced him with the music. So that they could summon him here tonight. But he didn't resent the conspiracy. He felt strangely grateful to have been chosen.

"The thirteenth comes to us a virgin, on the night she has become a woman," Sarah said, beckoning Jake closer. He could smell the jasmine woven into her hair. "Allow the Dark Prince to possess your body. Welcome Him, and through you He will initiate her."

Suddenly, before his eyes, the bonfire flickered with flames from years before. The Burning Man. Jake remembered the fanatic who had burned himself alive the night of Jake's disastrous concert at Lincoln Center, as part of some unspoken protest. But tonight the horror was gone from that vision of charred flesh. The image Jake saw in the bonfire before him was an angel with wings of fire, the Burning Man rising from the inferno. It struck Jake that his career, which had died that night, too, *had* to die, in order to be reborn tonight, to rise, phoenix-like, out of its own ashes.

"He needs your body, Jake. And you need His Power. Submit to Him and receive all you deserve," Sarah said quietly. "Yield to Him and He will exalt you as a composer. As a man."

The bargain. Jake would have refused it once, and yet

now his face creased with what he sensed was a drunken smile of acceptance. He was ready to sell himself. After all he had been through, he was thankful for the chance.

And what would he be giving up in exchange for all that he wanted? Would he be commiting so heinous a crime? The initiation—the act of violation—it would be done by another, really. The music throbbed in his ears, and he could feel a tingling between his thighs.

But the guilt? Where is the guilt?

He realized that he felt none, that it had been drained out of him by the music.

Praise Him.

The girls who had been circling the fire in the dance turned to him, and he let them strip off his clothes, their fingertips stroking his skin, arousing him. As they led him to the altar of black obsidian, he could feel that he was erect, from a power outside himself.

In the light from the black candle at her feet, he couldn't see who it was that lay there—only the chestnut hair that fell around her naked shoulders, the childlike body. The women urged him forward with whispers of encouragement.

One more step towards the altar.

"Cassie!" Jake's eyes snapped into focus when he saw her face.

Praise Him, a voice said from within him. *Praise Him*. But the voice was growing weaker, the ecstasy, the euphoria, replaced by something else. He inhaled deeply: for the first time he smelled the sweat of the naked bodies, the stench of sulfur and excrement, the metallic odor of blood.

"You'll be helping her, Jake," Sarah prodded. "Because once He uses your body to initiate her, she will be ours. She will feel pain, but only for a moment. After that she will feel no pain ever again, I promise you."

But it seemed to Jake that Sarah's voice had lost its gentleness, as harsh as the stench around him. His mind swam with images, images that cut through the haze that had deluded him: the cobwebbed, crumbling works of other men—other Jews?—who had been lured here in summers past, to live in that cabin . . . to give their bodies. What had become of them? Had they been exalted as artists? Had they won the recognition that had once been denied them? Or, as Murdock in the grocery store had told him, had they disappeared before summer's end without a trace?

Jake stared in dumb horror around him at the altar, the writhing, hysterical bodies, the carcass of the butchered ram that had been bled dry. He had felt such certainty a moment before. It had all seemed so simple. Now he was certain of nothing.

Robin and Iris held Cassie down on the slab of obsidian. As Jake stepped towards her, naked, she tried to break free once more, but their strength was greater than hers. Abigail handed Sarah a carved wooden box, holding it as carefully as if it contained jewels.

Sarah opened the lid.

A severed hand, a pallid green, the color of something covered with scales instead of flesh. The skin had shriveled until it stretched tightly over the bones, making the fingers spidery, hardly human. It was a hand that seemed to be neither dead nor alive, but lingering in some strange purgatory.

Yet Cassie saw proof that it *had* once belonged to a man: the faint mark of a tattoo on the wrist, reduced now to a dark stain. It was distantly familiar, like the hazy recollection of a dream: the effigies swinging from the Hanging Tree . . . the blood dripping through the straw. "*Runt*," she murmured.

"The Glory Hand was taken at midnight," Sarah said, "soaked in a brine made of mandragora and jimson weed. It was cured by moonlight, consecrated for this moment." As Sarah held up the Glory Hand, for the first time Cassie noticed the silver ring in the shape of a hand on her finger. "Tonight I'm wearing the ring," Sarah said. "The ring He gave your mother, the ring that can summon the power of the Glory Hand.''

She thrust her dagger into the bonfire. ''When the fingers of the Glory Hand have been lit, Jake, your body will be His.'' The steel blade flared like straw, and she touched it to the first finger on the Glory Hand. It burned, phosphorescent, a hissing blue flame, the smoldering flesh more foul-smelling than any candle of wax or tallow. And as the tip of the dead finger burned, the bonfire dwindled, as if its heat had been focused into the single needle of flame.

Slowly, of its own accord (*Cassie could not believe what she saw, and yet how could she deny it*?) the hand began to move, like something that had been long-frozen starting to thaw, turning toward the flaming dagger like a flower soaking up the light of the sun.

Sarah lit the second finger. The hand was moving, Cassie could no longer deny it, its fingers quivering with life. ''When all the fingers are lit,'' Sarah said, lighting the third finger, ''His power will be yours.''

She lit the fourth finger.

Cassie stared at Jake, praying that he would spare her. He seemed to be hesitating, his eyes darting from the Glory Hand to her, as though his mind were struggling to reach a decision just beyond his grasp.

And then, abruptly, Jake wasn't wavering any more. He stepped forward to the altar, and the women murmured approval at his eagerness. Cassie struggled to free herself—until she realized that he wasn't reaching for her. Instead, he wrenched the Glory Hand from Sarah's grasp.

''*Let's go!*'' He tore Cassie away from the girls who held her down and half-carried, half-dragged her towards the forest.

The music died with guillotine swiftness, and with the howl of a sudden wind that spun the fallen leaves into tortured spirals, the coven started after Cassie and Jake.

We can't run fast enough, she thought, fighting back the image of Runt, and the force that had mutilated and murdered him. And yet she *did* run, her bare feet bloodied by the thorns on the trail. Jake held the Glory Hand like a torch, the burning fingers shooting sparks, lighting the path in their glacial glow.

Only four fingers are lit, Cassie told herself as they crashed through the forest. *Only four. It takes five flames to summon Him*. She glanced at the Glory Hand in Jake's grasp, to reassure herself.

The thumb, with its claw of flame, was stretching out to light the fifth finger.

The thunder of trampled brush behind them ended. Cassie glanced over her shoulder—the women weren't chasing them any more. In the sudden silence, she could hear a low hiss. Green smoke billowed from the tips of the five fingers.

He stood facing them, blocking their path, the branches of the trees near Him smoldering from His heat, bathing Him in an aura that dazzled Cassie. She could feel His eyes admiring her, caressing her body, and she felt a strange and troubling spasm of pride: He recognized the woman in her.

He glistened, hard and lean, and though she knew she should run, she didn't want to. What terrified her wasn't the cloven hooves, the hint of horns at His temples. What terrified her was that she was attracted to Him.

He was smiling at her, a smile not of vengeance, but of recognition, as if He had been reunited with someone He cared for deeply—as if her dash to escape Him had really been a race towards this very spot, where they were to rendezvous, like lovers.

The look of wisdom in His eyes (and forgiveness, there was forgiveness in them, too), it forced Cassie back into childhood, towards a memory of her first longing, her first wish, an emotion she hadn't allowed herself to feel since the night on the *Pandora*: the overwhelming urge to go with Him.

No, He wants to hurt you . . .

But His eyes denied it. They were a wise man's eyes, gentle from having seen so much of life that nothing could shock Him, that all sins could be understood and forgiven. Beneath the visage of a beast, the face seemed as familiar as her father's. Hadn't her mother once loved Him, too?

But He'll hurt you . . . He'll fuck you . . .

And yet a louder voice within her said, *Go to Him.*

Jake thrust the Glory Hand into Cassie's arms and shouted at her to run. When she didn't move, glazed-eyed, he slapped her hard across the face. It cleared her head enough to see that Jake was picking up a fallen tree-branch to use as a club. He stepped towards the Burning Man and when she heard the low snarl coming from the face that had seemed so gentle, so wise . . . when she saw Him bare His claws, His pointed teeth at Jake, she broke into a run.

The face of the Burning Man . . . Jake could see that it was his own. The eyes of the Burning Man terrified him because in them he saw himself, his weakness, his selfishness. His lust. At least the struggle he faced would be a chance for him to redeem himself. If he had been a failure as an artist and as a man, he thought, then he would make up for it with murder.

Jake's body responded to his jolt of rage with memories from a childhood spent defending himself: the hammerlock, the choke hold he'd learned growing up on the edge of Harlem. But the Burning Man knew how to turn Jake's rage against him—the more desperately Jake fought, the more he felt his strength ebbing.

Go for his throat . . . But when Jake pressed his thumbs into the snake-smooth neck, it was he who felt all breath choked off.

Gouge out his . . . Jake dug his fingers into the bony sockets, but *he* was the one who was blinded.

Jake dimly perceived that he was destroying himself in the struggle. It was as if he and the Burning Man were really two halves of himself, tearing each other apart.

Yet in a sudden flurry of thought, his mind seemed strangely aloof from the pain.

Why did you turn down the bargain? Why did you say no?

For a fleeting moment it struck him that this was the first time he had done something that was truly brave, and that he had done it to crush out a part of himself. If he could kill the evil within him, and save the good . . . His hand slipped around the snake-smooth throat once more, and he squeezed, squeezed until the hot breathing gurgled to a stop.

Cassie groped for a handhold, scrambling down the steep rock face, and as jagged chunks of granite opened the old wounds from her mother's ring, she welcomed the pain.

Your mother died for you . . . Jake died for you, too.

Shivering in the night air, Cassie realized that the Glory Hand she carried to light the way shed no warmth. If only the Burning Man had taken her, back then on the *Pandora*, she thought, her mother and Jake would still be alive.

At the foot of the cliff a stream cascaded over rocks into a shallow pool. As she neared it, she was astonished to see a man kneeling on the bank, splashing water on his face, his skin as pale as the moonlight reflected in the water. "*Jake?*" He looked up at her and smiled weakly. "You're . . . okay . . ." she managed, through her tears.

He stood up to face her and she realized both of them were heat-scorched and naked. Her sobs turned into giddy, hysterical laughter, and she waded into the water towards him, to thank him for saving her—to thank him for still being alive.

But his face . . . the features were Jake's—the deep-set eyes, the full lips, the curly beard—but . . . what was it about him?

The eyes . . . cunning . . . malicious . . . They were not Jake's eyes. The face was only a mask, she realized.

And the body? She looked down into the stream: steam was rising with each step that he took towards her through the water. And a serpent, smooth and black, stabbed from the snarl of coarse hair between his thighs. It was stiffening, rearing its forked head, like a cobra about to strike.

The cry that rose from Jake's mouth melded anguish and triumph. In a helpless reflex, Cassie raised the Glory Hand before he took the final step.

EPILOGUE

"Make a right here . . ." Cassie said, but instead the driver skidded to a stop. He squinted through the ice-veined windshield at the turnoff and puffed on his pipe for warmth, stroking his coarse gray beard. "You've got to be kidding. This thing's a taxi, not a snowplow."

Cassie jumped out of the taxi and waded through the fresh-fallen drifts to the split-rail gates. They had frozen shut, and she pounded on them with her fist, her breath puffing white smoke from the effort. A final kick with her boot and the gates yawned open with the squeal of rusted hinges.

Strange, she thought as she climbed back into the taxi, that there wasn't a set of rabbit tracks in the snow. No hint of squirrel or deer—not even a single crow—as though with winter all life at Casmaran had ceased.

Grumbling, the driver fishtailed the Chevy off the icy blacktop, its chains cutting two scars across the white expanse. The taxi jolted through a pothole, and Cassie steadied the brightly wrapped package on her lap, then rubbed away the condensation on the window to watch the procession of bare branches, stark and dead against the sky. She took off her glove and ran her fingers through the fur collar of her coat, remembering her excitement when this tunnel of maples had been shimmering with leaves the day of her arrival at camp. The excitement she felt now was different, perhaps, but no less intense, the anticipation of something familiar. A long-awaited return.

Covered with snow, pure and still, Casmaran reminded Cassie of her mother, the way she had lain in the coffin, like a replica in white marble of someone who had once been alive. The once-imposing stone lodge ahead, the neat row of cabins, seemed smaller under the snowdrifts. Without the leaves on the trees, without the flowers, it was a bleak landscape, a lonely one, she thought, but she understood how the ice men could have lived here, through the long, cold months so many years ago. It was a season free of confusing summer shadows, free of the concealing mask of leaves. There was something crisp and clean, something certain about winter. And this winter she felt certain, at last, about many things. The reason she had come here today was as clear, as sharp, as the icicles on the eaves.

"Anywhere is fine," she said, as the taxi skidded across the frozen parking lot and lurched to a stop in front of the steps to the main lodge. The driver pulled the fur flaps of his cap more tightly over his ears and stared around him, taking in the stillness, pumping the accelerator pedal to keep the engine alive. "You don't have to wait," she said, fumbling in her leather shoulder bag for her wallet.

The driver rested his hand on the metal flag of the meter, but didn't turn it off. "It's fifteen below. No place to be stranded. I'll wait."

"It's okay. Really it is."

"This place is closed up like a tomb. Who's gonna take you the hell back to Bangor?"

"Thanks for the ride." She pulled her scarf noose-tight around her neck before she opened the door.

"I don't feel right about it," he said. "I don't feel right about it at all." But the crackle of the tens she slipped into his gloved hand silenced him, and she slammed the door behind her.

For a moment the wheels of the taxi spun helplessly in the snow. Then the gears ground into first, and the car churned back up the road. Cassie watched until the Chevy dissolved into the snow, the rumble of its engine merging with the wind.

She set herself a brisk pace, the stiff crust of snow crunching underfoot. Since summer, she had doubled the time she spent dancing, and her muscles were taut. But despite her confident stride, her fur-lined leather boots couldn't keep the cold from numbing her toes as she trudged past the main lodge. She walked faster, each step punching a hole in the icy gloss of the snow.

The doors to the arts and crafts building and the infirmary were padlocked, as if to seal in what was left of summer, she thought: the warmth of the sun, the scent of wildflowers. And the mischievous laughter. The camp was so still, so very still, yet somehow also fragile. Precarious. She wondered whether, like one of those crystal globes filled with snow, a single jolt would be able to shake it into a blizzard.

Behind the lodge, ice lacquered the gravestones on the way to the forest, making them look freshly polished, as though they had been chiseled that very day with the names of the dead. She shifted the package in her arms and watched her breath billowing in white smoke before her. Above the trees, the smoke from the chimney of Miss Grace's cottage was as pure, as white.

In the snow, the cottage looked like a gingerbread house, as though its gabled roof, its shutters decorated with hearts and cupids and crescent moons, had been frosted with icing. A snowdrift buried the steps leading up to the porch, and she waded through it, wiping her feet on the welcome mat. The wreath on the door gleamed with red berries, like holly, she thought, but the shiny, three-pronged leaves more closely resembled poison oak.

She tapped the brass knocker against the door, expecting it to echo like a gunshot in the silence. Instead, the sound was absorbed by the pine boughs, heavy-laden with snow, that hung over the house.

When there was no response from inside, she tried the metal knob. As usual, Miss Grace had left the door unlocked. She stepped inside quickly, like a fugitive from the cold, slamming the door behind her.

The warmth of the pine logs crackling on the hearth hung sweet and heavy on the air, and the fire bathed the parlor in an amber glow.

"Bless you, child!" The voice was sibilant, sharp, like wind whistling through a cracked windowpane.

Backlit by the fire, the old woman looked more frail than Cassie remembered. "It's good to be here, Miss Grace."

The wheelchair purred over to her, as softly as a cat coming to rub against a welcome visitor. "That *is* you, isn't it, Cassandra? You've grown so, I hardly recognized you."

"I almost didn't make it," Cassie said, holding out the package, "what with the weather so . . ."

"I never doubted for one minute that you'd honor my invitation. Tonight, of all nights, I'm glad you could come. The Winter Solstice is the longest night of the year, child. The night He first made Himself known to the long-suffering world. The night when we celebrate His power anew." She nodded for Cassie to put her package down beside a dozen other brightly wrapped boxes, near what looked like a crèche: the cottages of Casmaran had been fashioned of twigs against a snow-scape of cotton, with figurines of campers carved in fragrant sandalwood. In place of a manger with its Virgin and Child, was one perfect ebony angel a few inches high, its hand extended in blessing.

"Take off your things," Miss Grace said. "Let me get a good look at you."

Cassie unwrapped the scarf from her neck and unbuttoned her coat, eager to show the old woman how her body had developed since the summer—her breasts full beneath her Irish-knit cardigan, her legs willowy, her hips shapely beneath her jeans.

"You have matured nicely," Miss Grace nodded her approval. "And I've heard that things have gone splendidly with your dancing. They tell me you may be the youngest member of the corps they've ever had at the New York City Ballet . . ."

"It's still not final yet," Cassie smiled modestly.

"Congratulations are definitely in order. And for your father, too. All that talk now about his Presidential chances. Why, it must have been almost too much to hope for."

"We're very grateful," Cassie said. "We've been lucky."

"Yes . . . In life we make our own luck, don't we?" The old woman motioned for Cassie to be seated on the sofa. "With things so busy for you now, I'm most grateful you took the time to visit me."

"I wouldn't have missed it."

"Things may look dead in the winter, buried under snow and ice, Cassie, but nothing could be further from the truth. There's maple syrup in the trees, and fish hibernating in the lake with their eyes open, just waiting for spring to come. And it's taught me something. Why, if there's so much life hidden in the winter, then over there, on the Other Side, there's bound to be life too."

"I'm sure there is," Cassie nodded dutifully.

"Have you ever looked up into the night sky in winter? Why, it's so clear and cold you can see to the edge of the universe. You can almost see into the Beyond . . ." The old woman's eyes glazed over for a moment, her mind adrift. Then, as though she didn't like where her thoughts were leading, she changed the subject. "Do you like my new shawl?"

The wrap over the old woman's shoulders was a patchwork of bright colors, much too young for Miss Grace, Cassie thought. "It's lovely."

"You'll never guess who made it for me."

"I can't . . ."

"Iris! Iris crocheted it for me, all by herself. Now wasn't that a thoughtful gift?"

"Iris is very talented."

"My favorite girls have come up to visit me this winter." She nodded towards a cake plate on a side-table. "Robin brought me up some brownies . . . home-baked. You must try some. And Abigail sewed a quilt for my bed . . ."

"How nice of her."

"But you, Cassie dear, you were always so clever. I can't wait to see what you brought me."

"I can't wait to give it to you," Cassie said, and leaned over to pick up the package.

"I have a gift for you first. 'Age before beauty'!"

"You didn't have to . . ."

"Ah, but this is a time for giving. And you deserve it, child. You've *earned* it." Miss Grace glanced down at her paralyzed right hand. "But you'll have to take my glove off if you want it."

Cassie hesitated, then replaced her box next to the others beside the crèche, and walked back to the wheelchair. When she lifted the old woman's hand in hers, it felt as light and fragile as a sparrow's wing. She slipped off the glove of yellowed lace.

The silver ring in the shape of a hand hung loosely on Miss Grace's bony finger. "It was a gift to your mother from the Master himself," she said. "But of course He always intended that you should have it someday."

Cassie slipped the ring off of the old lady's finger and onto her own. It fit perfectly.

"It looks lovely on you, Child," Miss Grace sighed. "Because that is where it was meant to be." She smiled at Cassie. "You see how life is? The year that got off to such a dreadful start has had a happy ending after all. Spring will come again, and then summer. And then Casmaran will ring with laughter again, and we will all worship Him together.'' Her eyes widened, like a child. ''Now it's *my* turn for a present. Whatever could it be? Is it something you made yourself?''

''I'm afraid not . . .''

''Well, I bet it's lovely all the same. It's the thought that counts, after all, isn't it? I only wish I could open it myself.''

''I'm more than happy to do it for you.'' Cassie untied the red ribbon, careful not to rip the red and green paper as she unwrapped it. Then she lifted the lid off the box.

When Miss Grace saw what was inside, her eyes widened, and her mouth opened to speak. But she couldn't utter a word, as if something barbed had lodged in her throat.

The Glory Hand . . . Its flesh was a reptilian green, the green of death. When Cassie picked it up and leaned over the fireplace to set the tips of the fingers alight, they quivered with a life of their own. The fingertips hissed with blue flame, and the fire in the hearth dwindled, plunging the room into near-darkness.

At last Miss Grace's lips managed to shape a word: ''Bitch,'' she murmured. ''*You little bitch*.'' Her paralyzed hands began to tremble in her lap: ''The night of Lammas . . . How did you escape Him?''

Cassie unbuttoned her cardigan sweater, tore open the blouse beneath it. Even in the five months since that night, the wound had not fully healed, and the scar smarted as she ran her finger along the two red seams, the two jagged intersecting lines that she had burned between her breasts with the Glory Hand.

Miss Grace winced at the sight, shielded her eyes from the cross of scorched flesh. And with a shrill whine, the wheelchair whirred backwards, knocking over a table, sending the porcelain elves crowding it crashing to the floor. Cassie crushed the glass underfoot as she walked towards her.

I've waited so long for this, Miss Grace. I've waited so very long . . .

The old woman's body was twitching, as if it were about to succumb to a seizure. Her lips were white and pinched, shaping silent sentences, but only one word came out. "NO."

"I have the ring, Miss Grace. The Glory Hand will do what I want now."

The wheelchair could back up no further. It slammed against the wall, smashing into the shrine of photographs so that the silver and gold frames hung lopsided, or fell to the floor. And Cassie inched the five-pronged torch towards the yellowed pictures.

Miss Grace seized the moment to send the wheelchair racing towards her. Cassie stepped out of the way as it jolted into a rolltop desk, hurling the old woman onto the floor. The wheelchair careened into the fireplace, and the electric motor sputtered in a flash of sparks. Miss Grace's frail body lay curled, fetuslike, on the carpet. "You stupid child!" she shrieked. "You think you know everything, but you know nothing. *Your father . . . he was unbaptized, too!*"

Cassie groped to understand. Her father hadn't been religious, but . . . Was it possible? Had Grandfather Broyles, the freethinker who had told her that no one who knew the sea as he did could believe in God . . . had he refused to baptize his son? "What are you saying?" she whispered, her voice so faint she could barely hear it herself. "What do you mean about my father?"

The old woman smiled, seemingly relishing Cassie's confusion. Then she started to move. *But she's a cripple*, Cassie thought, *how can she?* And yet, Miss Grace was on her knees, pulling herself up on the leg of a table, her thin, bony arms imbued with a strength that only now did Cassie understand. It was written on her face: hate gave her the power, a hatred deeper than any Cassie had ever felt.

"The Master was too greedy for your soul," Miss Grace hissed. She stood upright, her eyes cold. "He should have known when your mother defied us that you would be poison, too. For it is her blood that runs in your veins . . . Her blood as well as *His* . . . The blood of betrayal. Cassie, how can you betray your father?"

"My *father*?" Cassie lashed out with the Glory Hand as if to fend off Miss Grace's words before they hit their mark. But the Glory Hand brought her back with brutal swiftness to a moment more distant than a memory, an image from a time so long-forgotten that it had merged with lost dreams:

A woman in bed with a man, locked in a hungry, urgent struggle, lit by the dim glow of . . . candles? No, it was a Glory Hand on the mentel.

And . . . was it a man in her mother's arms? If her father had never been baptized, had his body been possessed that night by another? Was it a man thrusting into her mother, sowing his seed in her?

Or was it Him?

It wasn't a memory; it went much deeper than that. It was the distant echo of the dawn of her own consciousness, the moment when she had been conceived.

"He spawned your life," Miss Grace said. "The spark was His gift. But you have lost the right to possess it." She took one unsteady step towards Cassie, then another, and locked her fingers around Cassie's throat. As Cassie reached up with both hands to tear herself free, she lost her grip on the Glory Hand. Its fingers raked her leg with fire as it dropped to the floor.

But Miss Grace's hands on her throat cut off the pain in her leg—cut off all sensation. With her oxygen choked off, Cassie felt herself blacking out, and fought against it, clenching her fist to feel the pain of the ring cutting into her palm.

Don't pass out. Once you go under you'll never come out again.

She groped for an image . . . any image . . . to keep her mind alive. Her mother's face . . . she could see her

clearly now, but not as she would have wanted to remember her: Ann, with that Hindu holy mark on her
forehead, that look of helplessness in her eyes.

They killed your mother . . . Cassie realized her
hatred matched Miss Grace's own. She was stunned to
see the Glory Hand responding to her surge of rage, the
flames from its fingers slashing out . . .

The old woman's grip loosened around her throat.
Cassie gasped for breath and saw that the blades of fire
had pierced Miss Grace's satin gown, that they were
feeding on the gaudy shawl that draped her shoulders.
Miss Grace tried to beat out the flames, but the sudden
movement only fanned them. They flew from her body
to the lace antimacassars on the armchairs, and to the
wallpaper; the photographs in the frames withered in
the heat like wilting flowers.

Miss Grace's silver hair was burning like straw.
You've killed her. The awareness stunned Cassie, until
she realized that she was wrong, that what was happening before her eyes wasn't a spasm of death, but a
transformation.

With horror and fascination, Cassie stared at the face
taking shape beneath the halo of blue flame, the features of another, emerging from Miss Grace's aged
flesh: Sarah's face, her hair shimmering more brightly
than it had in the summer sun, her skin blushing in the
heat with the glow of life.

"You . . . betrayed . . . us . . ." Two voices, one
parched and dry, the other strong and lilting. Or was it
just one voice, in youth and old age, as time had twisted
and distorted it? *"Betrayer!"* The voice echoed away,
like the last cry of someone leaping into a chasm.

The specters of Sarah and Miss Grace sank into a
single charred husk on the floor. Beside it, the Glory
Hand curled into a fist, dwindling, melting, devoured
by its own flames.

The fire had spread to the wood frame of the cottage,
and a ceiling beam crashed to the floor, blocking

Cassie's path to the door. Her eyes and mouth shut against the smoke, she leapt over the beam and fought her way out of the cabin.

Outside, flames were everywhere. It was as though the cabins, the lodge, the other buildings, had burst ablaze at the same moment, as if they could not exist without the old woman who had breathed them to life. Far from extinguishing the fire, the melting snow seemed to feed it, Cassie thought, like the gasoline that had drenched the straw men on the night of Consecration. Shutters exploded off the cabin windows from the heat, and doors burst their locks, leaving dark hollows that looked like blind eyes.

And did she hear screams? Or was it just the rusty hinges giving way? The roof-beams buckling? The shingles splintering apart? Unless . . . Could a place become as evil as the people who had lived in it?

At first, in the flames, the brooding December day shone as bright as noon. Then smoke and cinders darkened the sky. The air reeked of ashes, and of something else: the smell, she guessed, of something burning that had once been alive. She waded through the snowdrifts in the graveyard, brushing past the headstone chiseled "Choose Death," and remembering the fate of Iris and Robin and the others, she understood the epitaph.

Cassie veered away from the lodge and across the snowy expanse of lawn towards the frozen lake, her legs smarting from the burns. What was it about Miss Grace's words that had driven her here? Cassie wondered. *"There's maple syrup in the trees,"* she'd said, *"and fish hibernating in the lake with their eyes open, just waiting for spring to come."* Somehow Cassie sensed what the old woman had meant, even if Miss Grace had been too senile to grasp it herself: the hint of a promise Cassie could only dimly understand.

A ragged scar of ice marked the water's edge, and on the shore Lakeside cabin was burning, rocking precariously on its pilings, a flimsy boat on choppy seas. The frozen lake reflected the flames, ice and fire merging into one ruby-hard glaze.

Cassie stepped out onto the ice.

A chill assaulted her, but not from the cold. It was her mother's legacy afflicting her still, this nearness to the watery darkness. She could hear the ice starting to give way beneath her feet, cracking with each step as though she were walking on a mirror, and she didn't look down until she had counted a hundred paces.

Only when she reached the middle of the lake did she glance towards her feet. The ice was veined blue and green, translucent, like a thin slab of marble. And far beneath the surface . . . Was it only the way the light from the flames refracted on the ice? Or was there a form . . . a human form . . . lying there? A woman, as white as if she had been chiseled from ice herself? She lay on her back, her hands folded over her chest, her eyes open, staring at Cassie with a deathly melancholy. When she reached out a hand towards her, Cassie tugged at the ring.

At first it wouldn't come off, as if the metal were resisting. She had to pull so hard to remove the ring, it tore the flesh of her finger, but she didn't notice the pain. She held the ring in her hand for a moment, then dropped it towards the ice. It fell terribly fast, piercing the slab with a hiss and leaving a tiny hole, like one left from the impact of a bullet. Below the ice, the silver ring glinted for a moment, then vanished in the depths, along with the image of her mother.

With the crack of pistol shots, the ice was starting to break up under her feet, the thick blocks splitting, splintering, clashing like the blades of knives. Cassie walked calmly towards shore, walked with a sure and steady pace. She no longer felt the Chill.

The fire encircling the lake was dying, and the sky was black with smoke, as if a thousand crows had smothered the clouds with their wings. Cinders rained over Casmaran, as though to cover it in a final dark snowfall, descending as silently as dusk. Cassie trudged past the charred rubble of the cabins, and the scar on her chest felt tender and raw. As she started up the driveway toward the main road, following the tracks of the taxi, she realized she was limping from the burns on her legs. Limping, like her mother.

The flames had fanned a hot wind, and the air seemed terribly warm, so warm that Cassie could no longer see her breath in frozen clouds before her. A tear rolled down her cheek, as if a piece of ice that had been frozen inside her for a long time had finally melted. As if, after a long winter, there had been a sudden, startling thaw.

ABOUT THE AUTHORS

Paul Boorstin is the author of two previous novels, THE ACCURSED and SAVAGE. He has written and produced numerous award-winning television documentaries. Sharon Boorstin is the restaurant critic for the *Los Angeles Herald-Examiner*, as well as a regular contributor to many magazines. Although the Boorstins have collaborated on screenplays for television and motion pictures, THE GLORY HAND is the first novel they have written together. Paul and Sharon live in Beverly Hills with their daughter Julia.

BERKLEY HORROR SHOWCASE

Read Them Alone...If You Dare!

_____ ARIEL by Lawrence Block 05169-2/$2.95

_____ THE ALTAR BOY by S.J. Cassidy 05533-7/$2.95

_____ CAME A SPIDER by Edward Levy
04481-5/$2.50

_____ A GLOW OF CANDLES AND OTHER STORIES
by Charles L. Grant 05145-5/$2.25

_____ HOBGOBLIN by John Coyne 05380-6/$3.50

_____ THE LEGACY by John Coyne, based on a
story by Jimmy Sangster 05612-0/$2.95

_____ MAYNARD'S HOUSE by Herman Raucher
05079-3/$2.95

_____ THE PIERCING by John Coyne 05476-4/$2.95

_____ SAVAGE by Paul Boorstin 04938-8/$2.95

_____ CEREMONIES by Josh Webster 05466-7/$2.95

_____ THE SEARING by John Coyne 04924-8/$2.95

_____ SHADOWLAND by Peter Straub 05056-4/$3.50

_____ THE KEEP by F. Paul Wilson 05324-5/$2.25

_____ WHISPERS by Dean R. Koontz 04707-5/$2.95

Available at your local bookstore or return this form to:

B **BERKLEY**
Book Mailing Service
P.O. Box 690, Rockville Centre, NY 11571

Please send me the titles checked above. I enclose _____
Include $1.00 for postage and handling if one book is ordered; 50¢ per book for
two or more. California, Illinois, New York and Tennessee residents please add
sales tax.

NAME _____

ADDRESS _____

CITY _____ STATE/ZIP _____

(allow six weeks for delivery)   127 JL

Experience The Ultimate In Horror
By Bestselling Author

JOHN COYNE

Again and again, John Coyne
has proved to be one of the best
horror authors today. THE LEGACY,
THE PIERCING and THE SEARING
hit the bestseller lists when first published,
and have continued to be the choice of
millions of horror fans. And now— *HOBGOBLIN*
a totally new experience in horror, by the man
who made *THE EXORCIST* look like
a bedtime story.

_____ 05612-0/$2.95   THE LEGACY

based on a story by Jimmy Sangster

_____ 05476-4/$2.95   THE PIERCING

_____ 04924-8/$2.95   THE SEARING

_____ 05380-6/$3.50   HOBGOBLIN

Available at your local bookstore or return this form to:

BERKLEY
Book Mailing Service
P.O. Box 690, Rockville Centre, NY 11571

Please send me the titles checked above. I enclose _____.
Include $1.00 for postage and handling if one book is ordered; 50¢ per book for
two or more. California, Illinois, New York and Tennessee residents please add
sales tax.

NAME _____

ADDRESS _____

CITY _____ STATE/ZIP _____

(allow six weeks for delivery)

106 JY